One hushed Christmas Eve several years ago a woman sat in a darkened church. The greens, the carols, the beauty of the night—all contributed to the expectant stillness that filled the church. Suddenly she became aware of the strong sweet smell of the hay in the candlelit manger.

"It actually happened," she thought in wonder. "It happened to real people in a real place with real smells and sounds and sights. And that young mother was no older than my own daughter."

The impact of the discovery was overwhelming, and the woman left the church that night determined to tell the story of two real people whose lives were touched by God. The woman was Marjorie Holmes, and the story that was born in the scent of the hay was

TWO FROM GALILEE

Bantam Books by Marjorie Holmes
Ask your bookseller for the books you have missed

HOLD ME UP A LITTLE LONGER, LORD
I'VE GOT TO TALK TO SOMEBODY, GOD
LORD, LET ME LOVE
NOBODY ELSE WILL LISTEN
THREE FROM GALILEE
TO HELP YOU THROUGH THE HURTING
TWO FROM GALILEE
WHO AM I, GOD?

Two
From Galilee

Marjorie Holmes

BANTAM BOOKS
TORONTO • NEW YORK • LONDON • SYDNEY • AUCKLAND

TO Ruth Aley

TWO FROM GALILEE

*A Bantam Book / published by arrangement with
Fleming H. Revell Company*

PRINTING HISTORY
Revell edition published May 1972
9 printings through April 1973
Guideposts edition published March 1973
A condensation appeared in MCCALLS *Magazine December 1972*

Bantam edition / March 1974

2nd printing . . . March 1974	*7th printing . . . . March 1976*
3rd printing . . . . . May 1974	*8th printing . . . . . April 1976*
4th printing . December 1974	*9th printing . . February 1977*
5th printing . . . . . April 1975	*10th printing . . . . . April 1977*
6th printing . September 1975	*11th printing . . . . . May 1978*

17 printings through October 1983

18th printing . . . . March 1985	*20th printing . . . . March 1986*
19th printing . November 1985	*21st printing . December 1986*

ISBN 0-553-25936-9

Published simultaneously in the United States and Canada

PRINTED IN THE UNITED STATES OF AMERICA

KR   30 29 28 27 26 25 24 23 22

INTRODUCTION

Of all the books I have written, *Two From Galilee* will always be dearest to my heart.

It goes back, no doubt, to that magical Christmas Eve in a candlelit church when I sat next to my thirteen-year-old daughter, so close to the manger scene we could smell the hay. Real hay . . . its pungent fragrance transporting me back to the sweet-smelling fields and barns of my Iowa childhood. Filling me with a sudden, almost overwhelming sense of reality. For the first time in my life I realized, "*Why, this really happened!* On this night, a long time ago, there actually *was* a girl having a baby far from home . . . in a manger, on the hay!"

A very young girl, surely, for I remembered reading somewhere that in the culture of Mary's time every girl was considered ready for betrothal and marriage as soon as she went into her womanhood. And I thought, astonished: "When Mary bore the Christ child, she couldn't have been much older than my own Melanie here beside me!"

With this sudden awareness came a thrilling conviction about Joseph: He must have been a young man too. Old enough to protect and care for Mary and her child, but young enough to be deeply in love with her. *And she with him.* Why not? They were engaged to be married. Surely God, who loved us enough to send his precious son into the world, would want that son to be raised in a home where there was love—genuine human love between his earthly parents.

My feelings go back to the three years I spent researching and writing their beautiful story. Living with the characters, seeing them, hearing their voices, feeling their every emotion. They became as real to me as my own husband and children; not only Mary and Joseph but their parents, their families, the people in the village of Nazareth.

I could hardly bear to part with them when at last, with the tears rolling down my cheeks, I finished the final scene. I remember hugging the manuscript to my heart—a moment of both exaltation, and anticipation. All that I had experienced so profoundly, was now ready to be shared with the world. . . .

What followed next was only to intensify my impassioned faith in the book: For six long years I was destined to journey with Mary and Joseph from publisher to publisher, only to be turned away at the inn. No room, no room! "Nobody wants to read Biblical novels anymore," I was told. And, "You've made the Holy Family as real as the people next door! You can't *do* that."

"That's exactly what I meant to do," I pleaded, "to make people realize they *weren't* just statues or pictures on a Christmas card. They *did* breathe and hurt and hope and love just like we do. They too were human beings!"

Despite all these rejections, my stubborn faith never wavered. It was fortified by that of another fine writer, Patricia McGerr. "God's time is not our time," she told me. "When the Lord is ready this novel will be published—and have a great success."

Her prophecy was to be fulfilled. One final publisher did have the courage to publish *Two From Galilee*, Fleming H. Revell. And their courage was rewarded. Ninety thousand copies were sold in the first three months. It was soon on the *New York Times* best seller list, and became one of the ten best-selling novels of that year: 1972.

Fully nine years after that moment of revelation in the church on Christmas Eve.

But nothing makes *Two From Galilee* more dear to me than the avalanche of letters that have poured in about it. Beginning with the Christmas issue condensation in *McCall's* (a feature the editors told me "drew the highest readership of anything we have published all year—") and continuing ever since. Letters from men, women, and teenagers, from people in every circumstance, from all over the world. Not only letters but countless phone calls. . . . One girl telephoned from a distant state to tell me it was her thirteenth birthday. "My mother says I can have any gift I want. I told her all I wanted was to tell you personally how much I love *Two From Galilee*."

Phone calls and letters, saying that Christmas has taken on an entirely new significance for them; concepts of love have been changed, lives altered, faith enhanced.

One statement I particularly cherish came from a minister who had been discouraged: "You made me realize that if God would choose such simple, everyday folk for his great purpose, he surely has use for a humble servant like me. I have resolved to dedicate my talents anew to his service."

Two From Galilee has never been out of print.

But I am proud and happy that Bantam Books has published this book and its sequel, *Three From Galilee*. I am very grateful to the publishers who *did* make room for Mary and Joseph in their inn!

I

AND now she was a woman.

She was a woman like other women and her step was light as she hurried through the bright new morning toward the well. She knew she need not tell the others, they would know the minute they saw her. They would read her secret in her proudly shining eyes. And she knew she need not tell her beloved (if indeed he was still her beloved) though to speak of it would have been unthinkable anyway. He too would know. If, pray heaven, there were some way to see him before this day was past.

She must arrange it somehow . . . *would* arrange it somehow. Anxiety mingled briefly with her joy, yet her resolve was firm. Her parents would be shocked if they suspected—she was a little shocked herself. But somehow, some way, before this day was over she would see Joseph. Make him realize that at last she too was eligible to be betrothed. To be married.

For she was a woman now.

In the doorway, Hannah pulled back the heavy drapery which smelled musty from the long rains, and watched her daughter go. Her eyes yearned after the small lithe figure in the blowing cloak, balancing the jug upon her head almost gaily, despite the dragging pain that even Mary could not deny. "Let Salome go in your place," Hannah had offered, to spare her. But Mary had been

1

insistent. "Of course not, she's younger. It's Jahveh's way with women that's all. And all the more reason I should carry the water. I'm a woman now!"

"How long can I keep her?" Hannah grieved, watching her first-born disappear at the bottom of the windy hill. "How long will it be? Surely the Lord gave me the comeliest girl in Nazareth." She turned back into the house with a proud if baffled sigh. "Never did boys regard me with such longing as boys have regarded Mary from the time she first ran playing in the streets. Never did my own mother look thus upon me."

Mary was well past thirteen. Fortunately, her coming had been late. Something clanged harshly in Hannah. She herself had been barely twelve when given to the vigorous Joachim in marriage. . . . But no, she would not dwell on that. He had proved a wonderful husband in the end, and if possible he loved this exquisite daughter even more than she did. He would not be pressured into a betrothal even now; he would save Mary for the proper suitor. Sentimentalist though he was beneath that gruff exterior, Joachim would never yield to foolish pleas. When they gave over their Mary it must be to someone both rich and wise, someone truly worthy of so exceptional a bride.

The sun was fully up now, its pink light softening the objects in the rude, small room—the low table with its benches piled with cushions, the chest, the cold unkindled oven. She had better rouse the other children. But Hannah refrained a moment, savoring the thought of them sprawled on their pallets. *Mine,* she thought, and shuddered at the never ending wonder. Yes, even though Esau the eldest son was crippled and would never see the light of day . . . even so . . . out of these loins that were cold and empty so long, suckled at these breasts. . . .

And she pondered Mary's words—"the way of Jahveh with women." So bravely spoken, and so *vulnerable,* somehow. Hannah's breast ached even as she gave a cryptic little laugh. She began to call the children, crisply, that they might not suspect her emotions, and cracked a stick of kindling smartly across her bony knees. The hurt of being a woman—she would draw it into her own body if she could, she would spare her child the whole monstrous business.

But no, not monstrous, she sternly corrected. Simply the Lord's reminder that women were less than men. An afterthought, a rib. And it struck her as wry and startling that he should deign to honor one of them by making her an instrument of his great plan. For it was to be out of a woman that the Messiah would come. A virgin, a young woman. Not carved out of noble new-made clay like Adam, ready to smite the accursed Romans and bring Israel to her promised glory. Not flung like a thunderbolt from an almighty hand. No—as a squalling baby, the prophets said.

Out of one of these selfsame humble, unworthy, bleeding bodies. And thus it was that every Jewish woman cherished her body for all its faults and thought: *Even I could be the one.* Thus it was that mothers looked upon their daughters as their breasts ripened and thought—even she! But not really. No, not really. There lay in Hannah a practical streak as salty, flat and final as the Dead Sea. She was not one to pray overlong or fast and hear the fancied sounds of harps and angelic wings. She was not like her sister Elizabeth whose husband was a priest at the Temple and who consorted with the holy women there. She had Joachim and her five children and for her that was enough. When the time came (and it was near, many thought—after five hundred years of exile and slavery!) it would come, that's all, and have little enough to do with her.

There had been many children in the house of Hannah's father in Bethlehem and they were very poor. Though he was of the priestly line of Aaron, her father's limbs were twisted; and since priests must be perfect of body he was ineligible to serve. He had become, instead, a smith. He always stank of the forge and the fire, yet Hannah adored him, the tart acrid tang of him as she clambered over his dear misshapen limbs.

She was a wild little thing and her favorite memories were of running with her brother Samuel into the hills or along the busy streets. Bethlehem, now there was a town! No bigger than Nazareth, but always something doing. There was a great inn near the city gates. Its chambers and courtyards teemed with travelers on their way to Hebron and coastal cities to the south, or making a pilgrimage to nearby Jerusalem. Many of them were descendants of David, come to visit his birthplace. All were alien and exciting, drawing a noisy band of color across the provincial little Judean town.

Hannah and Samuel dove in and around their hairy legs like agile rats, feeling the rough bright robes that smelled of sweat and oil and musty spices and the dust of the great highways. They felt a boldness and a sense of special privilege as natives of this ancient cradle of Israel's greatest king. Jerusalem too lent them reflected glory. On clear days, tending goats on the hillside, they caught a glint of its dazzling colonnades, and the haze of its holy smoke paled the skies. You could even catch whiffs of the meals the priests were forever cooking on their altars to feed the vanity of God. The scent made the jaws leak, for meat was scarce in the house of a humble smith.

And then suddenly she was no longer a rowdy scamp running free when she should have been home spinning and learning of womanly things. A bloody hand had smitten her in the night. She hid her horror as best she could for two days, when her mother noticed her un-natural silence, her pallor, and put her mind ironically at rest. It meant only that she must leave off being a child, since she was now herself ready to beget.

The eyes that regarded her were filled with both agitation and tenderness. Their message was clear: "Though heaven knows what manner of man will have you." Then, hopefully, "Our kinsmen from Nazareth will be coming for the Passover Feast. It may be that their son Joachim. . . ."

It was accomplished with almost unseemly haste. Before the year was out she was setting forth with her new husband for the unknown hills of Galilee. "Whither thou goest I will go. . . ." The words of Ruth throbbed with new significance. Hannah turned wet eyes for one last look at Bethlehem, then put her small trembling hand into the big rough sheltering one of Joachim.

Joachim—huge, ruddy, leonine, with his thatch of dry

red hair. Saying little, either from shyness or reserve, and when he did speak, in a countrified accent. Yet a man with a queer dignity about him, and the look of deep and secret ponderings in his eyes. The look too of some recent pain. She was mad to know him completely, hurl all her energies upon him, possess him, love him.

Yet the shock of the marriage bed had been an evil dream. An evil dream all of it—the interminable journey to Nazareth, and having to live with Joachim's mother in the home of his older brother. Hannah had fallen ill, and when after many months she did recover, her womb was as frozen ground. If Joachim hadn't been a man of immense patience and devotion he would have divorced her. But bravely he had endured the disgrace of a wife who remained barren while all his sisters bred. He suffered no word to be spoken against her by his mother, who was certainly no Naomi (but then Hannah was no docile, doting Ruth). He even helped her with the water pots sometimes and brought her such small gifts as he could afford from the marketplace.

Why then she had often berated herself—why was it that she could scarcely bear his touch? For she had come to know what a wretched thing she was. And that for the first time she was completely loved.

At length Joachim's mother had died and the few acres they had tilled together belonged to his brother Simon. At first it seemed a hard thing, moving to this smaller mud brick house and striving to live on what Joachim could earn as a laborer until he could buy a little plot of his own. Actually, it had opened the sluice gates to happiness. Oh, the blessed silence after the clacking tongues. The joy of being mistress of your own house, however rude.

The house stood on the crest of a hill, commanding a view of the rich green pasture lands and orchards that made Nazareth the flower of all Galilee, as people claimed, even though it was but an insignificant hamlet, cut off from the main trade routes. Now, as she was slowly waking to herself as a woman Hannah wakened to the beauty of this place. The surrounding hills shimmered with the gold and bronze of grain in season, the purple-green tones of the vineyards, the silver of olive groves. White clouds coasted across the face of Mount Gilboa, trailing their ships of shadow. To the east lay the shining Mediterranean, and even nearer to the west, beyond Mount Tabor, the lovely flashing lake of Galilee.

One day Hannah stood in the doorway gazing upon all this handiwork of God. To her surprise, for it was midafternoon, she saw Joachim toiling up the steep path toward her, a young kid struggling in his arms. It was the first offspring of their she-goat which he had left off work to show her. And suddenly the sight of him, sunburned and sweaty, with the young thing bobbing against his chest, was as if all the heat of heaven had focused upon the chilled locks of her heart. Her breath came fast. And whereas she had been wont to gaze upon him boldly, without expression, now she lowered her eyes and wept.

"Hannah, what is it, are you ill?" her husband cried.

She shook her head but she could not stop weeping. She wept for all the lost years of unhappiness behind them and for the happiness to come. She wept for love.

Now came rapture, slow, insistent, tracking her down. Now a veritable explosion of rejoicing so violent it was like a pain. The sober, tough little face set in its patterns of defensive rejection began to break, unfold. She caught herself smiling as she worked; she sang. She felt lean and free and newborn; she stretched, she yearned, she gave. And then the miracle. It was discovered that Jahveh had at last blessed her womb.

Hannah bore a daughter, almost too beautiful to believe. They called her Mary. Despite the fact that she had failed to bring forth a son, friends and relatives came to rejoice with them, and the couple were beside themselves with pride. Hannah particularly. Joachim's happiness was tempered by his sense of obligation. It seemed to him that this child had been a direct answer to prayer, and as such must belong to God.

He pondered long in silence. But when it was time for his wife's purification he spoke to Hannah even as she wrapped the baby in the shawl. "When she is five years old it might be well to take her to Jerusalem and present her to the priests."

Hannah turned her back on him, appalled. "We have saved the redemption fee," she said. "Surely the Lord will be satisfied."

Joachim seemed not to hear. He was staring into the face of the sleeping infant. "As a ward of the Temple under the care of someone like Elizabeth she would receive so much that we can't give her. Who knows what high destiny God might have for her if we were only willing to make the sacrifice?"

Elizabeth. The named rocked Hannah with an ancient torment. Elizabeth had always been so beautiful, so fortunate. Elizabeth, barren even longer than she had been, yes, poor thing, but who had so much else to compensate. How could he even suggest that they give up their only treasure to someone like Elizabeth?

As for sacrifice! What kind of God was it that gave and then snatched back? Did the Lord with his multitudes have half the need of this hot little weight she held as either of them? But she dared not voice such blasphemies. She spoke tactfully, to protect her interests. She did not dream that she spoke as a prophet.

"Truly this is a child of God," she said. "But surely the priests and women of the Temple could never love her as we do, not even my own sister. Nor raise her more righteously. Nor even find her a better husband." Hannah gazed at the flower face in a greedy awe, seeing its sweet promise, yet tasting already the inevitable loss. "She's going to be one of the most beautiful girls in Galilee; she'll have any man she wants."

Joachim yielded. His own spirit was eased. And as time went on it was hard to say which one more passionately adored the child. Yet now that Jahveh had relented he made up for lost time. Hannah was soon expecting again, and subtly, swiftly, Mary was drawn to the father. He would swing her to the ceiling when she came rushing to greet him with her explosion of dusky curls and huge ecstatic eyes. Or he would carry her about on his shoulders, talking to her in a whimsical way that amused Hannah, while filling her with a vague contempt.

She was uneasy with the poet who dwelled so strangely
in this man of silence or blunt country speech.

Sometimes he would lift Mary onto the back of the ox
and let her ride as he plowed the rich if rocky fields. What
a little goddess she was, pagan almost, garlanded with
the wild cornflowers and narcissus that Joachim plucked
and braided for her. How she laughed and sang and
goaded the gentle beast by tickling its flanks with an
olive branch. Hannah argued and scolded—it was unseemly in a girl child even if she didn't come to harm!
But Joachim only laughed. Though he yielded to his
wife in most things, in this he had his way.

The second child was a boy, but their jubilation was
short-lived. For he was weak, very weak. And after the
long bout with fever when he was two they had to accept the burden of his blindness and his twisted limbs.
Hannah did so with all the intensity of her nature. He
was her heart. But now more than ever Mary became her
pride.

It exasperated Hannah that there could be anyone who
failed to appreciate not only Mary's striking beauty but
her other remarkable qualities. She lived in a perpetual
frenzy of comparison, choked and galled when her sisters-
in-law boasted about their daughters. To Mary's embarrassment, Hannah had to surpass them, she could not hold
her tongue. "Mother, please," Mary pleaded, "remember
what the proverb says: Pride goeth before a fall."

It brought Hannah up short. But she retorted, "See
that you remember that and never give us cause to hang
our heads."

This morning, slapping the cakes onto the now glowing
coals for breakfast, Hannah smiled a trifle guiltily to
remember. As if Mary could ever cause them shame.
For Mary was all the things she claimed and more, things
that, maddeningly, you could not convey to outsiders.
Even sweaty and laughing from play as a little girl, or
grubby from toil, there had always been this queer delicacy
of her person, this quality of gentleness, as if she were
truly a king's child. She was patient and helpful with
the younger children; her wit brightened the darkest
days.

If she had faults they were but the kind that gave her flavor. A fierce allegiance to her father, sometimes shutting Hannah out. A tendency to dream over the spindle. And she was not content with the old songs and tales (this worried her mother most) but would make up songs and stories of her own. "If she were a boy she might have been another David or Solomon," said Joachim. But Hannah had small patience with such imaginings. A girl should never be anything but the mouthpiece of the truth.

The truth. Sternly Hannah examined her own concept of Mary. Even allowing for prejudice, surely if ever a daughter was well nigh perfect, that daughter was her own. And most of the village knew it. Certainly the young men knew it. Not one of Mary's cousins could claim such impressive suitors as had already approached Joachim.

Hannah tallied them up: Abner, whose family traced their lineage to the first high priest of The Land, but who supported themselves as sandal makers. Abner—tall, gaunt, sweet-natured but rather remote, forever poring over his books. His parents had scraped up the money to send him to Jerusalem for study. He aspired to be a priest and serve in the Temple and it seemed likely he would succeed. Hannah could not but be tempted as she visualized Mary living near its splendors, her days heightened by its constant procession of holy and important people.

And Cleophas. Son of Reb Levi, a town elder and its richest citizen. He dealt in silks and spices and fine stuffs which most of Nazareth was too poor except to admire. He was forever sending Cleophas on trips to K'far Nahum and Sidon. Joachim's relatives buzzed that the family dealt with agents of Herod, although Hannah marked that up to jealousy. Certainly Cleophas was a handsome if somewhat wild and arrogant boy, and he doted on Mary. Sought her out at the grape tradings and sheep shearings and dancing at wedding feasts. Hannah's blood quickened as she thought of the fine house of stone and cedar wood of which Mary might one day be mistress, the gems and elegant fabrics that would surely enhance her loveliness.

Joachim had put both fathers off when they sounded him out last year. Not wishing to admit that Mary was not yet nubile he had said merely in his brusque, authoritative way: "We need her. There's plenty of time."

Yes, time. Plenty of time even now, Hannah reassured herself. For she had wearied already of thinking of suitors —she could feel one of her headaches coming on. No, she would not allow herself to think of others. Especially not one.

Yet Joseph's tall splendid body seemed to invade the tiny room. His sea-gray eyes seemed to haunt her, demanding, insistent. And so she must cope with him. Jacob, his father, was also of the stock of Jesse, she had to admit, but poor, and a wine-bibber, it was rumored. A squat, merry, loquacious little man who sang and joked as he mended the carts of passing travelers, leaving the shop that adjoined their mean little cave of a house pretty much to his eldest son.

Unlike his father, Joseph was rather sober, albeit he had a quick smile and a radiance about the eyes very pleasant to behold. Called forward to read the Scriptures on the Sabbath, he came on a light, quick, pounding tread that seemed to stir all the girls seated in the gallery. Even Hannah felt his strong masculinity throughout her whole spare yet vital being. She did not miss the little tremor that ran through them, the unconscious leaning forward. All but Mary who sat locked in her quiet poise, betrayed only by the half-smile on her lips, the fixed and shining look in her great eyes.

He was older than Mary by some six years. He should have long since taken a wife. But that he'd been waiting for her daughter Hannah knew with a helpless sense of dismay and stubborn rejection. Many times over the years he'd come by the house on unnecessary errands —to deliver a yoke that Joachim could have picked up himself, to bring an offering of his mother's fig cakes, to mend a trough. And he invariably lingered with Mary. Pictures plagued her: Joseph patiently picking out nutmeats and popping them into Mary's innocent mouth. Fourteen-year-old Joseph hoisting the basket of olives to his own shoulder as she struggled up from the common orchard behind the town. And once when unexpected clouds had sent down an avalanche he had picked her up and carried her bodily across the swirling waters.

Hannah would never forget their laughter or the look of his streaming face as he set her down on her own doorstep. And though Mary had been scarcely eleven then and he almost eighteen, Hannah had felt a sense of dark outrage.

"Never let such a thing happen again," she had said severely. "What would people think?"

"That it was pouring and the streets were such a torrent that I might have been swept away and drowned."

"Swept away indeed!" Swept away . . . and away . . . into youth and longing and dreaming and foolishness and the mistakes that were forever waiting to overtake those who imagined themselves in love.

But she had guarded Mary well. She had made it plain in many ways not only to Joseph himself but his parents —yes, and the soft-hearted Joachim—that a match was out of the question. They had not had the effrontery to ask. But until Joseph had settled on another girl and the banns were announced Hannah would not rest easy.

Mary, their Mary, was meant for a finer fate than toiling and bearing children for a poor young carpenter.

II

THE pink light was claiming the sky. The very breath of God was tinted as mists drifted down from the hills, across the fields, blurring groves and vineyards. Foliage sparkled with last night's storm and petals gemmed the streets. In all the little houses people were stirring, and the singing that always signaled the beginning of a good day in Nazareth joined that of the birds. There was the smell of bread baking. And passing the big public oven dug near the well for the use of the poor, Mary could feel the heat of the coals as the crone Mehitabel slapped her loaves upon them.

"Mary!" Other girls carrying jugs or skins or leading livestock to drink at the trough, cried out to her. And it was as she had expected. Her cousin Deborah, who missed nothing, pounced on her secret and made it news. Above the creak of rope and bucket, the slosh of water being poured into pitchers and jars, the mooing and blatting of sheep and cattle, the ripple of it ran through the crowd. "Mary's a woman now!" Offering a mixture of congratulation and commiseration, they made room for her nearer the head of the line. Old Mehitabel joined them, her cackle splitting the bright fruit of the morning. "I say it's just the beginning of a woman's misery. A heavy price to pay, I say, because Mother Eve ate an *apple*. Now if it had been a pomegranate or a melon! . . ."

The women laughed. They could see a joke. For wasn't

their entire existence based on a proud if almost ludicrous anomaly? Here were the Jews, God's chosen people—yet none had known such bitter hardships. And their land for generations had been occupied by heathens to whom they must pay tribute, but whom they would not deign to touch. There was something crudely cleansing about Mehitabel's audacity.

Another voice spoke up. "But nobody's really a woman until she's lost her maidenhood. When that happens let us know, that's when we'll celebrate!"

Mary flushed. You must be thick-skinned to be a Galilean woman. You must not mind these jokes. Modesty quarreled constantly with this brash discussion of the state they seemed to value above all else. The coming to bed with a man, the loving and begetting. But how could she blame them when her own thoughts could dwell on little else? Cleophas, Abner, the others, but above all, Joseph. Adored as a child, dreamed of as she grew older, scarcely daring to hope. Her friend, yes, but perhaps her friend too long. One day she had summoned the courage to ask him, "Why haven't you ever been betrothed?"

"Can't you guess?" he smiled. "I'm waiting for you, little Mary."

After that it was their secret, almost too precious to discuss. Yet a baffling change had come over him these past months; he avoided her, she never heard his voice except in the synagogue. Wherefore? she thought in mystified desolation. Why, *why?* Had she done something to offend him? Or was he bowing to Hannah's snubbing, too proud to beg for what he thought he could not win? Heartsick at the prospect, Mary swung the bucket over the worn stone lip of the well and drew it up. Or had he changed his mind? The prospect was staggering. Could it be that Joseph had at last found somebody else?

Hoisting the moist weight of her jug to her head, she fell into step with Deborah, who had shooed her little sister ahead so they could talk as they climbed the hill. The child was plainly disgruntled, and although Mary felt sorry for her she was grateful. She was anxious to question Deborah, whose high white forehead and long elegant nose seemed almost to sprout antennae, so alert was she to all the latest gossip. Deborah would have heard.

But Deborah was also vastly filled with herself, and today she babbled of Aaron, her betrothed. He was just back from Magdala and had brought her a cashmere shawl. "And he's ordering a chest made for me, of the finest camphorwood."

Mary swallowed. "Who's making it?"

"Now wouldn't you like to know? Who else but Joseph? Aaron wouldn't trust anybody else." She moved along with the grace of a mountain cat. Her cool alert yellow eyes toyed with Mary, seeking her reaction. Then she rushed back to Aaron, the stone house he was going to have ready in the fall, what an importunate lover he was getting to be.

How she runs on, Mary thought, with a kind of pitying impatience. How she exaggerates. And she thought of Aaron, pudgy and slow-witted, despite his high good humor and his generosity. People loved and despised him vaguely, including Deborah herself.

She said with a shade too much enthusiasm, "Aaron will make a splendid husband. You're lucky your parents chose such a good man for you. As for the chest," she blurted, "when is Joseph starting? You'll want to see how it's coming, won't you? Let's go together to the shop."

"I knew I'd trap you!" Deborah turned on her in triumph if not in sympathy. "Come now, Mary, you can't go hanging around after him when it's plain there'll never be anything between you."

"Why is it so plain?" Mary demanded. Her whole body ached from the weight of the cold jug. "Do you mean you've heard something I should know?" She had an almost superstitious faith in the powers of her cousin. Better even to face the worst than go on enduring this mystery.

"If you mean have I found out he's asked for someone else? No," Deborah admitted flatly. "There was nothing to that talk about Leah. I got it straight from Aaron who got it from Joseph's brother. Leah's father wanted the match and frankly Joseph's parents would have been relieved. But they yielded to his argument that he wasn't ready to marry. Not ready," she scoffed, "at twenty-one

and past." Again she darted a tantalizing glance at
Mary. "Though if he takes after his father he'll never
be able to provide much for a wife. And he's never laid
anything by for a marriage."

Mary bridled. "He's been helping his family. The household is swarming with younger ones to be fed. How
could he save anything?"

"How you defend him. Well, I don't blame you,"
Deborah said disarmingly. "He's the most attractive youth
in Nazareth. Even comelier than Cleophas in some ways."
She gave a dramatic sigh. "The way he moves—and that
voice, those eyes! Or maybe it's because he's kept himself
from women that makes him seem so appealing. Whereas
Cleophas—he's like the Greeks."

"Where there is money there is always more temptation."

"You can't put me off by defending Cleophas. It's
plain you're mad for Joseph. But then so are a lot of
girls. He'd have been married years ago and the father
of a large family if they'd had their way. But you, Mary.
. . ." Deborah regarded her cousin with wry resignation. No amount of maternal rivalry could alter her affection for Mary or her own curious pride in her.
"You're the only one he's ever had eyes for. If he's not
to have you I wouldn't be surprised if he never married."

"But that would be a disgrace," Mary protested. "And
a disappointment to his family."

Deborah shifted her pitcher, here at the corner where
their paths parted, and continued to hold Mary with her
look of open envy, speaking these tart truths too obvious
to quarrel with. "Anyway it's you who are far luckier than
I am. It's a rare thing to be loved so steadfastly by such
a man, whether you ever lie by his side in marriage or
not."

"Thank you, Deborah." A great love for her cousin
surged up in Mary. "That's a generous thing to say. But
why," she pleaded, "why then is it so certain that this is
not to be?"

Deborah shrugged impatiently. "Don't be a stupid
donkey. Aunt Hannah, of course. Do you think she'd ever
give you up to someone like Joseph after all her boasts
about the grand matches you can make?"

She turned, graceful and catlike, and went her own way up the winding alley, while Mary stood hesitant, torn. Hannah would need the water, she ought to go straight home. But now more than before she was assailed by that high desperate resolution at the well. The conversation with Deborah had only made it more imperative. *She must see Joseph.* Not now, of course. It was too early to discuss so grave a matter. But perhaps if she just walked by his house, brushed however lightly against the worn stone doorstep, her nerves would be fortified for that later encounter, her hungering heart would be appeased.

Turning swiftly, as one driven, she headed for the short street where the carpenters plied their trade. Yet as she drew near her blood began to race and she regretted this rash compulsion that would only make her look brazen and foolish should any of his family be about. She wished desperately that she had veiled her face.

Then, as she plunged hastily along, she heard her name. "Mary!"

The voice rang out like a bell. And looking up she saw him just above her on the incline of ground behind the half-cave of the house. He leaped the fence and came striding toward her, impossibly tall in his rough dark sleeveless tunic, his astonished face alight.

"What are you doing here so early in the morning?"

"As you can see, I am on my way home from the well. I'm in a hurry. If you'll but let me pass. . . ."

"But I must know why Mary has taken the street of the joiners if she's in such a hurry? Her usual route is much quicker."

"Aren't the streets of Nazareth free for the choosing?" she said, mimicking his courtly tones if not the smile behind them. "And isn't Joseph forgetting his manners to waylay a maiden like this and risk being seen talking to her on a public street?" She spoke sharply, to belie the terrible pounding in her breast. She had not planned it like this; she felt startled, stricken.

But when he said her name again—softly, softly, like a slow caress—something went very still within her, and she lifted her eyes to meet his.

"You're right," she said. "My friend has guessed my motive, though it's not very gallant of him to force me to admit it. I came by his house because my heart was sore for a sight of it, since it has been so long since I've seen Joseph himself."

"Mary." He said it again, his clear gray shining eyes still fixed on hers. He reached out and took the jug from her shoulders and drew her into the shelter of a clump of almond trees. The ground was strewn with their white petals, and a few more coasted down. Mary watched him place the jar on the ground—it was tipsy and she worried lest some of the water spill out.

"Wherefore?" she demanded, beyond pride. Her hands, still damp and cold from clutching the vessel, were pressed tightly together. "Wherefore is it that you no longer find reason to come by my house, Joseph ben Jacob? Why do you always disappear after the services at the synagogue without a word to the family of Joachim?"

He plucked a blossom from the tree, studied it a second, then handed it to her. "Surely the family of Joachim feels no loss."

"I do." The words hung vibrant between them, yet it was as if words were superfluous. What she said or did not say had little to do, actually, with this charged atmosphere between them. She rolled the bloom between her fingers, crushing it. "I miss you, Joseph. I miss you so much."

He turned and gave the tree a violent shake, as if deliberately to withdraw from the spell in which they both were caught. His tone changed too. "You're not a little girl any more, Mary, that I should carve you dolls to play with, or sit picking out the nutmeats for your mouth." He began brushing the new cascade of petals from his shoulders. "You're not a child to be taken up in my arms and carried about."

"I wasn't a child then," she told him gravely. "I was nearly twelve. I have never forgotten. From that moment until this I have never forgotten what it was like to be held in Joseph's arms."

He drew a deep breath and dragged his gaze back to hers. And now in amazement she saw his suffering. She remembered Deborah's words, congratulating her on

Joseph's faithfulness—which if it were not to be fulfilled could only mean his grief.

"Forgive me," she whispered. "Believe me, the last thing on earth I want is to hurt you, Joseph."

The muscles in his throat tightened. He said, "I know that, Mary. But if your courage in speaking to me as you have is painful, it's nothing compared to the joy your words have also given me."

"Then why?" she implored again. "Why do you avoid my house?"

"I haven't slept," he said wearily. "Not in weeks."

"Truly?" she said. "That's a pity. But you haven't answered my question. Why is the sight of me and my people so distasteful that you turn from us as if we had some dread disease?"

"It's too early in the morning to be so cruel, Mary. You know very well why I'm trying to dwell on other things. The son of Jacob is not welcome in the house of Joachim."

"Your lack of sleep must have affected your mind that you should think such a thing. Come tonight," she invited before she could even consider. "Come to eat the evening meal with my father so that I may prove how foolish your words are."

He gasped and so did she, but there was no retreat. And a radiance came into his lean brown face that was indeed ravaged from lack of sleep. He laughed. "Does your mother know of this?"

"My father will inform her. He'll send one of the children down to confirm the invitation this afternoon. Or come himself."

"You seem very sure of this."

"My father loves me."

"I'll count the hours," he told her. The faint ironic twinkle had returned to his eyes. "If you're sure I won't encounter any representatives of the family of Abner or Cleophas presenting their case for Mary's hand?"

She started, but held her ground. "If Abner and Cleophas want me enough to goad their fathers into pleading their cause then let Joseph—whose sleep is so strangely disturbed, he claims—let him want me enough to bestir his father to enter the picture before it is too late!"

She took up her jar then and fled. A vast astonishment lent wings to her feet as she flew up the cobbled steeps. It was as if she had been carried boldly over unthinkable crests, and was soaring now to forbidden and joyous heights. She wanted to laugh, to shout. To join in the singing that now rang out from countless courtyards: "The heavens declare the glory of God and the firmament showeth his handiwork. . . ." Joseph! she thought. His handiwork—that strong high forehead, those serious shining sea-gray eyes, that sensitive mouth.

Her womanhood arose in her and flowed from her, not as something submissive and weak, but as a force, a release. Joseph was still her beloved, he had always been. And now the time was come when all things might be achieved. For she was a woman at last, truly a woman, and she would take things in her hands, however untried, and make it all come about. She was not even afraid of Hannah, who would resist, of course and make things difficult. But who would yield to her husband because she must.

Not once did it occur to Mary that Joachim might offer resistance of his own.

Her father stared at her from under his rough red brows. His heavy face was troubled. "Here, this night? To break bread with us?"

Mary nodded. Until now it had seemed so simple, even inevitable, such had been the urgency of her desire. Several times during the morning she had been tempted to speak of it to her mother. For to her surprise, Hannah had not been angry about the long time it had taken her to fetch the water. And there had been a precious harmony between them, grinding the flour. A curious new feeling of unity as their hands moved in the familiar rhythms on the mill, pulling the handle back and forth.

Before, the rasp of the stones had often seemed to her like the very air that hovered sometimes between her and Hannah—gritty. Yet this morning the millstones had made a kind of homely music as they ground the grain, and they smiled at each other through the little haze of dust from their mutual task. And when Mary spilled the meal, rising too abruptly to dump the fine soft cone into the bin, her mother had said only, "Don't worry, we can grind more. A woman's hands do tremble somewhat at this time of the month."

Oh, Mother, Mother, that is not the only reason my hands tremble. These hands touched those of Joseph this morning. He loves me—I know it, I know it, but he's too proud to humble himself before us. He fears your rejection. Oh, Mother, so bright and full of vigor, in many ways so dear—don't give him cause to avoid and deny me any longer! . . . But Hannah's very patience stayed the words. Mary could not bear to spoil this rare mood that sifted so exquisitely through her reverie.

And again, threading the loom, the smell of her mother's flesh bending over her as Mary's fingers fumbled for the strands—a dry, faintly acrid yet tingling scent of herbs and curds and vinegar that exuded from her wrinkled skin—this together with the heat of her mother's quick breath, stirred her to an almost insupportable need to speak. To tell her, in desperate tones if necessary, how lately her whole being was like a parched field thirsting for a sight of Joseph. . . .

Surely you were young once, Mother, surely you've felt the heat of the blood, the terrible longing. You're vividly alive in every bone and sinew, you've mated and borne children. Though desire seemed preposterous between her parents, nonetheless her imagined argument rushed on: If ever you have loved anyone, love Joseph too. Make it known to my father that you won't oppose his taking me to be his wife. . . .

"You *are* clumsy this morning," Hannah fretted, retrieving the dropped shuttle and deftly correcting the mismatched threads. But she brushed a rough little birdclaw hand over the bowed head. "You'd better lie down a while, I'll put Salome to the weaving."

Her kindness unnerved Mary. "No, no, I feel all right. Only the love I feel for you and—and for others, seems very close to the surface today. I want to laugh and to cry over nothing. The spilled flour, the tangled threads, I want there to be harmony in all things. When two people grind the flour that makes the bread of life together—they should never be pulling against each other instead. And the loom, the patterns interwoven on the loom—"

Puzzled, Hannah saw that Mary's eyes were luminous and wet. "If only lives could themselves weave smoothly in and out, joining and strengthening each other instead of so often tangling and breaking apart."

Her mother gave a short uncomfortable laugh. "Truly I do think you should lie down and rest," she said. And she turned and gave a brisk, comical little kick to the loom. "This old loom belonged to your father's mother. I'll never forget the miserable hours I struggled over it when I lived with them. Perhaps it would be well to be rid of it, have some carpenter build us a new one. Then you and your sisters will have less cause to weep over tangled threads."

Mary gazed at her, shaken with temptation. Some carpenter. And while they were at it. . . . But no, wait. Take this matter up with her father. Then all would be well.

But now that she had stolen in to where Joachim was sprawled on the cushions for a slight rest after the midday meal, her confidence deserted her. He had roused up, bracing himself on his haunches, scowling as if he hadn't heard aright. He was very tired and sweaty and she saw that she had chosen a bad time.

"Wherefore?" he demanded. "Have you spoken to your mother?"

"No. I haven't dared. You know how she feels about Joseph, she's made it only too plain. For some reason she considers him and his family unworthy even to consider as . . ." Her voice shook, she plucked at the fringed shawl he had thrown across his eyes, curiously ashamed—"as possible relatives."

"No, now, it isn't that she finds them unworthy. It's just that when the time comes there are likelier candidates."

"Likelier in what ways? Surely you can't believe that how much a man owns or even the amount of his knowledge are what make for happiness. Better a dinner of herbs where love is than a fatted ox and hatred with it."

"Yes, yes, there's a proverb for everything. It is also written that children are to obey their parents, particularly to respect their mothers."

Mary let that pass. "You never went beyond the village school, Father, but you've studied, you're wise in the things that matter. You'll never own a camel or a fine house but you've given my mother more important things. Kindness and devotion and . . . love." Her voice broke. It was hard to name it like this in the cold glare of midday. "The kind of love that Joseph and only Joseph is prepared to give me."

Joachim smiled crookedly and locked his blunt fingers behind his head. "Mary speaks out of her youth and inexperience. Living together in peace and joy is not a matter of passions but of patience. It's like nurturing a seed that has been planted, often in unyielding ground— waiting and tending and wondering sometimes if love will ever sprout at all."

Mary said quickly, "Truly that is often the case when parents choose their children's mates. But when love is already full blown between two people the painful waiting is avoided."

"Now, now," he said, startled. Yawning, he turned his back, burrowing deeper into the cushions as if to escape this painful discussion "Why are we speaking of such things? You are still a child and dear to us. And yes, still needed. There's plenty of time."

"Forgive me, Father, but I'm a child no longer. I haven't felt like a child for more than a year. My friends and cousins are betrothed and are being married, while I—for all my mother's foolish boasts, I'm forced to dangle like poor fruit on the vine."

"Poor fruit!" Thumping the pillows, he turned back to her, laughing, but stopped abruptly at the expression on her face.

"I am almost fourteen, Father," she said, "and I have become nubile this day."

"Truly?" He was astounded that she should confide in him. The news should have come from her mother. Embarrassed and touched, his eyes filmed. "Truly?" he muttered again, and passed his hand in a gesture of mute wonder and denial across his jaw. "It seems only yesterday that you were a babe in your mother's arms. Our firstborn," he reflected on the never-ending wonder. "And then riding the ox into the fields with me. Remember, Mary?" He stretched out a hand and awkwardly fondled her wrist. "Remember the little songs and games we used to play?"

"Yes, Father, I remember," she said, trying not to sound impatient. It was all so inconsequential and long ago; he must not think to divert her with such memories. Time was fleeing, he must rouse up and go back into the fields. "But about Joseph, please say that you will bid him join us, and what's more speak to Mother urging her to make him welcome here again."

He got up, grunting, and focused his attention on fastening the leather girdle at his waist. Why, he's stalling, she realized, dismayed. He's trying to think how to put me off without letting me know he's afraid of her too.

"You know we seldom have company except on the Sabbath Eve. And your mother has many children to cook for, Mary."

"Hospitality should not be confined to only one day of the week. Tell her that I will prepare the meal."

"And it's hard to cross her. Remember that she is your mother, to be honored as the commandment says."

"Is she not also your wife, and commanded to obey?"

Both were on their feet now, their glances locked. Joachim sighed heavily. "Mary, Mary—is this matter of such consequence to you that you would come between mother and father to achieve your ends?"

She didn't answer for a second. Unconsciously her hands had come together in a fierce attitude of supplication. She said, "I love both of you, Father, it grieves me to think of hurting either of you. But as you have just reminded me, you and I have been close from the time I was a little girl. While women—two women, alike as we are in our bodies, there is often a great difference in how we feel. If I were to speak out there would be a clashing of swords. There is often a clashing in the air even when I keep my peace," she said regretfully. "But with you I can speak freely."

The words were true, yet she recognized their element of blandishment. "Joseph and I love each other, Father, and it is not a thing sprung up overnight. It has been growing between us for years. But I also love you. And if you tell me to put him out of my heart I will speak of him no more. But if you understand even a little bit how it is with me, then you will at least open your mind and try to see his qualities before you order me to cast him aside."

Joachim stood pondering. The column of sunlight that had slanted through the room was beginning to recede. There was the shrill sound of children's voices coming from the yard. A stray dog seemed to have joined the games. They could hear it barking in a gay frenzy. "I have no objection to Joseph," he said finally. "He is a fine young man. No doubt he would be a good husband. But I have been able to give your mother very little, and she has always taken such pride in you. To make what seems such a poor match for our eldest—I needn't tell you, it would be a sorry blow for her."

"And is my mother's pride of more value to you than my whole life's happiness?"

He shook his head. He drew his hand once more in a gesture of defeat and weariness across his mouth. "It is a hard bargain you drive, Mary. Your way with words is a trap and a snare. But I will do this much for you. I will send Esau down to ask Joseph to come up tonight, and I will tell Hannah to bring forth the best wine."

"Oh, Father, Father!" She flung herself against his chest. "And could we have meat for a change? Could we prepare a kid?"

"Don't press your advantage, we can't spare a kid even if the rabbi would kill it for us."

"A fowl then? Say a duck whose blood has already been drawn, at the market?"

"No, no, no. A fish perhaps, if the peddlers have brought in any that are fit to eat." He thrust her roughly yet amiably aside. "Go now and look after your brothers and sisters, they are quarreling. Quarreling is something that has always sickened me."

Thrusting back his shoulders, Joachim tramped off to find his wife.

III

IT was Joachim who went plodding down the cobbled streets. A great irritability goaded him, together with other emotions he found it hard to sort out. Yet this was no errand for a blind child, as Hannah had made plain. "You must be out of your mind to suggest such a thing!" And he sensed her consternation that their son, sightless and halt, should come groping into the inferior house of Jacob on such a mission. Well then, Joachim had retorted, he'd go himself.

Hannah's protest that this would only lend more significance to what could otherwise be passed off as merely an invitation to discuss a loom, simply made firmer his determination. Just when the loom had entered the discussion he didn't recall, except that Hannah, seeing he was not to be dissuaded, had cleverly worked it in.

"Certainly we can't have Jacob thinking we're so hard put to find suitors for Mary that we would go making advances to any young man. Least of all his son!"

He had refrained from the arguments that sprang to his lips. He had long ago learned that the best way to handle his acrimonious little mate was to let her seem to have her way. Let her prate and scold, he thought with a kind of grudging admiration. So long as he did not stoop to contending with her, he retained his stature as a man and his will prevailed.

Joachim stomped along, his dry red beard bristling in

the sun, dreading his mission, yet feeling an irascible satisfaction in it too. He had a private sympathy for Joseph; he too had been forced to leave the village school at an early age to support his mother and sisters. And though Joachim had been a slow scholar, he loved learning. In a secret part of himself he fancied he'd have made a good rabbi, and had suffered the scorn of his family by poring over the few books he owned.

He particularly loved the Scriptures that spoke with such certainty of the coming of the Messiah. He would come, he would come in all his glory! Perhaps even in Joachim's lifetime. The dream made tolerable this life of toil when you were only robbed for your sweat in taxes. It had been appeased those first raw years of his youth when he had suffered such torments over the unattainable Abigail.

A faint amusement came into his blue inscrutable eyes. *Abigail.* And those distant days when he had believed it would be better to be strung up by his heels by the Romans than never to have her. . . . He remembered the undulant roll of her hips going down to the well; how he would rise up from the shamed bliss of his dreams to watch from the half-moon of his window. And her eyes, round and moist and lush with secrets. The color of ripe grapes, he recalled with a sweet start. Purple, like the grapes they had once tramped together, joyously, both a little drunken from the wine.

Would he have had the courage to kiss her otherwise? . . . The kissing had made it worse. The kissing and the clutching, those few stolen times together. It had seemed that he could not endure it when it was announced that she was being betrothed to a rich landowner.

Joachim remembered only too vividly that stunning pain. Though he wished not to. Not on this fumbling errand to appease and gratify Mary . . . No, now, he had been a dutiful son, loyal, patient, and innately cheerful. Striving to banish all thoughts of Abigail when he had journeyed to Bethlehem with his people and returned, a man betrothed. Bound to a wild little Judean who had become, withal, so dear to him.

Well, but he must set his mind to the business at hand.

Banging somewhat imperiously on the door with the heel of his hand, he stooped and thrust his big shoulders into the shop of Jacob the carpenter. There seemed to be no one about, and he felt again that plaguing irritation. Hannah was right; he was on a fool's mission. Humor Mary if you must, but remember that Jacob's son must not be encouraged.

Sunlight flooded the room, painting stripes of light and shadow across the implements which hung from beams or lay in corners. Some were quite dusty as if long unclaimed, others but half-finished. Joachim ran critical palms over the handles of a plow. The workmanship was good but the metal share was bent. It was a common, almost fond plaint of farmers that if you depended on Jacob your fields would soon be fit for only the crows. He'd rather waste his time on elaborately carved chests and tables for which there was small market. Those who adhered strictly to the Law considered them pagan. ("Thou shalt make no graven image.") Most Galileans were notoriously lax when it came to the Law, but this impiety of Jacob's only further irked the more strait-laced Joachim. Or Jacob would spend hours on the cart of some traveler, who might joke and share the wineskins with him, but never come this way again.

The place smelled of sawdust and chips and curly yellow shavings. Impatiently Joachim sifted its mealy dust through his fingers. Some people could afford to laze the afternoon away, but he had work to do. He was about to leave when he heard the commotion. The shouting and laughter and the frenzied squawking of a hen. In a minute the curtains that led into the adjoining cave parted and the shop became a wild flurry of feathers, children, and flying chips. In hot pursuit of them all was the object of his quest.

Joseph had been laughing when he plunged in, but at sight of Mary's father he sobered. His pleasant face flushed. "Forgive me." He threw back his shoulders, almost imperceptibly his cleft chin jutted. "I'm afraid we didn't hear you enter. As you see we're trying to catch the hen." The bird had flown to a beam just over Joachim's head, where she was scolding them in frenzied clucks. "It was given my father for mending an axle,"

Joseph said. "Since it's my sister's birthday, Mother intends to make it into a stew."

Joachim cringed in his own bones at the youth's embarrassment. Explanations always troubled him. "A birthday celebration, ha?" he said overheartily. Relief quarreled with his vexation at failing Mary, now that he had come. "Well, no matter, since I've only come about a loom. My wife would have you look at the old one to see if it's beyond repair. And we had thought. . . ." He cleared his throat, "Perhaps you'd prefer to come late in the day and be our guest for the evening meal. But no matter," he added hastily, "perhaps another time."

The joy in Joseph's eyes was almost too much to countenance. Joachim looked up. The distraught bird above him was flapping her wings, raining dust down on his tunic. Joachim grabbed her.

"But if the loom needs attention let me give it at once," Joseph said. "My family will excuse me from their celebration."

Joachim handed over the fat protesting hen. "I'm afraid we won't have so royal a feast as you could be enjoying here."

"I wouldn't have the wife or daughters of Joachim trouble themselves over what is served," said Joseph. "The honor of being asked to my lord's house is more than enough."

Joachim winced. Yet the words were so warm, so anxious, yet fraught with such dignity that he stood for a moment regarding Joseph. So this was the object of Mary's desire, he realized in a baffled protesting. He had paid scant attention to the village youths. Like Hannah, he had simply been unwilling to visualize the hour when Mary must leave them. And while fathers did the bargaining when that time came, it was usually the mothers who had subtly but firmly accomplished the first vital weeding out. If Hannah had dismissed this one as unsuitable, he had thought, then so be it.

But now almost angrily the question struck him: Wherefore? Unconsciously he took a step forward, studying Joseph boldly in his zeal to know. The fair young passionate face yet had a steadfast look. The sea-gray eyes that returned his gaze, unflinching, were to be trusted. The mouth, with its full sensitive lips was gentle. The body, hard as an axe, was also supple and neat. Glancing about the untidy shop it bore in upon Joachim: He is shamed by it even now but too loyal and proud to betray it. His own shop will be a good shop, well-ordered and dependable.

"Until this evening then," he said curtly, to cover his astonishment, and turned on his heel.

Striding back up the hill, he veered right, toward the market. It was late in the day; such few fish as there had been were gone and there were never many fowls. Even so, he found a fat duck which he bought and carried determinedly to the home of the rabbi to be blessed and killed. If the family of Jacob could eat flesh when it was not a feast day, he thought, then so could his.

Joseph watched the burly departing figure with a sense of amazement. Even the thrilling encounter with Mary this morning had not had the impact of this visit. He braced himself where he stood in the door. It was an attitude of flight, almost; it was also a position of restraint. For this was more than a bid to the house of the girl he had loved from his earliest memory. It was as if Jahveh himself had stepped down from whatever remote throne he must occupy in the mysterious reaches of heaven, to place a reassuring hand upon his shoulder. To confirm some bargain made with his servant long before.

Then he told himself not to be foolish. Everyone knew that the Lord of Hosts did not hear such private entreaties as Joseph had been making so long. Everyone knew that God was but the vast unknown, nameless yet omnipotent, all-powerful, who in his own good time would deliver The Land once again from bondage—this time forever. But as for the bondage of his poor weak sons to their desires, what was that to him? No, for that one should be a Greek or Roman worshiping at the altars of their all too human deities. Or a heathen Canaanite performing obscene rites before that god whom even a good Jew blushed to mention, Astarte. Jahveh, hope of Israel, was neither friend nor father but fearful master, who had bigger fish to fry. And yet, Joseph could not help it, he had uttered his humble insistent prayers almost from the day he had first become aware of Mary, daughter of Joachim.

At first they had taken the form of sheer grateful adoration. "Praise be to Jahveh for fashioning her for me." Innocent, callow, straightforward, there had not been the slightest doubt. She was his, that radiant little being whose great eyes became so enchanted when he tossed her a ball to catch, or sailed the little boats he had made for her, after a rain. Joseph thought of those early years of his own ingenuousness with a tender incredulity now.

Just when the prayers had turned to desperate imploring he didn't recall. Was it when other boys first began to notice Mary, discuss her beauty among themselves, vie for her hand in the dancing? Even then, though he had been assaulted by a fierce jealous sense of protest, he had been fortified by the almost serene conviction that no outer force could alter: God had given her to him. Yet he had begun to pray with a kind of stubborn assertion tinged with anxiety: "She is mine. Oh, Lord, surely that is your intention." (He almost said, "You promised.") "One day she will truly be mine."

Yet God did not communicate with his yearning children. If the Lord did not send down plagues and scourges upon the enemy as he had done in Egypt, or call forth his promised Messiah to spare his tortured people now, why should he heed the voice, however desperate, of one young man in love?

Joseph thought of the massacres that prostrated Jerusalem under the vassal king, Herod. The outrages that happened sometimes even in outlying provinces. Romans were seldom seen in Nazareth, but when they were, in their red cloaks and flashing helmets, people fled from their uncleanness and the terror they revived. For who could forget the horde that had once come charging through the streets, whipping dissenters and suspects before them to be crucified?

Even then Jahveh had stopped his ears and averted his eyes. If he saw or heard the rearing steeds that trampled the crowds, the neighing, the screaming, the blood and dust and the vileness—the girls dragged from their houses like little white kicking rabbits to be violated in the ditches—if he had cared about the crosses where men writhed in agony, then Jahveh gave no sign.

All this Joseph knew. Yet he could not leave off wrestling with that dear dread figure, as if to wring from it some visible warrant that his life's wish was to be realized.

Outwardly he had remained composed. He had evaded the issue of marriage with ancient quips and ironic jokes about its miseries. "Besides, I'm so poor who'd have me?" Whistling, he had gone on carving the spindles of the cradle he was building for a well-to-do bridegroom friend.

"Also, you're waiting for someone, isn't that it?" his father prodded. Jacob's merry, sly little eyes shone in their darkish pouches. "If Mary, daughter of Joachim, was old enough we'd see, you'd be anxious enough even if it meant lying with her in the storage cave."

The image, so stirring yet so unspeakably put, filled Joseph with a blind fury. But his mother's words, however kindly, were almost more insufferable. "Well, if that's what's keeping you from marrying and bringing grandchildren into this house, my son, I fear you'd best forget it. Hannah sets great store by that girl."

Timna hesitated where she sat sewing in the company of her men, there amongst the pleasant litter of sweet smelling cypress shavings, planks and tools. She was a large-faced white-haired woman, bland, serene, undisturbed by what people said about her chaotic household or even her husband's weakness. For she knew that he couldn't help it; it was like a sickness. It sprang from some secret sickness of the spirit that no one else suspected beneath that jocular exterior, and that no man could heal. She bore it with the same quiet courage that she had borne the loss of three children. In other ways Jacob made them happier than most. His effusive love, the contagion of his humor. She was a self-assured, benevolent woman.

"As well Hannah should be," Timna added, biting a thread. "That dear child came late and has been a blessing ever since. I don't wonder that Hannah might well want to cling to her."

Jacob leaned on his saw. "What about Joachim?" he

blustered. "What about grandchildren to brighten their old age? He sets great store by Mary too, but he'd find it a sorry thing to have a spinster on his hands."

Timna sewed on, gentle, generous, not wishing to hurt others, unaware of the hurt she was dealing her son. "All Nazareth knows that Mary's a choice flower. If she's not plucked early it is only because such was her parents' choice. And when they do betroth her it will surely be to someone who has more to offer than we can." Troubled, she gazed at Joseph's stricken face. "Son, I beg you—if indeed you do have any such intentions, put her out of your heart. I've heard it said at the well that Reb Levi is going to speak to Joachim for Cleophas. Also that the parents of Abner aren't loath to consider her for him."

Joseph's eyes blazed. "Am I then so poor a thing in the sight of my parents? Do you think that either of them would make Mary a better husband?"

"No, now, you know better than that," protested Timna. "That's not the issue."

"Your mother's right," said Jacob with his usual quick amiable resignation. "We're as well born as the parents of Mary. Why, we all come from the royal stock of David," he declared, vaguely marveling. "But for some reason they think awfully well of themselves, those people. They've set their sights high. Now me, I wouldn't care to compete with either Reb Levi or Reb Saul in this matter. It would only mean further humiliation for this family and for you. Come on now, stop brooding and wasting your time." Playfully he jabbed the outraged flesh of his son. "You're a strapping youth and fair in the eyes of all the maids."

"Yes, and estimable in the eyes of their parents," said his wife.

"Choose someone else, it won't be hard," Jacob went on. "Take Leah, her cousin. She's been mooning after you. Just say the word and we'll ask."

Joseph could bear it no longer. Blindly, scarcely knowing what he was doing, he had flung off his leather apron and run out into the streets . . . *Abner*. The thought of that cold thin-necked creature ever laying his skeletal hands on Mary filled Joseph with such revulsion that he almost retched. *As for Cleophas.* He caught up a rock and hurled it savagely over a precipice.

The handsome face taunted him. The heavy-lidded eyes, the seductive, gaily jeering mouth. Again Joseph heard the remark that Cleophas had made about Mary one Sabbath on the way to the synagogue. It had set Joseph at his throat. One minute friends, the next murderous enemies, they had rolled in the dust, dressed though they were in their best garments, battering each other. Then, panting, both were on their feet. and Cleophas, with an expression more of surprise than anger, was staring at the blood that spurted from his splendid purpling nose.

"Just look what you've done to my robe," he'd scolded, grinning. "Now I'll have to go home and change." He glanced about, alert for his reputation. "Fortunately nobody saw us. And for her sake I won't speak of this if you won't."

"For *her* sake!" Joseph had cried, furious. "What of the vile thing you said about her?"

"Oh, that. Come now, don't tell me you haven't thought of her that way yourself?" Suave even in his dishevelment, he had mopped his face with the skirt of his striped linen robe. "Or is it milk that flows in your veins instead of good red blood?" Cleophas laughed again richly, flinging out his hands—"Of which I seem to have no lack!"

"What you lack is a decent tongue."

"True, true," Cleophas admitted cheerfully. "My tongue has been colored, no doubt, by the talk I hear in the ports of Tyre and Sidon. But I assure you I meant no offense either to you or to our pure and beautiful Mary." He had even slapped a jaunty hand on Joseph's taut shoulder. "And now let's go before the gossips come along and ruin all of us."

His rival's casualness only increased Joseph's indignation. From that day the mere thought of the merchant's son had been enough to make his fists clench. And now it was he, even he, his mother said, who was about to seek Mary's hand.

In his frenzy Joseph had paced the fields and forests, scarcely knowing where he went. But in late afternoon,

thirsty and spent, he had flung himself down under a tere-
binth tree and slept. And when he awoke it had been with
a curious sense of release. The sun was setting, laying a
banner of flaming orange across the sky. Overhead a
hawk was lazily wheeling. He could smell the dry toasty
wheat that rusted just beyond the fence, and the rich
black earth beneath his head. He could hear the crunch
and rattle of stones as farmers trudged the roads that
led home, sickles over their shoulders. His tongue was
dry, his bones stiff, but the feverish thirst with which
he had dropped to the ground was gone. One hand
over his eyes, he lay staring into the vast blueness, now
turning to lavender, and considering his lot.

His parents were right. He was in no position to compete with anyone. To press his cause would only result
in failure and humiliation for his family, and distress to
Mary's. For several years, in crisp, firm little ways,
Hannah had been making her attitude plain. She never
returned his mother's offerings in kind—cakes or flowers
or wild honey. She managed to hasten her children off
when they would have lingered to mingle with those of
Jacob after services. And seldom had Joachim brought any
business to his shop. A subtle yet very real barrier
had separated them, a barrier as forbidding as if Mary's
people had been wealthy and highborn.

"Is it never to be then?" he demanded of the empty,
uncaring space above. He searched it vainly a moment
for some sign. And Joseph's eyes were wet, in part for the
immutable loss of Mary, but in part for the loss of his
faith. He thought with shame and bitterness of the long
communion that in his desire he had conjured up. He
had given himself the answers all the time! Now he
saw that the true worshiper does not expect answers. The
days were long past when God summoned Moses up onto
a mountain, or revealed himself through a burning bush
or a ladder of stars. This was a new age and a new era,
where the true believer did not expect such evidence from
Jahveh. Least of all should he expect personal favors.

"So be it."

He watched a lizard dart up the tree, its iridescent
blue whip of tail quivering. He sat up and plucked a
leaf from a low bough and bit down hard upon it. Its

taste was bitter, like life. But it existed. It was. As he was and would continue to be. Even without her who had gradually become his primary excuse for being, he would survive. But how? How? The prospect was scalding.

His first thought was escape. The desert monastery of the Essenes, holy men who fasted and prayed the better to draw near and know the unknowable one. Joseph winced. As he had bitten the leaf so he set his teeth against his own brown, salty flesh. He did not want to deny it, to beat or starve it into submission, he wanted it to be fulfilled as a man must be fulfilled. He wanted it to live and to beget further life. But if he was not to have her, his heart's true wife?

He flung himself over, brought his fists down savagely upon the hard unyielding earth. "Oh, God, my God, if this be thy will then so be it. Thy will be done!"

And then the peace of his first awakening came over him and he lay quiet once again. He lay regarding his lifted hands. Scarred though they were he knew their strength and skill. They could fashion things, good worthy instruments for the business of living. Plows and wagons and yokes, benches and tables. For he would prove that celibacy need be no disgrace. He would build the houses and furnishings for the married; some day he might even build the cupboards and railings in the synagogues. And that would be his manner of worshiping the Lord of Life. He would be a good man, a good carpenter, better than his father, better than anyone perhaps in all Galilee. Such would be his aim and his purpose, his method of making amends to the God Jehovah for having dared in his brash and passionate youth to presume that God had somehow made with him a covenant.

He had risen that day many months ago and brushed the earth and leaves from his tunic and come back into the village curiously cleansed and freed. His parents, sensing some change in him, did not badger him further. They were strangely quiet about Mary, though the news had gotten about: her betrothal was not imminent after all. Evidently it was as Timna had predicted, no suitor was considered up to Hannah's expectations. At least Joachim had found excuses to put them off.

Relieved though Joseph was, he had gone on hammering nails into boards, hammering his own hopes back into subjection. For he must turn his thoughts elsewhere, avoid her at all costs. He knew there would be others; the hour had merely been postponed. He must practice the detachment and self-control he would need to endure it when it arrived.

But now—this day. . . . Staggered, he watched the departing form of Joachim. And it was as if the thick shoulders in the faded brown tunic, the staff that almost truculently struck the stones, were bathed in a small burning cloud of glory, belying his hard-won knowledge that no more did Jahveh mingle in the affairs of men.

Joseph's face was slightly dazed as he turned back into the shop.

His father waddled in, rosy and puffing from his own merry chase of the hen. "What ails you, son?" he asked. "You look as if you'd just seen a vision."

"Perhaps I have," Joseph said. "That was Mary's father. I have been bade to his house to share the evening meal with them."

IV

THE meal was almost ready.

The bread had been baked and was cooling, the table was set. Anxiously Mary surveyed the bowls of curds, the dishes of dates and raisins, the squat earthen mugs of wine. In a few weeks there would have been fresh vegetables from the garden, she thought with regret, but no matter, the duck would compensate. Its aroma roasting on the spit outside intensified her affection for her father. Wiping her hands, she raced into the yard to turn it once again. The fat dripped into the fire, smoking and hissing, the flesh was turning a golden brown.

"Matthew!" she summoned. "Come keep an eye on the duck, don't let it burn. Esau, your sense of smell is keen, you warn him when it's ready to be turned."

She flew inside, glancing at the table with a start of pride—its white linen cloth, and the best goatskin rugs and cushions which she had spread down beside it. Then she climbed the ladder to the loft to freshen herself. But first she pulled aside the drapery and looked into her mother's room. Hannah lay huddled on her pallet, one hand flung over her eyes.

Mary tiptoed in. "Is your head any better, Mother? Let me sponge it for you."

She knelt and dipped a napkin into the basin of water and vinegar that stood on the floor. But her mother turned away. "No, don't bother yourself. You have more important things to do."

"Nothing is more important than the health of my mother. It grieves me to know that you're suffering."

"It's nothing," Hannah said tightly. "There are worse pains."

Yes, worse pains, Mary thought. Worse pains than this sourness that had come between them again and hung as sharp as the vinegar in the room. But no, she would not let herself be troubled, not tonight.

She sprang up, since Hannah would not accept her ministrations. What if Joseph arrived before she'd changed her spattered tunic or brushed her hair! She caught her breath before the enormity of his coming; its miracle sweetened the fetid air. "Then forgive me, Mother, if there's nothing more I can do I'll go to prepare for my father's guest."

Hannah lowered her hand, gazed at her daughter, so excited, so flushed. "Your father's guest," she said drily. "In the middle of the week, not even the Sabbath, and flesh roasting. A *duck*. And you speak of your father's guest."

"Would that he were to be your guest too," Mary said. "Would that you felt like rising and freshening yourself and coming down to greet him."

"I'm ill." Hannah turned her face once more to the wall. "There are hammer blows on my head and nails in my heart, and nobody cares. Neither you nor your father. Nothing matters but the coming guest."

"I care, Mother. I'd stay with you if I could. But since I can't let me call Salome."

"No, no, go on. If I can't have you I don't want anyone. Go and make yourself fair," she said. "For your *father's* guest!"

Mary bathed swiftly from her own basin of soft cistern water. She longed to linger. Her body was hot and sweaty from the rushing around. She longed to lavish on it the care she had given the food, to annoint and perfume it and bid it be still for the coming of Joseph. But he might be striding up the hill even now, and the water for his own handwashing wasn't drawn. Thank goodness the cistern was full from the rains, but this very water in which she was sponging was brackish and gnat-filled. It would never do for Joseph—was there enough clear well water for the purpose in the jugs?

And the children—she could hear them shrieking as they pranced around the duck. What if they upset the spit and it fell into the coals? It might be burning—there was almost too crisp a smell of it coming through the window slit.

She kicked aside her stained tunic and pulled a fresh one of pale blue over her head. Its cool touch against her skin was calming. It helped to stifle the resentment that had come out of nowhere and had been smouldering, gaining strength, until now it too seemed to be burning deep in her vitals. This is my mother's house and these are her children; wherefore is it that she leaves me alone to cope with them when I have already prepared the meal? No, no, my mother is ill. . . . But she had to bite her quivering lips. For it was surely tonight's event that had brought Hannah's illness on. And if one visit was enough to drive Hannah to her bed, what of more serious demands?

A sudden desolation came over Mary. She stood very still for a moment, giving herself over to the hopelessness. Then she brushed and bound up her damp dark hair and went below.

He came early, in his eagerness. He arrived before Joachim was in from the fields. The children, who had been perched on the step watching for him, ran shouting the news to Mary, who had brought the duck indoors. It was indeed burned on one side, she saw, stricken. Well, no matter, she would carve the other side to be served the men; she and the young ones could eat the bitter side later. A flat dull resignation had replaced her earlier nervousness. He was here. She had assaulted him brazenly on a public street this morning and then bullied her father into inviting him, and now dutifully he had appeared. Only to find her mother absent and her father still not home. It served her right for her folly, this humiliation that seemed symbolized in the charred, half-ruined duck. But since there was no undoing any of it, go now and get it over with.

Head high, she went to greet him. "Peace be with you," she said. "And please forgive my mother's absence. She bids you enjoy the hospitality of this house, which she regrets she can't extend to you herself since she is ill."

He murmured something—she was too troubled by her subterfuge to heed. And the water, here came Esau proudly bearing the basin and jug, his sweet face wearing a bright fixed smile, his twisted leg hobbling carefully so as not to spill it. He must have strained it through a cloth, she noticed gratefully, for it seemed clean and clear. A sudden rejoicing sped through her, a blessed recklessness. Joseph had come, he was truly here. He was standing before her, washing his hands, taller than she had believed, remote and grave with his tense cleft chin, and even more fair.

She longed to search his eyes, to see if his mood matched that of the morning, but she did not dare. Instead, she fastened her gaze upon his hands. How large, how rough and fiercely beautiful were the hands of a man. A little forest of black hairs grew on Joseph's long fingers, sturdy and brittle like the fragrant seas of brushwood that ran triumphant over rocks and fields. Look at me! they seemed to boast—both the brush and the bristling hairs. I will survive despite drought and wind and battering rains, I am tough, I am strong! But his nails were blunted and bruised; there were callouses from the hammer and saw. A mute pity went through Mary. Vaguely she sensed and was awed by the tremendous burden of being a man.

Even as she was thinking this, she noticed that the hands were not quite steady. Joseph was trembling. In astonishment and pain for him she saw that he sloshed the water on the floor and dropped the towel.

"Forgive my clumsiness." Joseph bent to retrieve it, silently cursing himself. To be here with her, a guest at her father's table and have his very limbs betray him. His suffering gaze met Mary's. Was she laughing at him or trying to console him? Impossible to tell for she turned abruptly away, startled by the voice behind her.

"Peace be with you, Joseph. Here, don't use that towel, we have more." Hannah stood there, holding out another. Her small sunken eyes were distant and chilling, her mouth tight for all its courteous words.

She had caught Joseph at his worst, the awkward groping for the dropped linen, the strong assertive face gone scarlet with embarrassment. And the hands that had so moved Mary—she was newly conscious of their scars. But the main thing was that Hannah had risen. She had put on fresh garments and twisted her hair into a hard little knot and come down.

"I'm glad you're feeling better, Mother," Mary gasped. And scarcely knowing what she was doing, she snatched the abandoned towel and ran with it. Outside she leaned limp against the wall for a moment, the scrap of cloth pressed against her cheek. It was still warm from his touch, it bore the marks of his hands. Oh, let her father come soon and make Joseph truly welcome, and let her mother be in an amiable mood after all, kindly and entertaining the way she could be if she wanted. An amused tenderness came over Mary. She might have known that her mother would join them, if only because Hannah couldn't bear to miss anything.

There now, her father was coming along the path from the olive grove. The sun had already vanished behind the mountains, but for a moment before the darkness fell its scarlet enflamed the sky. And against it, between the shimmering silver of the trees and the small crouched shed she saw him and the ox in silhouette. Tired beasts both of them, heavy and stolid, pushing hopefully toward the evening's rest. And wonder and gratefulness flooded her afresh, akin to the wrench of awed pity she had felt at sight of Joseph's hands.

Stuffing the little towel impulsively into her bosom, she ran to help her father with the ox. "Oh, I'm so glad to see you. Joseph is here and Mother's feeling better and now surely all will go well."

In the house Joseph sat playing with the children while Hannah rattled bowls and vessels and darted about in a burst of perverse animation, correcting the meal. She snatched off a dish of dates that seemed to her too dry and added more curds. Where were the onions? No meal was complete without onions! She thumped and rearranged cushions. As for the duck, the near-tragedy that had befallen that rare indulgence struck her as both fitting and devastating. How had they let it burn? "I can't turn my back a minute. Esau, Salome, somebody—stop those children from clambering all over our guest."

"Oh, but I'm used to children. Remember, there are even more of them at our house." Joseph caressed the curly fluff that covered the head of three-year-old Judith. It was like Mary's; it too would strive to escape its braids some day. His eyes sought hers where she knelt by the hearth. "I love children." And the words, however open, bore a message for her alone.

Joachim had come in and washed himself. He greeted the guest cordially but with a trace of something restrained, vaguely on guard. The two of them sat down while Mary and her mother served the food. The silence was uncomfortable at first as they dipped their bread, each groping, Mary sensed painfully, to find something to say to each other. Then gradually their voices rose above the click and rattle of the bowls. The gruff, weary and opinionated nasal of Joachim, and the respectful golden tones of Joseph, discussing the subjects on which men could always grow heated—taxes, tributes, and the latest atrocities of Herod.

"A man in my father's shop brought word that he's not only still torturing and murdering people around Jerusalem, he's put another of his own sons to death."

"Good riddance," Joachim said grimly. "They're all a nest of vipers. How can they help it—the issue of a man who's neither a Roman nor a true Jew? An Idumaean," he said with vast derision. "A circumcised Arab."

"Even so, there are some who claim he's done a good deal for us," Joseph found himself saying. "He's restored the Temple, and rebuilt our ruined cities. And he's kept the peace."

"Peace!" Joachim exploded. "You call this peace, this milking us dry to adorn those cities, build his heathen palaces and theatres and Coliseums? This bloody tyranny?"

"At least it's not civil war," Joseph persisted, against his better judgment, while Mary despaired. "As it was when we first appealed to Pompey for help in settling our own terrible conflicts. That's the irony of it," Joseph said earnestly, "that our conquerors are here by invitation. Because we didn't have the wisdom or unity as a people to settle our own affairs. Maybe we deserve them."

Joachim stared at him, astounded, grudgingly impressed. It was indeed a smudge on the glorious history of Israel, that ancient feud between the Pharisees and the high priest Jannaeus, who in his own way was as much a monster as Herod. A man who had feasted with his concubines while eight hundred crucified prisoners were forced to witness the slaughter of their own families as they hung dying. And after his death, the mortal combat between his sons, tearing the country asunder. Little emphasis was put upon this sorry fact when teaching the young. If people knew about it they submerged it in the larger fact of their own cruel suffering under Rome.

Restraining his mild, irked approval, Joachim carved another choice slice of duck and put it on Joseph's plate. "Surely you aren't defending this rape of our country?"

"No," Joseph hastened to assure him, "only trying to get it in perspective. And this madman who's trying to represent both our people and the heavy fist of Rome. When will Rome itself realize that's exactly what he is? Insane. A man who'd murder his own wife, drown his own nephew, his children. . . ."

Joachim grunted. "Yes. As the joke goes—it's better to be Herod's pig than his son, for at least he makes the gesture of not eating pork!" He leaned forward, liking the youth who did not sit in mute agreement, however anxious he surely was to make a good impression. "And Rome. Do you think she'll ever spit out this vassal and send us a better successor?"

"He can't last long," said Joseph. "He's not only possessed, they say he's dying of some awful affliction. . . ." *Herod*, he thought wretchedly, perspiring. Why had he ever brought up the ugly subject? Instead of being tactful and diffident before an elder he'd blundered, tried to overcome his nervousness by saying far too much. At least he might have hit upon something more pleasant for this meal at Mary's table.

"But his successor," Joachim prodded. "Do you think Judah will ever enjoy better days under any Roman emperor?"

Joseph hesitated before the challenge. "There is only one real hope for the land of Judah," he said. "And that is the coming of our own ruler. Even he that has been promised us so long."

"And you believe in this Messiah? That he will come soon?"

"As a good Jew I believe in the prophets who have told us that one day he will come. But when?" Joseph made a helpless gesture. "We've endured so much for so many generations, and each time the people thought they could endure no more. Just as we feel we've reached the limit of our endurance now. Surely if the Lord truly intends to send us a deliverer the time is ripe, for our travail is as great or worse than at any time since our forefathers left Babylon."

"Maybe the Lord is testing our patience as the prophets also warned," Joachim said. "Making us wait until we are worthy of our own deliverance. Wait until we have come to understand more of the true nature of Jahveh before the Messiah comes."

"But how shall we know him when he does?" Now it was Joseph who demanded an answer. "How can we be sure? The false prophets, those who honestly think themselves the Saviour—we have seen what happens to them, and to the poor souls who in their desperation follow them."

Joachim nodded and wiped his fingers. "We'll know," he said. "The Lord will give us a sign."

It depressed Mary to hear them, and the dumb compassion rose in her once more. Surely it was hard enough to have to provide for a woman and her children, to know that upon your shoulders rested the responsibility for their food and shelter and their spiritual welfare, as well as the responsibility to keep them safe within the Law. But worse, it seemed to her, was this cross that each of them also began to shoulder as they approached adolescence—this awful concern for their whole people, Israel.

Boys who had been pleasant playmates became bowed

with it; their eyes became enflamed when they spoke of
it. It was almost an obsession. And it was true, all true,
these things they said. Once when she was small her own
village had been ravaged. Joachim had reached his family
in time and carried them off into the hills, but she would
never forget the blood in the streets when they returned,
or the acid odor of burning wood. Worse were the crucifixions. Zealots who dared to defy the power of Rome,
false prophets such as Joseph had mentioned. Whether it
was at that time or later Mary couldn't remember and
didn't want to, but Hannah, in a fierce mixture of
curiosity, drama, and protest, had taken her to one. A
spectacle so horrifying that she had fled screaming
through the crowds and dreamed of it ever since.

Sometimes she could still hear the man's sick yells,
pleading with them to take him down, crying pitifully that
he couldn't stand it; and most ghastly of all, the apologies
to the Romans, to all Israel, for realizing too late that he
must have been mistaken or God would not have let such
a thing happen to him. Though she had muffled her ears
with cushions and beat her head against the wall, she
could hear him long after she reached home. And she
sometimes heard him still.

Yet there was this about being a woman. A woman
could speak of other things. Because, for all man's
greater responsibility, his superior strength and knowledge,
it was through a woman that the deliverer would come.
From a virgin, the Scriptures said. A young woman.
Mary shuddered softly, newly conscious of her ripened
body and its sweet weight of love.

And he would heal all these bloody wounds, the
prophets taught. Every injustice would be avenged. The
Romans would retreat in disgrace. The kingdom, so wide
in the days of Solomon, would expand again. He would
reign in majesty and infinite wisdom, and all the world
would recognize that the despised but proud and mighty
Jews were right, theirs was the true religion. Soon, soon!
"Oh, Lord, how soon?" the mobs kept crying—along
with the priests in the Temple, and the rabbis in the
synagogue. The cry was a ceaseless supplication. And
God in his mystery gave no response. But Mary knew.
All women knew—and this too was what gave them a cer-

tain serenity, detachment and power over the more impassioned men. They knew that it would not be long.

The men stood up, brushing away the crumbs. It was time for the women to clear away the cups and bowls and bring the children and sit down. Mary kept her eyes averted as Joseph moved past to follow her father to the roof, for the night was unseasonably warm. They would continue their discussion under the stars. But she could feel his presence strongly, and she knew without even lifting her gaze that his whole being yearned toward hers.

Later, stepping into the yard to empty the dishwater, she could hear the voices continuing overhead. "The Sanhedrin has no power. . . ." "The effrontery, to put a golden eagle on the very Temple to mock us, and putting the torch to the people who tried to remove it. . . ." An affectionate exasperation shook her. Oh speak of something else! Speak of youth and love and marriage, speak of me. . . . The towel still lay cradled between her breasts. She could feel it like a caress as she bent to toss the water over the last red coals of the spit. They hissed and sputtered and sent a plume of white smoke coiling toward the roof.

For a moment she stood watching it, aware of him who might notice and look down upon her, small and desirable in the firelight as she performed her task of drying out the vessel. Slowly, in a sweet lassitude of love, she moved back into the house that was still redolent with the scent of food and the flickering oil lamps. She wished that Joseph knew that the towel nestled against her heart, that she would sleep with it beneath her cheek this night.

Sleep was a long time claiming her, however. At first she was too excited by the evening, whose wretchedness in the beginning seemed to enhance its gradually mounting harmony. She lay reenacting it, from the first shattering news, "He's here!" on through his every gesture, every word. Joseph's charm with the children, the gentleness of his manners at table (surely not lost on Hannah). The very assertiveness she had deplored seemed to have won Joachim's respect. And the way he'd responded to her mother when the women drew shawls about their shoulders and joined the men on the roof.

Warmed by food and wine and the certainty that only by her appearance had the evening been saved, Hannah had unbent. She had in fact become expansive, telling impish tales of her childhood that made Joseph's laugh ring out. He had matched them with stories of his own. "I remember the inn," he said. "Though I was only about three years old when my parents moved from Bethlehem."

"That's right, you were born there," Hannah exclaimed. "I'd forgotten. The City of David," she added—and this too seemed to confirm some subtle new bond between them, reminding her as it did that they were all of David's stock.

Everyone was smiling by the time farewells were being said. Hope flared as high in Mary as the torch which Joachim insisted on handing to Joseph to light his way down the dark winding streets. How foolish her earlier apprehensions, she thought. And how infinitely fortunate that first incredible impulse to seek out Joseph this morning, despite the shameless way she had hurled herself at him.

But even as Mary lay marveling, the muffled voices came to her from beyond the curtains. She lay stiff, scarcely daring to breathe. Her limbs, aglow a moment before, began to chill. Her parents were quarreling. In whispers that blurred their words, yet only made more appalling the impact of those she heard.

"No, no, he's not right for her, no matter how pleasant he is. That bright nature—it's like his father's. Light without substance, that may brighten a window but never cook a meal."

"You misjudge him, Hannah. He has a very serious side as well. Didn't you hear our discussion of Israel? He is deeply concerned."

"Ha, all men are concerned. It's the fashion to be concerned, small good that it does any of us. Let men concern themselves with their wives and children and how to provide for them. Especially if they come seeking our daughters in marriage."

"Our fate as providers depends upon the fate of Israel. When taxes take the very bread from the mouths of our families."

"Don't think to divert me from Joseph. Like father like son. He comes from a poor household."

"It's a happy household, Hannah. I was there today and felt their joy in one another. Even the children—"

"Did you also feel their ribs?"

"The ribs of Jacob's children are no thinner than those of mine. And there is other food, Hannah. The spirit too needs food, the food of love."

"Love!" Her voice broke rawly. Accused, "You speak as if there is small love in the house I have made for you."

"No, no. How you twist things. I am only trying to show you that Joseph's background is not so impoverished as you think. Love compensates for many things. And while it's customary and right that parents arrange such matters, how much better for everyone when two people love and want each other from the very beginning."

"Unlike us?" Hannah challenged. "You didn't love me. I was a poor bargain picked by your mother for heaven knows what reason, and a sorry disappointment in your bed."

"Must we rake up old miseries?" Joachim begged. "I loved you almost at once."

"No. No, you only pitied me."

"Yes, that too, but pity is close to love, Hannah, and in protecting you, taking care of you, you know how much I came to love you."

"There was another whom you loved before me. Your sisters told me. A woman named Abigail. Would it have been better had you married her instead?"

"You'll never know how thankful I am that I didn't."

"Then so it is with Mary. One day she'll thank us."

"Not if we give her to someone she hates and fears. Joseph loves her deeply, Hannah, and she's beside herself with love for him. He'll make her happy. She knows him so well, she'd never be afraid of him as you were afraid of me." Joachim's rough hand stroked the thin gray hair. He attempted to draw her spindly body closer, but she twisted away. "That was the hard part, Hannah, that you were so terrified of my love, when I only wanted to be united with you and to give you joy as well. Think,

Hannah, think how much sooner we might have found happiness had it been with us as it is with them, had you loved me from the very start."

"How do you know?" Hannah demanded. "Joseph, yes—the way he's hung about her has sickened me for years. But Mary," she protested, "she's young, she's given little thought to marrying. And if she has, certainly she'd prefer to do better than this."

"You're wrong. She loves him so much she will have no other man."

"How do you know?" Hannah cried again.

"She told me."

Hannah jerked upright. "Told *you?* I'm her mother. Why hasn't she spoken of this to me?" She began to shake with dry wild sobbing. "Am I then so poor a mother that my own daughter confides such matters to her father's ears instead of mine?"

"Perhaps she felt it would hurt you too much, knowing the high ambitions you have for her."

"And I'm right! She could have any man in Nazareth."

"Examine your conscience, Hannah. Is it truly your daughter's happiness that drives you, or only your pride?"

Hannah didn't answer. She had flung herself back upon the pillow and given herself over to the sobbing that ripped through the curtains, beating upon Mary who had crept from her own bed, past her sleeping sisters, and now stood at the little window staring up at the clouds that quilted the sky.

"Hush, you'll wake the children," Joachim ordered. His voice was stern, to keep at bay the assault upon his senses that her tears always made. "Hush now, be still." He patted the heaving shoulders, bony and sharp under the thin shift. "One further thing you must consider. Have you thought how it would be should we give Mary to someone like Cleophas? Surely we are far more humble in the sight of Reb Levi than the family of Jacob is to us. Do you think that once Mary and Cleophas were wed we'd be welcome in their fine house? Or the homes of their kinsmen?"

"Mary would never consider herself too good for us."

"As the wife of Cleophas she would belong to his family, not ours. And she would obey him. I've thought about this a long time, Hannah, and even if it weren't for Joseph I wouldn't give our daughter to anyone as spoiled as Cleophas. We would lose her. And we would lose her just as much if we gave her to Abner."

He waited for some reply, but she was too far gone in her grief. His reasons could not penetrate this damp devastating curtain she had thrown up between them, he thought angrily. Nonetheless, he drove stubbornly on. "If Abner succeeds as predicted, he would go to Jerusalem and Mary with him. Except for the annual pilgrimages we would never see her."

Ah, but it was no use. No use trying to talk to her when she became like this. He rose from her side and crept downstairs and outside to the ladder to mount to the roof, where his big feet paced up and down, up and down.

Mary could hear their dull thudding overhead, jarring the ceiling, quivering through her own flesh. Their tremors joined force with the sound of her mother's weeping. And it was as if she were being rent asunder between them. "Jahveh forgive me for bringing such strife into this house," she whispered. She reached out and pulled back the dry tangle of vines, the better to see the moon. It had risen late and was running, running, face half-averted, yet smiling at some secret within its own white burning heart. And the clouds pursued it, their effulgent veils trailing seductively across the mystery of its shining, or falling away like garments cast aside. And winking in and about and all around the lovely race were the stars.

Steady, singing night sounds came up to her; dew had stirred up the fragrance of the earth, the trees, the almond blossoms. She was dazed and shaken. It seemed to her incredible that there should be sorrow and dissension on such a night. It was too beautiful. God's world was simply too beautiful to countenance ugliness and agony, whether it be on the epic scale of Israel's prostration, or the sheer stabbing torments of the human heart.

And it seemed strangest of all that love could be the cause. Hatred, yes—it was hatred that accounted for the cruelties of Rome. But love! . . . Her parents loved her, both of them, just as she loved them. And she loved

Joseph and he loved her. And yet in the strange contortions of human affairs, somehow this mixture of love had given birth to the anguish that now assailed them all.

Without realizing it, she still clutched the small towel that Joseph had dropped. Now she used it to wipe her wet eyes, and pressed it an instant against her mouth. Then she lifted it up in a little gesture of sacrifice. "Jahveh forgive me," she whispered again. "If it be thy will that I think no more of Joseph, let me know, and let me be resigned."

There was no answer. The stars continued to dance and blaze in a fashion at once friendly and remote. There was naught but the dry rattle of the vines in the breeze, the soughing and gentle threshing of the palms and the olive trees beyond. Sometimes, when she was very young, she had felt such an intensity of communion with the unknown, inconceivable presence, that it had seemed to her that she had actually heard it speak. "Mary . . . Mary! . . ." Even at times as if a majestic yet infinitely tender hand had touched her hair, her cheek. Enthralled, eager, innocent, she had rushed to confide these experiences to Hannah, who only looked dismayed.

"Don't be deceived," her mother had warned. "You have an unusually vivid imagination. See that you learn to discern between that which is only pretense or a dream."

Yes, to distinguish the true from the false. To know the actuality from the dream. Yet when the first breath one drew in the morning belonged to God, when no morsel was eaten without first asking his blessing, when it was he who ruled not only the universe but the smallest fragment of your life—how was it possible that he did not draw literally close to you at times? Flow in and through and around you, making you even more fully one with him? And that he did not move you so deeply in so doing that you felt his almighty hand upon you, heard the impossible voice speak?

She could not express it. There were no words in which to make this mystery plain. But dumbly, blindly, beautifully, the unreasonable conviction remained. Jahveh did love and communicate with his children. Perhaps only the very young children who were sufficiently pure and simple to be receptive to his touch. Those who were not yet corrupted by the emotions that beset us as we grow older—jealousy and worry and selfishness. And the desires that lashed her even now as she stood by the sill, striving for peace.

Joseph. *Joseph*. . . . But beyond the whitewashed walls her mother wept, and overhead her father paced. . . . She longed to be as a little child again, untouched by the pains of her womanhood. She longed with a sharp nostalgia for the blessed peace of the presence of God. "Thy will be done," she whispered one final time. "In this matter of Joseph, let me only obey."

All was stillness now. She could no longer hear her father's footfalls or her mother's sobs. A lizard scurried up the walls. Somewhere in the cupboard a mouse gnawed. Yet the sounds only accented the quiet of the sleeping house. She could almost hear her own blood pounding as she waited, searching the stars. Her feet on the bare floor were chilled; she was shaking. She knew that she should creep back into bed; yet it seemed that if she but remained here long enough the voice would speak. Only this time God would address her not as a child but as a woman grown.

"Marriages are truly made in heaven. Long before you were conceived, or Joseph son of Jacob, you two were one. This love that you feel for each other is not of your doing but mine. No one shall put you asunder, neither father nor mother nor neighbor nor friend. Go now to your bed and rest."

No . . . the words, however clear, were born of her own desperate longing.

And yet as she turned away a great new peace not unmixed with joy enveloped her. Her trembling ceased. Drawing the body of her little sister up against her to warm herself, Mary fell asleep.

V

TIMNA'S foot paused on the treadle. She cocked her white head the better to hear her son's song. One of the many that had rung through the house since the night he had come loping down the hill, his face almost as bright as the torch that had led him home. She and his father, uneasily waiting, had known both relief and dismay at his expression, so plainly did it signal the course that they would now be forced to take.

"What about the loom?" Jacob had tried to forestall what he secretly dreaded. "Did you fix it?"

"The loom?" Joseph laughed, clapping one hand to his brow. "Nobody mentioned it and I forgot to ask."

"And how is Hannah?" Timna had probed, with apprehension.

"She's well and she asked for you. In fact, she was the liveliest of the lot. You were wrong about her, Mother. All she wants is her daughter's happiness."

"Ah, now now now," Jacob protested. He jutted his plump weak lip. "Surely matters aren't suddenly so changed at Joachim's that they are forced to cast out nets?"

Timna recoiled at his tactlessness, but Joseph was too elated to take offense. "Forced? They wouldn't dare, the nets would break." He was smiling in triumph. "They're just good humble people even as we are, who respect their daughter's wishes. Oh, Father, don't make me wait," he said earnestly after a minute. "I know, that other Jacob, the one you're named for, had to wait fourteen years for his Rachel. But I—I'm afraid I'm not that strong. Forget your fears and your pride and speak to Joachim for me before it's too late."

So it seemed there was no help for it. Though his father had fussed and hedged and put it off for days, in the end he washed himself and donned fresh clothing and submitted to Timna's trimming of his wild cascade of beard. Watching that squat figure go trudging off, Timna's breast ached. Compared to many men he had so little to offer, this dear sorry jocund husband. She was afraid that he would be half-brash, half-apologetic and try to cover his lacks with a joke. And that this would not set well with Mary's parents. Also, despite their own lack of wealth, they managed somehow to convey an air of superiority.

Thanks to Joseph's own savings, Jacob would be able to provide the marriage portion of fifty dinars as the Law required, and little more. For the sake of appearances they would draw out the bargaining; but if Jacob's suit was agreeable then the arrangements should not take long. Yet Timna shared her husband's concern. Baffled and privately hurt by Hannah's long aloofness, now it seemed to her incomprehensible that Hannah should suddenly have so changed.

And yet it seemed equally improbable that Joseph could make such a grave mistake. It had been only this past year that he himself had seemed to be resigned, however grimly, to losing Mary. An abdication, in fact, of all women that was grievous in one still so young and vital. But something had bestirred him now. And while Timna rejoiced, she had also been building defenses against the hour when the cruel blow might fall once more.

Yet when Jacob came bouncing back down the hill he had brought the hoped for news: Joseph was acceptable! The terms would be worked out later. Let the wine be poured, let the family celebrate. And Joseph's songs gladdened the air above the brisk rapping of the hammer and the rhythmic music of the plane, the saws. He carried the children about on his shoulders, his sea-gray eyes shone.

"After the betrothal I'll start building our house. That other cave just beyond the one you use for storage would be a perfect spot. An extra room in case of storm—I could build our house above it. We'd still be near the shop but we'd be alone. . . ." *Alone.* In a house that would be a credit to his darling. He would hew the stones out of the hillside himself and fashion its furnishings. Already he had begun wresting a few stubborn stumps from the fields and hauling them home to be sawed into boards. He was dazed by the wonder and awe of what had befallen: She was to be his, after all. To come unto him as his wife to protect and provide for—and to love.

How could he wait? How could he bear it when he had already waited so long? Yet each step must be taken decorously and in order. The announcement in the synagogue this Sabbath, followed by the receiving of well-wishers that afternoon. The betrothal in the middle of the month on the fourth day of the week. The betrothal, which meant that they were man and wife before the world, linked by law if not yet in the flesh. According to the customs of Galilee, that final union must await the formal wedding, which could be all of a year later, although Joseph was already determined that it must not be that long.

His senses surged blindly ahead toward that blessed hour when he could with honor carry her into his house. How could he endure the interminable months that must lie between the betrothal and the wedding? Yet there was so much to be done. Therein would lie his salvation: the house to be gouged out of the earth and cut into building blocks, the wood to be lovingly carved and joined into the things they would use together—benches, cupboards, a cradle. . . . His hands trembled. He whistled and sang to express and yet to still the mingled glory and fear of his own good fortune. It seemed, at times, almost too much. And yet paradoxically there drove through him the old intense conviction: God had never meant otherwise. God moved in mysterious ways.

Mary awoke that Sabbath morning with a sense of something tremendous impending. What? She could not, for a moment, remember. Then the sweet knowledge smote her: this day Joseph would stand beside her, publicly revealed as her chosen husband.

Not that the village did not suspect. There had been rumors almost from the hour when Joachim had sought the rabbi at such an unlikely time for the ceremonial killing of the duck. Her cousins and others had accosted her with it the following morning. And throughout the negotiations speculation whetted the appetite of the little town. Joseph and Mary! Evidently there was to be a match. But why? How was it that Joseph had suddenly emerged as a suitor, cutting out his astounded rivals? And what of Hannah? the women asked, particularly Mary's aunts. Bursting with curiosity, they had hastened to see her, only to be met with the news that Hannah had taken to her chamber with so severe a headache that she couldn't see anyone.

On the third day, however, Hannah sprang from her couch. "There's much to be done if we're to receive guests in your honor this Sabbath," she announced. And she set about the cleaning and baking with a zeal matched only by her fervor in now convincing Nazareth that, of all its youths, Joseph ben Jacob was the finest. In fact, the only one she would deign consider for her daughter.

Mary could not resist a smile of gentle irony. But so intense was her relief that she banished the memory of her parents' bitter quarrels and these last dark days of sulking.

Hannah was already up, rousing the family, for this day would be full. They must make haste to wash and dress and be about their devotions. She scurried about giving orders, goaded by a wry anticipation. On the strong tide of her vitality they were swept to the synagogue.

The day was bright and sparkling. Light washed the familiar rose red stones of the building, set upon the highest point of the city so that none might look down upon it, its face turned east toward Jerusalem. The light enhanced the multicolored Sabbath robes that flowed into the place of worship like a wind-tossed tulip garden. Mary felt dazzled by it. Leading the younger children, she followed her mother into the women's gallery. A bustle of interest followed her; she could feel her own beauty, quickened and enhanced by love.

Hannah was beside her, eyes lively, in proud defiance. Below them were the men in their fringed prayer shawls; the women relegated to second position and yet above them behind their wooden screen, like angels smiling down. Regarding the men who were so mighty, had such power, and yet were as nothing, as lost sheep, without the women. The rich male voices rose in the chants and psalms.

Joseph was beside his father. Not far from them was Abner, who seemed even from this distance the picture of wretchedness. His eyes were redder than usual—had he been weeping? Mary wondered sadly. Cleophas and his father were toward the back, richly robed, the gold on their dark wrists and ankles gleaming. She yearned toward them too, roused and distressed. To be so cocksure and wealthy and then to suffer this baffling indignity. What an outrage! Reb Levi had made that plain, storming into the house of Joachim.

"How is it that you put me off last year," he demanded, "and now are bargaining with that ass Jacob without even giving me notice? You must be mad—don't you realize I'm prepared to pay almost anything?"

Joachim's reply only incensed him further. "My daughter is not for sale." No, not for sale this sweet newly awakened flesh. Though had it not been for Joseph she would not have objected to Cleophas, whom she'd always liked despite his jaunty insolence. He was engaging and exhilarating, that spoiled young traveler, though his way with girls was well known. If that handsome face was sardonic to hide his suffering now, it would not be so for long. But again it struck her as sad that love should be so divisive, lashing this person to that against another, lacerating those whom it must cast aside.

It was time for the reading of the Torah. The candles in the seven-branched candelabra shone with pointed tongues of flame. The curtains at the back of the dais were parted, the holy chest unlocked. The priest brought forth the sacred scrolls, ivoried with age. The congregation waited for the seven chosen ones. Mary waited too in a soft dream. Surely today my father; surely today my Joseph.

And indeed they were summoned, together with Jacob in honor of the occasion. Joachim on his heavy tread, to solemnly deliver the Hebrew passages, which the interpreter translated into Aramaic, the language of them all. Then Jacob, looking humble yet carrying the peculiar essence of his jocularity, as if to lighten and reduce to their level the weighty words of God. And finally Joseph, striding gracefully forward, his face grave yet unable to resist one shining glance upward.

His last words had fallen, he lifted the parchments high. The old rabbi rose, clearing his furry throat and plucking at his vestments. Expectantly the congregation leaned forward. Mary clutched the railing of the balcony. Dimly she heard the words of the required announcement: Joseph ben Jacob, well known to all here assembled, desired the hand of Mary, daughter of Joachim, whose lineage was likewise of David. "If any here present have just cause to question this union, let him come forth now and make his protests known."

In the stillness you could hear the pigeons cooing and scratching on the roof. Hear too your own blood beating like the flutter of their wings, as they wheeled off. Someone coughed, there was a stirring toward the back, and Mary's heart raced for it struck her as not inconceivable that Reb Levi might stalk forward to make public the indignation he had vented on Joachim. Half-smiling, the old gray leader waited a moment more before lifting his hands for the blessing.

But even before it was pronounced, two figures moved into the aisle. Robes billowing, Cleophas and his father strode from the synagogue.

Men surged forward to congratulate Joseph. The rude departure only added zest to their words, for they were mostly poor and it delighted them that a mere carpenter had bested the richest man in town. Upstairs the women crowded around Mary and Hannah, eager for details. But Hannah squirmed through, impatient to get home. She'd be unable to concentrate on the Scriptures for fretting about the food. Would there be enough to go around? After that little scene, no doubt the company would be considerable, and Hannah shrank with anxiety for the deficiencies of her little house.

She had one terrible final pang at the image of those grandly departing backs. As if she were being forced to witness the literal withdrawal of some glittering fulfillment almost within her reach. But no—she set her sharp little teeth. She must cut the garment to fit the cloth. Joseph was all that her tormented pride had driven her to proclaim. Down in some dark locked cupboard of herself she had known it all along. . . . Oh, she was a vain and wretched woman, unworthy of this rare and exquisite daughter, this noble if humble youth who was to become her son. Let her be punished and shamed in the streets if ever again she muddied the vessel of their happiness.

Cora, Deborah's mother, stood with the other sisters-in-law trying to protect the cheeses and fruits and cakes, spread out on tables in the yard. The flies were bad and the children almost worse. Both must continually be shooed away. Meanwhile all about, guardedly lest Hannah overhear, was the tentative buzz of tongues.

"It's still hard to believe Joachim would not give in to Hannah—she dominates our brother in everything else."

"Well, you know his weakness for Mary. A wonder she wasn't spoiled."

"Not spoiled?" Cora gasped. "What about now? 'The eye that mocks a father and scorns to obey a mother—'" she began, but halted before the shocked reaction of the others that she should choose such a cruel proverb. For Mary was their niece and the family ties were strong. Cora was irked at herself for betraying the resentment that had smouldered within her for years.

She was a massive, strong-jawed woman, who had borne seven children, five of them sons. As the eldest sister, she had tried to champion Hannah when the family first became saddled with that impudent waif from Bethlehem. She had made a great show of counseling and commiserating with her in her barrenness; yet she had felt fortified by her own fruitful loins, armed against Hannah's quicker mind and sometimes vitriolic tongue.

It had galled her when Hannah finally conceived. Galled her further that her brother's wife had failed to be

properly humble that the child was a girl. Mary's undeniable beauty had been a blow. Jealously examining
her own daughters, Cora had found them wanting.
Deborah had an agile catlike loveliness. Esther was
pretty in a pudgy, dimpled way. But Mary's was the
kind of beauty that people turned to gaze at on the street.

Thus from the beginning Hannah was armed, a
voluble little adversary with whom you could not compete. And Joachim was almost as bad. It was amazing
that Mary wasn't ruined. Yet Mary only grew more
radiantly appealing with the years. Cora was baffled and
aggrieved.

Outwardly unctuous, creamy with praise, even forcing
her own daughters to yield to Mary when it came to toys
or games, she bided her time. Often she used Mary as an
example: "How soft-spoken your cousin is," she sometimes corrected the strident Deborah, "can't you be more
like her?" Or to the untidy Esther: "Mary would never
leave the pots and pans in such a state." Even so, she
had failed to generate any real dislike between them.
Though they had their share of quarrels, she knew that
they loved and admired their cousin and wished her happiness.

Nor would Cora begrudge the child. Especially not today when she had been delivered of a vexing, unworthy
but long tormenting burden—that Mary would surpass
her daughters in marriage. Live in a greater house, have
servants, travel, shop in the bazaars of exotic cities. She
had not missed the final plaintive look on Hannah's face
as Cleophas and his father swept from the synagogue. As
for her, it was as if they carried with them her heavy
accumulation of dread.

Cora hastened to correct the impression she had made.
She could afford to be generous. "It still seems a pity." She
plunged the knife into her own breast. "The chances
that girl had."

"And beauty fades so fast," said Ruth, Joachim's
small dark intense middle sister. "I shudder to think
what a few years suckling the babes of a poor joiner may
do to her."

"Yes, I'm afraid they'll all live to regret it," Cora said.
"For her own sake her parents should have been firm.

Now Deborah had plenty of other chances too," she claimed. "Some that might have pleased her more than Aaron. But Deborah's obedient, she's been trained not to question what we deem best."

There was a quick change of subject as Hannah came out. They didn't want to spoil this day for her, poor thing; they knew it was hard enough for her already. They had a grudging respect for her spunk, the way she always bounced back. Even now Hannah couldn't refrain. "Did you ever hear such a moving reading of the Word as Joseph's this morning? He should have studied for the priesthood. But he knows you can serve the Lord in other ways—by being a good husband, a good father. A good carpenter!" she declared, daring them to doubt. "You should see the table he's making for Mary—why, it would be a credit to the Temple."

They agreed, with the loyalty that overrode their differences. How was it that Hannah always managed to be right? they wondered. Yet they wanted her to be right in this instance, if only because they were all of the self-same family. Whatever befell one of them befell them all.

Upstairs, Deborah was helping Mary unbind her hair. She yanked the pins from the dark coronet and impishly began to tumble it about. "Come, now," Mary protested, laughing. "Hand me the comb. It's a maid my loosened hair is supposed to symbolize, not a wanton."

Deborah held the comb wickedly away. Her slant green eyes were dancing. "What a glorious joke *that* would be, to sit demurely on the bench with disheveled hair all day, knowing that you were no virgin as the visitors believed, but wild and wanton."

"It would be dreadful I should think."

"I thought of it at the time of my own hair's unwinding. I didn't feel demure and virginal at all, but wanton. I thought how it would be if I had lain with some of the boys I'd kissed, and almost wished I had!"

Mary smiled at her cousin's self-dramatics. "But what about Aaron? Don't you love him?"

"Plenty of time for Aaron when he leads me to the marriage bed." She attacked with the comb, so vigorously Mary winced. "As for love, you tell *me* what it's like.

How does it feel when you look at Joseph, what is it like when you kiss?"

"We don't kiss," Mary said softly. "Not yet."

"You will. You'll find they're all alike, they can hardly wait. Even Aaron—this betrothal has been one long struggle. Don't you tell," she warned. "It's legal, of course, but still a disgrace. I wouldn't think of it. But then I'm not tempted." She shuddered. "His lips—they're like kissing a sausage."

Mary gasped, shocked if amused. A sausage was heathen food. "Oh, Deborah, no, it shouldn't be like that! When Joseph looks at me it's like drowning sometimes, almost too lovely to bear. And his touch, even his hand on mine! I dare not even imagine what the rest of it will be like."

"Well, you're lucky." Deborah took up the wreath of blue forget-me-nots. She could hear the other girls coming with their garlands and she wanted to be first. She felt very possessive of Mary; she wanted to claim and crown her, this cousin whose beauty had always been a thorn in her side, who seemed born to be loved. "But you'd better be well chaperoned, you've got a long wait ahead."

Mary too could hear the patter of her friends' feet approaching. Her hair spilled over her shoulders in a sweet cascade, the shining hair of her maidenhood. A thrill of longing pierced her as she thought of the impending hours, months of waiting. Waiting for the beloved to come unto her. Yet surely there was reason in postponement; surely it would only enhance the time when they could truly be one.

She smiled at her restless, importunate cousin. "The Lord will give both of us strength," she said.

VI

THE betrothal had been fixed for the Wednesday three weeks hence, when the moon would be full for good luck.

Each night Joseph watched for its rising, and often he was still awake as it set. By the light of the moon and a single saucer of oil he worked on his gifts for Mary: A sewing box. A pair of slippers from some doeskin bought in the bazaars at Sepphoris. And his table. The moonlight poured across the doorstep, for he had flung the door wide; it made him feel closer to Mary. Everywhere things were blooming and bearing. The fragrance of almond and pomegranate blossoms drifted in, mingling with the odor of shavings and the cedar oil that he was rubbing into the table. Deeply, lovingly, with all his force to make it shine for her.

The moon plated it with silver. The moon was like a maiden itself, at first frail, fine-boned, but growing, nightly fleshing toward the fullness of love. Or it was like one of the ships that coasted across the blue lake of Galilee, too fragile, it seemed, for its cargo. But when the wind caught the sails how they billowed and strutted forward with their precious freight. The moon was like that, it drew his love along as it rose and nightly swelled. God's own moon watched over his labors and gave them light.

He no longer sang. A great silence had come upon him. The music within him was too mighty for words, even those of David or Solomon. He could make music only with his hands, working for the beloved.

"You should get your rest," his mother worried, holding him with her bright penetrating gaze. "You'll be worn out before the betrothal, let alone the wedding."

And the children taunted him. "Joseph's sleep-walking—see, see, he doesn't hear a thing, Joseph's in love!"

He laughed good-naturedly; they were all remote from him, outside the borders of his private journey. He was on his way to Mary.

He had scarcely seen her since the Sabbath when she had sat surrounded by other maids, with her hair unbound. . . . That hair. The scent of its rich dark tumbling tide . . . he had had to turn away lest he press his face into it, disturb it with his fingers, make a fool of himself. And since then he had not dared draw near her house. For one thing, it was considered more seemly; for another, her parents were so busy. Hannah had hauled everything out onto the grass and was whitening the walls afresh. But most of all, he was restrained by his own desire. The image of her sitting, eyes downcast, so small and lovely in the intimate tent and shelter of her hair, was to rouse up such passion in him that he was afraid.

God had kept faith with him. He could not even imagine the consequences should he break faith with God. . . . As for Hannah! Joseph felt a flash of amused alarm. Or Mary—Mary herself. At this he had to retreat from his own tormented thoughts. For he saw her eyes, large with love. He saw her parted lips.

His heart stopped as it smote him how easily he might have been someone else. But she, a slight girl, had shown far more courage than he, standing up to her parents, an almost unheard of thing. Before the spectacle of his own blind wasted year, Joseph was appalled. Now he resolved to make it up to her. He would protect her from the emotions that sprang like lightning between them. He would keep himself distant. He would not suffer himself to touch her, not even a finger, or a strand of that sweet temptation of hair. As for the fine gifts that he could not bestow upon her, he suffered. Yet in his wretchedness he was also proud.

Weighing himself against them, he realized that Abner had his scholarship, his devotion to the Law. Cleophas had his wealth, his travels, his other women. He, Joseph, had only his love for Mary. She was his Temple, his wealth and his wisdom. And to her he would bring all that he possessed, every stitch, every penny, every eagerly hewn bit of wood. Every fiber of his strong young body, every thought that did not first belong to him who had made her for him, their God.

He was awed by the honor of his undertaking, but he was not humbled. He knew that the gift of total commitment is never small.

Josph worked feverishly even the day of his betrothal. It would help to pass the hours until sundown. Furthermore, there had been a slight upsurge of business, as if already his union with the house of Joachim might become an asset to his family. He did not want to be found wanting, and he wanted to prosper. Soon he would have a wife to support.

Suddenly he could not believe it. The daze of sheer blind yielding, moving forward, ever forward in harmony with his fate deserted him. Something might happen even yet. Hannah might still hurl herself between them. Or some awful caprice of God might strike. His mother had gone up to help with the baking; any moment she might rush in, her eyes cold with horror. Or Timna would never return at all. The day would simply go on forever, with Mary ahead of him like a mirage on the desert, or a port toward which he was forever doomed to sail.

"My darling, you're still working?" His mother's hand parted the curtains, her concerned face peered through. "It's growing late, I'll fetch the water for your bath and lay out your garments." Flushed and perspiring but smiling, she pulled off her kerchief. Hannah had bade her come up with the aunts and other kin to join in the joyous preparations. Kneading the dough and baking it in the ovens dug in the yard, setting out the vegetables that were now bursting in such abundance, polishing the bright fruit, checking the wine. And all the while they worked, caught up in the glittering net of women's talk.

They had praised each other's efforts and each other's children, favoring her especially, as mother of the groom.

Home now, she looked about with her familiar anxiety for her husband. But Jacob was fine, Joseph assured her; only sleeping. "Good," she sighed, "he'll need the rest. We'll be up late. You should have rested too." She pressed his arm.

Joseph bathed and dressed and annointed his hair with olive oil. His confidence was returning. As the water had washed away the grime and sweat, so it cleansed him of his nervous, foolish imaginings. He felt the splendor of his own body in its pure white linen; he felt the wonder of his youth pulsing, urgent and eager. One small thing troubled him exceedingly—his hands. Although he scrubbed them nearly raw and rubbed them with the precious oil, he could do nothing about their callouses or the scarred, broken nails. He wanted to be perfect for Mary. He did not want his hands to be harsh, clasping hers, or to snag the betrothal veil.

His father puffed in and out, bumping into him, borrowing things, asking Joseph's help with the tying of his girdle. Jacob could never manage and his wife was busy with the girls. "And do I have to wear shoes?" he pleaded, exhibiting his poor swollen feet with their bunions. Squat, ruddy, his wispy hair combed futilely over his baldness, he looked uncomfortably clean and dressed up and rather pathetic. Yet it was he who reminded Joseph of the things that in his agitation he might forget: the purse of long-hoarded silver dinars, the ring, the presents.

Together they set off at last, Joseph lugging the heavy table. Jacob limped along in his unaccustomed sandals. A brisk breeze set the palm trees clashing and blew their robes about their legs. The dusty cobbled streets seemed strangely empty, as if life had been suspended for this gravely impending hour. Behind a tumbled-down rock fence a camel lurched growling to his feet, a donkey worried a bucket and brayed. They trudged along the steep narrow corridors in a strange silence. They were miserably aware, the nearer they drew to their destination, of the inadequacy of their offerings.

Ahead of them in the fast falling darkness they saw the newly whitened bridal house in its clump of prickly pears.

Fluttering from it like a beckoning arm was the pennant that proclaimed its festivities to passers-by. As they approached they saw that Joachim had stepped outside to light the torch of pitch-soaked rushes at the step. It blazed up suddenly, revealing his face with its unguarded look of grief. However quickly he jerked his head there was no denying that naked sorrowing. Because of me? Joseph wondered, or only because his dearest child has so little time left to be under his roof? Promptly Joachim recovered himself and turned to welcome them. Courteously ignoring the gifts they carried, he led them inside.

The room had been transformed. This was no house now, but Eden; the women had gathered up armsful of Eden and brought it inside. The white walls struggled to hold up its colors—the shining green of dampened leaves, and blossoms that rose in a bright riot, to wind even into the rushes of the ceiling. Purple iris, scarlet carnations, pink and blue cyclamen, the ruddy cups of tulips, heavy-headed poppies, already beginning to swoon in the heat of the lamps that stood like little floating stars.

The largest lamp, burning the finest oil, was placed at the head of the table where the bride and groom were led. Joseph found himself there as in a dream. Mary seemed unreal beside him, though her sweet flesh at times brushed against his. The scent of her was more heady than the overpowering fragrance of the flowers. He was stiff with guarding his emotions, remote from her, afraid. Her eyes had a fixed shining, she was smiling, smiling, laughing and smiling before the lavish compliments that each guest paid as he laid his gifts at her feet. Bolts of cloth, baskets, jugs, skeins of flax, countless tools for keeping house. The guests deposited them and then returned to their seats which were bedecked with olive boughs.

Finally an expectant hush; the scribe came forward. The rabbi nodded to Joseph, whose heart was large in his throat. With unsteady hands he drew from his girdle the purse containing the marriage fee, and turned to Mary, whose face floated before him. Not smiling now, but grave and as white as one of the pure white roses in her crown.

"And have you brought a token to give the bride to signify that this covenant is made?"

Nodding, Joseph unwound his girdle. His eyes did not leave Mary's as the rabbi took it and placed it across her uplifted hands.

"And have you other gifts?" the rabbi asked.

"Yes." If only there were more. . . . But nobody seemed to think ill of them, the shawl he had for Hannah, the fine hand chisel for Joachim. And for Mary—ah, for Mary, the sewing box, the soft little doeskin slippers, and the table that would be the first piece of furniture for their house. Plainly she loved them all, especially the slippers. She cried out with delight and thrust out her feet to their measure. There was an awkward moment for it seemed as if she would have him kneel there in the presence of everyone to put them on her. He flushed and people laughed at his discomfort and the rabbi made stern noises in his throat. For the scribe sat waiting to pen the terms of the contract.

And when it was finished, Joseph spoke aloud the prescribed words: that he would work for her and honor her in the manner of Jewish husbands, and that all of his property would be hers forever. Thus did he openly take the vow already made within his heart.

It was over now, all but the draping of her face with the betrothal veil. But the children must first be called forward. They had been bouncing with impatience for their treats; now the rabbi beckoned, and the mothers who had been restraining them let them go. They came in an eager swarm, shrieking, hands outstretched for the nuts and cakes. The eyes of Mary and Joseph met, and between them ran a shining thread of wonder, for despite its festive nature, this too was a grave thing, this matter of bestowing the sweets. For it symbolized the fact that she had kept herself for him.

In the commotion he almost forgot the veil. "The veil, the veil!" various ones were whispering. "Quiet the children." An aunt shepherded most of them outside, the others clung to their mothers, eyes focused with a placid interest on the bride.

As Joseph had feared, his fingers caught on the delicate gossamer stuff, and his hands shook placing it with anguished care so that it fell before her face. Yet pride upheld him. This was his victory; he knew that he stood before them tall and comely, humble yet mighty, a man claiming his true bride.

A vast tenderness swept him, and a great reverence. Now she belonged to him and her face was his to shield. In regret and joy he draped her, his personal Torah, which now must be returned to the ark to await their covenant.

Mary could not sleep. Affectionately she had thanked her parents for the betrothal feast and bade them good-night and crept into the chamber from which they had removed the younger children, in deference to her new state. Long before the revelry was over the little ones had collapsed one by one, to be carried, limp as the drooping flowers, to pallets in various corners of the house. There, heavy with food and spent with excitement, they slept the deep sleep of the innocent. Her parents slept too at last! She had lain rigid during the long hour when they had murmured together. But finally the voices and the creaking of the mattress ceased. There was heavy silence broken only by Joachim's snores.

Slowly, luxuriantly, she let her knotted fists uncurl, her whole being go limp. And as she did so the memories came flooding in . . . Joseph. *Joseph!* The proud tilt of his head throughout the ceremony. The trembling of his hands—she marveled that he hadn't dropped things as he had once dropped the towel. She ached for him; all that he did was inordinately precious and must be looked at in the fresh new light of herself, alone in her chamber and yet bound to him, awaiting their hour.

And it was all mixed up with that longing which made her toss and turn, which is why she had held herself back until her parents slept . . . Joseph! The grave little smile upon his face as people shouted blessings and wished them well. And his eyes upon her in the glare of the torches in the garden. Those passionate, pensive gray eyes. And the songs that he had sung only for her, quietly, next to her at the feast table, looking straight ahead almost as if she were not present. Singing to her softly, secretly, wooing her with his lips and his remoteness while the others danced and sang.

"Thou hast ravished my heart, my sister, my spouse;

thou hast ravished my heart with one of thine eyes. . . .
How fair is thy love, my sister, my spouse! how much
better is thy love than wine! . . ."

Some of the village boys had brought up lutes and a
timbrel, and they too sang and danced, but like shadows,
a spectral chorus whose faces flared and fell in the roister-
ing light. Abner had been among them, a trifle tipsy with
wine even before he came, striding about making noise,
which was alien to his shy nature, and by that giving
his heartbreak away. Poor Abner. And poor Cleophas,
who had gone off to console himself in Magdala, she had
learned. She grieved for them, yet always her being turned
back to Joseph. He was the only one she had ever wanted,
and he was hers. Hers by law. If he were to die she
would be his widow. And if she were to die he would be
her widower. And if she were to betray him he would
have to give her a bill of divorcement.

But no—no, how could she entertain such thoughts on
this night of her betrothal when the moon was shining
for good luck? It was still fairly early; the working people
of Nazareth could not spend much of the night in celebration, for they had to rise at dawn. The moon was still
so bright they had scarcely needed torches going home. It
was flooding her little room and she couldn't bear it, this
restlessness, fed by the moonlight.

By night on my bed I sought him whom my soul loveth;
I sought him, but I found him not.

I will rise now, and go about the city in the streets, and
in the broad ways I will seek him whom my soul
loveth. . . .

She found herself at the window. The moon possessed
the sky. It traced every tree and twig and bush and
branch in silver, laying inky shadows, giving everything
a stark clarity seldom seen by day. "Joseph. *Joseph!*" she
whispered toward that blandly smiling and triumphant
face. Was he sleepless too, perhaps pacing alone in this
unutterable light, or gazing up in a frenzy of longing?
And all because she had indeed set forth on the streets
like the bride in Solomon's dream:

. . . but I found him whom my soul loveth: I held him, and would not let him go, until I had brought him into my mother's house, and into the chamber of her that conceived me. . . .

My dove, my perfect one, is only one, the darling of her mother. . . .

Hannah. Poor brave beaten little Hannah, who had been finally reconciled. Who slept in the next room by her husband's side. While the bride . . . the groom? Mary shuddered and pressed her hands to her breasts.

"A garden enclosed is my sister, my spouse," Joseph had gone on singing from those selfsame songs, *"a spring shut up, a fountain sealed."*

Joseph. Joseph. She gave herself over to the final memory, held back to savor utterly. The moment in the garden when both her mother and father had been busy with the guests and they two had drawn a little apart. He had gripped both her hands within his own. "Would to heaven this were our wedding night!"

"Yes. Yes," she whispered, swaying toward him. "But we must be patient, and it won't be long, I promise. Just as I persuaded my father before, I'll surely be able to persuade him not to postpone the wedding for long."

Yet even as they gazed at each other in the nakedness of their yearning, she had begun to shrink from the task ahead. Having yielded thus far, her parents might feel it a point of honor not to yield again. Besides, they loved her, she was their firstborn. She knew that they would keep her with them as long as possible.

VII

JOACHIM saw his daughter now with a dumb aching resignation. It was done. Her spirit had fled the house, she belonged to another, so let her go, let her go. His wife, however, was adamant. The wedding would be in the fall, shortly after the Feast of the Tabernacles, and not a moment before.

"It will take Joseph at least that long to finish a proper house. Otherwise you would have to move in with his family."

"You did," Mary reminded.

"Yes, and a sorry day that was." Hannah's needle stabbed the cloth she was stitching. Her face was determined. She knew that she was wounding Joachim with her words, but so be it. It was necessary these days to wound someone in order to ease her own constant sense of defeat and loss. Mary had won, she was going to marry the man she wanted just as she had always gotten nearly everything else from Joachim. Now it gave Hannah a queer, fierce delight to have her way in the matter of the wedding.

Actually she felt she had been generous in not making them wait the entire year. Now Mary's impatience, and the fact that Joachim was obviously suffering at the thought of losing her—so much that he was even anxious to have it over with—such only enhanced Hannah's obstinance.

"Come now, surely it was not so bad living in the house of my mother," Joachim said.

"You know yourself we had no moment's peace or privacy. Not until you took me to a house of our own did we truly know happiness."

To avoid the taunt in her eyes he betook himself to the yard, where he paced in his misery. Truly his wife's love had been a long time coming; but it was not so in the case of Joseph and Mary. They would need neither peace nor privacy for what they felt for each other. A blur of pain enveloped him. He was jealous of Joseph—his youth and his love that was so richly returned. Yet if she must be given to someone, let it be a good gentle man like Joseph, and let it be soon.

Hannah had no idea what it was like to be a man—this waiting. No woman could comprehend physical passion. Even Mary, with her great eyes starry with longing, her lips drooping before Hannah's decision. She was but a child; she did not have the faintest concept of the demon-god that entered a youth's loins at puberty and gave him no peace thereafter. That drove him, a whip goading, lashing him sometimes beyond all reason and honor. Six months, Hannah had compromised. He snorted. Six months could be an eternity when you are enflamed by a woman and already bound to her.

He felt deeply for Joseph. He was rankled and saddened before the fact of it, but he was also sympathetic. And concerned. He was very much concerned. . . .

Hannah sewed on, taking satisfaction in the soft fall of cloth across her knees, the thread so neatly binding the seams. And in Mary, dreamily embroidering, and Salome, a slow careful round-eyed child, working earnestly away at the loom. These were women's tasks, to spin and weave and bind and impose order upon the importunate men. When Mary went into the house of Joseph she would not be found wanting by her mother-in-law, she would take a full chest. Six months were scarcely enough—she thought of the bedding, the tablecloths, the towels, the draperies for the doorways. Hannah yanked the cloth impatiently, her fingers dipped even swifter. Yet she felt a keen thrill of sheer organization. She felt her own brisk control. And this mounting stock of linens—weren't they proof of her devotion for Mary? And underneath this surface of vigorous, practical activity ran a river of rebellion that surpassed Joachim's. And an incessant secret wailing: *Mary. Mary!* My blessed, first fruit of my fallow womb—how can I bear your going?

Already the house seemed stripped, emptied of the precious presence now committed and focused upon a new house and life of its own. You could not reach Mary, however you shouted at her and bade her be still for the fitting of garments. You could not shake her into an acknowledgment of you who had borne her, slaved for her, well-nigh worshiped her. She thought only of Joseph, the hour when he would come to work in the garden beside her, or sit with the family making polite conversation, while the thing that was between them chimed and quivered and lent discomfort to all.

No, no . . . it would be a good thing when they were safely married. Joachim was right, it would be a relief. Yet she clung to her decision. And it was only sensible with all the preparations, Joseph's as well as theirs. She could not have her daughter going to live in that hovel with his parents, not after all her fine talk.

Hannah cringed sometimes to remember. Well, the Lord had seen fit to chasten her. Perhaps because she had loved Mary too well. For the Lord their God was a jealous God, and there was no denying it, she had loved Mary next to God and perhaps more. More even than Joachim, more than the other children that had come to bless their home. Even her passion for Esau was intricately bound with pity, whereas Mary—Mary was her pride, her obsession, imposing a burden of love so intense that she almost longed to be rid of it. She should be almost grateful to Joseph!

Yet she was not. She could scarcely abide the sight of him striding up the hill, that comely, gray-eyed face of his aglow. She could not bear the sight of them murmuring together on pretext of weeding the garden or feeding the ass. She must hasten out, intrude herself, insist that they come inside for a cool drink of juice or wine. And she must sit with them, guarding them, guarding her child against this invader, this fair youth who had come to rob her of her dearest possession.

That it was unnatural, even wicked to feel so, she re-

alized. She examined her conscience and found it squirming with evil. You would have kept her a callow lass
forever, she castigated herself. You prayed that her de-
velopment into womanhood would be slow. And God
answered those dark and secret prayers. God stayed that
fertile flow signifying that she was finally ripe for seed—
seed that might well be holy seed. For wasn't every marriage bed the potential seedbed of the coming Messiah?

The marriage bed . . . was it that which made her
heart shrivel? She wasn't sure. At great cost to herself,
for she was innately shy despite her aggressive demeanor,
she had warned Mary. "I was only twelve and my mother,
dear soul, had never told me about the ways of a man. I
want you to be prepared. The suffering and shock will be
less if you understand what is expected of you."

Mary had gazed at her, bewildered. "Oh, Mother, no.
This thing that we feel for each other, surely its expression
could never be anything but beautiful."

"*Beautiful.* You'll find out." Hannah jerked the mill-
wheel savagely in her embarrassment. "Later—it's better
later when you've lived a while together and come to trust
each other. But in the beginning it's no pleasure for a
woman, and I won't have you thinking otherwise."

Mary hadn't believed her, of course, and Hannah felt
that she'd botched the whole thing. Well, she'd done her
duty. If she'd affronted Mary she couldn't help it. Or
could she? Had this too been an unconscious part of the
resistance, the clutching, the evil toils in which she herself
was writhing? Had she been striving to strike the stars
from those dark eyes, bash that reminiscent smile, strew
such doubt and fear that she might even yet rush in and
reclaim that which she knew was lost?

Thus did Hannah torment herself, thus did she bleed
and lash about inside that pert little frame that was openly
so vigorous. She never ceased praising Joseph to others or
to his face. Never ceased claiming that she was happy
about the union. And all the while, on quite another
plane altogether, hung a shadowy wing of premonition.
It hovered there, apart from the dozen devils that dwelled
within her and were chasing her, giving her no peace. It
had nothing to do with her possessiveness as a mother.
Shadowy, indefinite but strong, its chill threat followed her.

And she was afraid for her child. She was desperately afraid.

Mary had never been so happy. When she awoke it was as if the new day had been ripened and polished and given gaily into her hand like a piece of choice fruit. The sunrise had never seemed so rosy, the women at the well more friendly. With them she laughed and gossiped and discussed her wedding plans. The wounds of Israel seemed distant and impossible. When her father discussed them she scarcely heard; it was an old song, too dreary to have any place in the life of a girl recently betrothed. Nothing lay ahead but delight, the hour when she would at last belong to her love.

Meanwhile, Joseph wove in and out of her life as much as possible under her mother's hawklike watchfulness. And sometimes she and her father would walk down to inspect his progress on the house. It was rising fast above its cave to keep them safe from earthquakes and stable the ass. Joseph's brothers were helping, and they sang as they mixed the mortar and fitted the stones, a merry lot. It would be sturdy and cozy, filled with the furniture Joseph was building long after he should be at rest.

Occasionally Timna or a sister would come out and invite them into their house for a cup of wine and a piece of cake. Joachim found excuse to demur but Mary went, and they would sit visiting, and worrying about how hard Joseph worked. "Try to persuade him not to drive himself so hard," his mother said. And Mary could only reply, "I have but it's no use." And they smiled at each other, feeling the closeness of women who love the same man, sharing the futility of trying to change him. And this too was warm and delicious, a part of the day's sweet fruit.

With Timna she felt at peace, loved without being devoured. There was none of the rivalry that stung the air when Joseph came into the presence of Hannah, only this sense of acceptance as the future wife. Joseph's wife— with its implications of intimacy already, sitting here with his mother who washed and mended for him, smoothed the linens of his bed. Mary's flesh sang.

For they had kissed now, several times. When two people loved this much they were deft and resourceful, there were ways. And the stolen kisses were unbearably sweet. A sample of joys to come. Poor Hannah. Mary felt only pity for the bungled warnings of her mother. Poor scared little Judahite carried away by a stranger, no wonder. And Hannah so confused, so energetically trying to manipulate other people's lives and emotions ever since.

Mary felt protective, almost as if she were the parent and Hannah the child. She wished it were possible to calm her, put her heart and her bustling little body at rest. But no, this was Hannah's nature, her outlet, her release —building toward the hour of the wedding just as Joseph was building his house. And her mother was not wrong, Mary realized. It was better to set a thing aside and work toward it, for surely the goal was dearer for the very discipline imposed. Wait, savor the dream yet a while longer.

Meanwhile the spinning, weaving, sewing, the drying of herbs and cheeses upon the sunlit roof, the making of the clay pots she would need. Hannah was right about this too, she must not come to her husband with empty hands. And it was all so womanly, her half of the partnership that began with the rapturous union of flesh and went on through all phases of life so that they might comfort and give joy to each other.

She had never been so happy, so poised upon the brink of wonder. She felt a tender ecstasy in every living thing: her parents, the hobbling grace of Esau, the very beggars on the street. The little silver-gray donkey in its stall, the blunt-nosed sheep. And the inanimate—the fecund, seedy smell of newly wakened earth—how could she bear its fragrance? The odor of bread fresh from the oven, the raw tangy scent of clay drying on her hands.

She would lift them sometimes and gaze upon them in amazement. To be alive was a miracle, a holy thing. To be alive and roused to your being as a woman. At times she could not sleep. She would rise up from her couch and go out to the places where Joseph had kissed her, under the silvery olive trees. Or she would climb to the roof and lie gazing at the infinity of stars. And the words of the psalm would rejoice in her.

When I consider thy heavens, the work of thy fingers, the
moon and the stars which thou hast ordained;
What is man, that thou art mindful of him? and the son
of man, that thou visitest him?

The singing silence of God was overpowering. He
would speak to her any moment now. He had a message to give her before her marriage. A blessing perhaps,
or an admonition surely; for to marry would be to leave
childhood behind. The innocent bliss of its unquestioning acceptance. She had an instinctive knowledge that
once she became totally a woman, a wife, she would
feel God's presence so completely no more. . . .

Yes, Lord? . . . Lord? . . . It was too late even now;
the pure channel of childhood was closed.

Then one day toward sundown she had gone down
the path a little way, into the stable cave to water the
ass. She had emptied the skins into the trough and the
stubby creature had bent its head to drink, when its
pointed ears laid back. It shied and made an odd whim-
pering sound. "Hush now, what's wrong?" Mary stroked
its quivering nose to gentle it, following its blank stare
toward the doorway where a shaft of sunlight poured
through.

Mary.

She heard her name, and at its sound the little beast
reared.

"Yes, Father?" she said, though it seemed strange that
he should be home from the fields so early. "Here I am. In
the stall."

Mary!

Suddenly she realized that it was not her father's voice
that called. She could not place it, nor the source of it,
though she went to the low leaning doorway and peered
out. The yard and the grove and the adjoining fields lay
quivering with the falling light, peaceful and undisturbed.
There was no one by the old stone cistern, no one by the
vine-covered fence. Strange.

Puzzled, she turned back to the donkey. It had bent its
prickly nose again to the water, but only hovered there,
not drinking. Its sides were heaving. She could hear its

uneasy breath. And now her own heart began to pound. She clutched its dry fur for comfort. "We must be hearing things, you and I," she said.

Then she saw that the shaft of light pouring dustily through the doorway had intensified. It had become a bolt, a shimmering column, and in it she dimly perceived a presence. Neither man nor angel, rather a form, a shape, a quality of such beauty that she was shaken and backed instinctively away, though her eyes could not leave that living light.

Mary. Little Mary. . . The voice came again, gently, musically. *Have I frightened you? I'm sorry. Be still now, be at ease, there is nothing to fear. I am sent from God, who has always loved you, don't you remember? He has watched you grow from childhood into womanhood, and now he has a message of great importance. So listen carefully, my child, and heed.*

"I am his unworthy servant," Mary whispered, though she scarcely believed her own voice. She was trembling. Could it be that her recently heightened awareness had affected her senses? Why was she speaking thus, alone with only the beast in the sun-white stall? "What . . ." it was difficult to form the words, "what is it that the Lord would have of me?"

There was a second of silence. Then, in clear ringing tones the answer came: *Behold, you will conceive in your womb and bear a son and you shall call his name Jesus. He will be great and will be called the Son of the Most High. . . .*

"The *Messiah!*" Mary gasped. Involuntarily, she shrank away. "I? *I* am to bear the Messiah?"

Even so. And the Lord God will give to him the throne of his father David, and he will reign over the house of Jacob forever, and of his kingdom there will be no end.

"But I am unworthy!" Mary cried. She was grasping the nibbled manger; she felt her bare feet upon the gritty earthen floor. The sweat poured down her face. "I have many faults. I have rebelled against my parents, I often envy my cousins, I have impure thoughts. How can I be the mother of this long awaited child?"

God knows the secrets of his handmaiden's heart. He does not expect perfection. This child that he will send

*you will be human as well as holy. The Lord God wills it
so, in order that man, who is human, can find his way
back to God.*

"But I am not yet married," Mary protested. "How
can this thing be when it is many months yet before I
come to the bed of my husband?"

With God all things are possible, the voice said. *Al-
ready he has quickened the womb of your aged aunt
Elizabeth, so that soon she too will bear a son. Now the
Holy Spirit will come upon you, and the power of the
Most High will overshadow you; and the child that is
born unto you will be the Son of God.*

"I will strive to be worthy," Mary whispered. It was a
moment before she could go on. For one stark, appalling
instant she could feel something fleeing from her, something precious. She felt a sense of incalculable loss. "Behold, I am the willing handmaiden of the Lord."

She closed her eyes, still gripping the donkey's fur,
the stall. When she opened them again the little beast
was quietly drinking, and though the shaft of light still
slanted through the doorway its intensity was diminished,
the voice of her destiny was gone.

But something else remained—some quiet consciousness
that told her she must be still and wait now upon God.
If he had sent his messenger at this quiet hour of
evening, then surely he must be near, perhaps gazing at
her even now. Soothing her, calming her, bidding her
be still and yield to this astounding command. Again,
for the flick of an instant, she felt the whiplash of dismay.
Not fear, but sheer human bewilderment.

Joseph! What of Joseph, my beloved?

There was no answer. Only the breathless quiet,
heightened by the beast that had dipped its head now
contentedly to drink from the trough. The stillness, laced
with birdsong. The trembling, pervading stillness that
comes with sunset after a hard day's work, when the
body aches with weariness and yet is alive, alert, the more
receptive to love. Mary stood waiting, humble, bowed,
flowing out to it, whatever it was. As the glory of God
had possessed her in childhood, so it would possess her
now in whatever manner it saw fit. Hers not to question,
hers not to fear, hers only to submit.

And even as she waited, it happened as the angel had said. The Holy Spirit came upon her, invaded her body, and her bowels stirred and her loins melted, her heart was uplifted, her whole being became one with it—the infinite, the unknowable, the total fusion that is the bliss of God. Beside it even the kiss of Joseph was as nothing, even the dream of becoming his wife.

"My God, my God!" she cried, and the sweat ran down her limbs.

And so it was that Mary knew God and was one with God and became at once his child, his mate and his mother, and the miracle was achieved.

VIII

IT had happened.

She had not dreamed it. Nor was it but one last sweet conversation with the Most High before she shed forever the innocence and trust of her maidenhood. It was a thing apart. And if it had been impossible ever to convince Hannah that such things were not untruths to be punished, or at best feverish imaginings, how then would it be possible to convey to her this astounding thing?

Yet it had happened. The finger of God had touched her, the presence of God had consumed her and kindled life within her. As surely as if Joseph had taken her unto himself.

Joseph . . . she scarcely dared think of him. He had become one of a company of strangers. Her parents, her family, people on the street—all laughed and spoke and prayed and toiled and moved in the usual way, so commonplace as to be well nigh terrifying. They did not know, they did not suspect, they could not see the awful veil that hung between them. They did not recognize the mark of God upon her.

But the time was fast approaching when they must.

She was newly nubile. Her blood should flow freely every four weeks—this much she knew. Yet twice now the moon had waxed and waned. Her breasts were swelling, and the nipples stung like little apples bitten and browned by the frost. Sometimes she felt so dizzy it was all she could do to creep to the chest for her clothes. And the smell of certain foods was nauseating. Once, straining the curds with Salome, her face went as white as the soured milk and she had to rush for the basin.

"What's the matter, Sister?" Salome asked. "Are you nervous about the wedding?"

"Yes, that must be it." Mary wiped her clammy brow with her apron. "It's nothing. Please don't tell Mother."

Again she had gone into the cave to fill the lamps. And suddenly she could not bear the rich rank smell of the slippery oil. Her hands shook, she dropped and broke a little pink lamp that Hannah had carried all the way from Bethlehem, one that she always kept burning in her room at night.

In a panic Mary knelt to scoop up the fragments, knowing already it could never be mended. Even as she was trying to think what to say, she heard her mother's brisk step. "Oh, Mother, forgive me," she pleaded. "I'll make you another. Though I know how much it meant to you, that it can never be replaced. The last thing I want is to grieve you."

She could hear her own foolish lamentings while Hannah only stood shaking her head. But her mother's eyes in the dim half-light of the cave were sharp upon her. "Rise, child," she said. "You shouldn't be kneeling on the cold floor like that, it's nearly the time of your outflowing." Hannah squatted to pick up the last shreds of the lamp, tucked them, these pitiable precious bits of clay of Bethlehem, into her handkerchief. "It's not good for a woman to take a chill, it can hold her back."

So she was watching, Mary realized. Counting the days. And in her dread already providing excuses to stave off suspicion, forestall a possibility too monstrous to credit. Yet the time was fast approaching when Hannah could be put off no longer. Spiritual though the child in her womb might be, God had seen fit to grip her flesh and give it substance. Purely human symptoms that would soon be evident to all eyes. Her parents. Joseph. His people.

What then? What then?

She was frightened and confused. She did not understand. She could only pray blindly: "Help me, help me

to be worthy of this thing that you have done unto me,
oh my God. And these others who are so dear to me—
when the time comes that they must know, help them to
understand. Don't let them cast me out!"

Meanwhile Joseph continued to come to the rooftop,
a fervent young shadow still preparing for their wedding
day—by which time she would be deep in shame. (Or
glory? Oh, God, sustain me, give me courage, let me
not drag around drawing puzzled attention in my ignorance and wretchedness; let me grasp thy purpose, let me
lift up my head and be proud!) Meanwhile her mother
continued to guard her daughter even more zealously
against the temptations of youth. And to watch. To watch.

One bright morning when the cistern was full and the
sun hot for drying, they carried the linens into the yard
to soak in a wooden tub. Hannah loved to wash. She
enjoyed the pounding and flailing and wringing things
out with her sturdy little red fists. And when she shook
them and spread them to dry on bushes and grass and
fence, it was as if she had personally come to grips with
all the problems and evils that harass a woman, and
bested them. She had made them clean and smooth. She
was in a buoyant mood. For this day she was determined
likewise to cleanse the air and banish forever the dark and
delicate thing upon her heart.

"Go now and see about the bees," she bade the children. "Salome, you take them and see if they're about
to swarm. We'll need honey aplenty in store for the
wedding. Take care now," she warned as they trooped
off down the path. "Put your kerchiefs over your faces
if they come near, don't get stung." Her eyes followed
them fondly a moment, then with a conspiratorial air she
turned to Mary. "I thought it well to be rid of them while
we soak our stained cloths." A reminiscent look came
into her eyes. "Ah, daughters, daughters," she mused.
"How well I remember my mother making the same
request of me. Though she usually did it for me. I can
see her yet bending over the tubs."

Mary rose slowly from her attempts to make the fire
in the pit burn brighter by fanning it. She had carried
out coals from the oven but the sticks were green, they
only smoked and sputtered. Now the smoke coiled be-

tween her and her mother, separating them further. She shrank back into the protection of its bitter blue-gray screen.

"It's a task I'm afraid you won't have to do for me," she said. She drew a deep breath, for now the time was come and she must be calm. "Mother, I must tell you. It has been three months now since my loins have bled." She waited, heart pounding, her eyes fixed upon the face that fell suddenly, as if a blow and struck it, then slowly drained.

Hannah began to wipe her hands on her tunic. It was a faded blue washday garment; absently she rubbed her red hands on it, and then, moving carefully to a wooden bench under the tall date palm tree, she sat carefully down. It is nothing, nothing, she firmly informed herself, gripping the sides of the seat. Girls are often irregular in the beginning; they miss their periods for many causes—sleeping in a draft, getting their feet damp in the fields. I warned her about that, she thought in exasperation, but no, she wouldn't listen, she will run about barefoot, old as she is.

Thus she pounced upon pique and annoyance to postpone and assuage the sick fear. It's nothing, nothing, she went on, so why should the blood pump so painfully in my breast and my bowels run thin? Yet now it came surging in upon her, all the signs she had refused to notice. Mary's strange change lately—she often sank into deep silences. Where the laughter that once rang out so freely? Where the quick bright word, the singing? And her step. Hannah had noticed her daughter coming from the well with the jugs, or up from the milking with the bulging goatskin bags on her shoulders; instead of the flowing gait that had always given Hannah such pleasure, Mary had been slow-footed, bowed, as if the weight of the vessels was almost too much to bear.

All this flashed through Hannah's consciousness as she sat there, managing a fiercely determined smile. She thrust aside her wretched and unworthy alarm. "We'll brew some herbs," she said. "We'll fix you a potion."

"Don't pretend, Mother," Mary said. "I know what you must be thinking." She had moved away from the smoke now and stood before her, clearly revealed. There was something pleading about her, and yet unflinching. There was about her the cold calm of the innocent. "But you need have no concern. It is not true. I have not lain with any man."

Hannah flinched. Never! Never her Mary . . . even now, betrothed, the thought of Mary thus was a laceration. "Not even Joseph?" The words came spewing out before Hannah could stop them. She caught a fist to her quivering mouth, wishing them unsaid. But there was no calling them back and she could only await their answer.

"Joseph is a good man, Mother. He would be crucified before he would bring dishonor on me or my family."

"He loves you," her mother said helplessly, yet with a certain grimness. "And you love him. There's no denying such things, it is all too evident. He's been waiting for you all his life, and to wait for you now is torment—he can scarcely keep his hands or his eyes away from you. I can see now that forcing you to wait even this long may have been a mistake."

"You mustn't blame yourself, but above all you mustn't blame him," Mary said. "Joseph is an honorable man."

"But you love each other," Hannah cried out. "And heaven forgive me for saying this, but the flesh is weak."

"Yes, yes, we love each other. Postponement of the time when we can honorably come together has been agony for both of us. But whatever you may think of Joseph, Mother, he loves me too much to bring any scandal upon me. And whatever you may think of me— how can you think me so weak, so wanting in respect for you and my father that I would give myself to him as his wife before our actual marriage?"

"How can I?" Hannah moaned, and rocked back and forth on the bench. "Because I'm a woman, and I've lived a long time, Mary. I know that respect for parents, respect even for the Law are sometimes not enough to keep two people apart who love each other."

"Then you don't believe me?"

Hannah had been sitting with her eyes shut. Now she opened them and gazed a long moment at her daughter. "Yes, Mary, I believe you," she said "Heaven knows if I didn't! . . ." She shuddered and shut her eyes once more, as if to escape it. The disgrace. After all her boasting. If now, on top of the humiliation of stepping down, there were to be no proper wedding, but merely a shamed public acknowledgment that the marriage had been consummated in secret—legal as that was, it was still ignoble, degrading. People sneered and made contemptuous jests. No, no. She had been punished enough for her vainglorious claims; God was surely going to spare her this.

As for that other possibility—it was too appalling to consider. *Adultery.* Cleophas was back. High-spirited, impetuous Cleophas who also had loved Mary and was accustomed to snatching what he wished. For Mary there had been only Joseph, nobody but Joseph, yet she had been fond of Cleophas, and she was kind. . . .

These fantastic thoughts lashed through Hannah as she sat trying to regain her composure, her command of the day. The devils were battering at her again: how much do we really know of those close to us, they asked? How much does even the most careful mother know about her child? Look at her, this beautiful small daughter standing before you, a very princess, alien to all you ever were. She harbors a secret still. She is rich and full with a secret thing.

And the devils whipped their tails and screamed: "Adultery means death by stoning! Shame, divorce, death." Even if a man had pounced on her out of the hedges as she came home one night from the meadows, she would be sullied, defiled. Even Joseph would not have her; no man would. . . . Hannah saw her beloved crouching, begging for mercy, heard the stones raining down. She saw the white body bruised and bleeding, perhaps hurled over a cliff. . . .

Hannah sprang up, grabbing at the garments to be plunged into the steaming tub. She must scrub them and cleanse them and spread them out in God's clean thirsty sun. She must again grasp the garments of life and force them into patterns of neatness and precision. What folly to sit wasting time over nothing.

"Come now, let's get busy," she said. "I'll make you a potion that will make your blood flow once more. But first we must finish the washing."

"Mother, wait," Mary reached out a restraining hand.

"You had better sit down again. There is something more that I have to tell you. And this—this I fear will be even harder for you to believe."

Joachim let the ox rest at the end of the furrow. The beast had been with him so many years that he regarded it as an old friend. He often talked with it as he plowed or scattered the seed. He was far too law-abiding a Jew to spare it by harnessing it up with the ass, as some of his neighbors did. But he never used the goad except to prod it gently, and at night he always allowed it to cool off, rubbed it down, and washed out its mouth with wine before giving it water and hay.

He stood by it now, regarding his thriving fields. Thus far Jahveh had been merciful. No hail had riddled the early crop of beans and lentils and barley, which soon would be ready to reap. Those inevitable pests—caterpillars, beetles, mice—a host of enemies whose insatiable jaws could spell ruin, had been remarkably scarce this year, and the wheat looked to be plentiful this season. Even considering tithes and taxes, it seemed as if God meant to grant one of his dearest wishes—that he be able to give his firstborn a fine wedding.

He took off his hat and mopped his steaming forehead. Overhead the sky burned hard and blue, a shimmering tent spread over the flowing greens and golds of the hills that seemed to speak of ancient patterns, rhythms that could lead only to eternity and fulfillment with the author of so much beauty. The land of milk and honey. The earthly paradise to which they, God's chosen children, had been led. Joachim's being burned with it, flowed into it, feeling its harmonies along with the constant agitation in his breast.

The wedding feast was the prerogative of the bridegroom's family, but Joachim knew with a certain satisfaction that Jacob simply could not manage; he would have to have help. If Jacob balked he would persuade Joseph himself that this was no occasion for false pride. For Mary's sake there must be musicians, groaning tables, plenty of wine. Hadn't she been the most sought-after girl in town? Hadn't he reminded them of that when they came begging for her hand? How then could they wish to embarrass her by any lack of wine?

He caught himself up at the absurdity of the imagined argument. Surely there would be no such cause for words since the problem must be solved and he was able and glad to do it. He felt almost a fervent need to do it, if only to impress upon everyone that he and Hannah had no regrets about giving their rare jewel of a daughter to the carpenter.

Yet he was impatient to be about it, have done with it. Three months had passed since the betrothal; three months more to go. They had reached the halfway mark, and he sensed that it was a time of crisis, some mounting intensity and challenge. He wished that it were over, that she were already safely married.

Safely? It troubled him that the word had even entered his thoughts.

"Well, friend," he patted the patiently waiting haunches, and set his brown hand once more to the wooden plow, "this is no way to harrow a field."

As they started down the next furrow he saw Hannah's small figure hastening toward him. At once the familiar reflex of gladness smote him. He could never see her like this, his raw little sparrow of a mate, without a sense of blessing. It seemed to him always that she came running to him with her hands outstretched. Always in his secret nature he would anticipate a gift that was probably the more precious because it was so rarely in her power to bestow.

"I'm over here," he shouted as she halted, shielding her eyes from the glare. Joachim pulled back on the ox and plodded toward her, surprised at not seeing the napkin of bread and cheese or the skin of water that she sometimes brought. Then he saw that she gasped for breath, her eyes were huge with alarm, and her face was tear-streaked.

"Hannah! Hannah, what is it? Come sit down." He could feel her convulsive shaking as he led her into the shade of a fig tree. "Are you ill?"

"No. No, it's Mary. Mary—you must come quickly." The world was rocking, she could scarcely see him. "She's the one who's ill, very ill I'm afraid."

"What sort of illness?" he demanded. "A fever?"

"Yes. Yes, a—a fever of the mind. She seems to be possessed!" Hannah clutched at her throat which felt dry and taut and enflamed. "Possessed of an evil spirit."

"Come, now. Our *Mary?*" He laughed shortly, yet he knew that his wife's terror was real. "Get hold of yourself, Hannah, tell me what makes you think this preposterous thing."

"She's having illusions. Fantasies. You remember how she used to have them when she was a child? I punished her for them then, but she's too big to be punished now for these lies!"

Joachim said bluntly, "I told you then and I tell you now, our Mary would never lie."

"No, you wouldn't believe it, you'd never believe ill of her," she accused. "Where Mary's concerned you'd defend her no matter what, you've always been so blind. Maybe if you'd done your duty as a father to her then, if you'd chastised her, made her realize the sin of falsehood, we wouldn't be facing this madness now."

"Madness? Hannah, watch your tongue."

"It's true. Only a mad woman, a person possessed of a demon would tell such a story as she's just told me."

"What story?" In his own mounting fear his tone had become harsh. Now he gripped his wife's shaking shoulders, trying to crush into her some calm. "Hannah, Hannah, quiet now, quiet—tell me—what is this thing she claims?"

Hannah caught her breath, bit her trembling lips. She gazed for a second over the blurred but shining fields, trying to find and shape the words. "She says that she is with child."

"With child?" It was torn from him in a startled cry. His hands dropped. "Whose?" he demanded. *"Joseph's?"* And when she did not speak: "I'll kill him."

"No! No, that I could understand," Hannah told him. "They're in love, it would be natural—an outrage, yes, but natural. That I could bear somehow. But Joachim my husband, listen. Our daughter claims that it is an unnatural child she is going to bear. A—a holy child. That an angel came to her and announced it unto her, and that the seed of Jahveh himself has entered her womb."

Her voice had dropped to a whisper. Her little eyes, raw with fear, were fixed upon his face. Under its roughness, ruddy from the sun, it was going ashen. His lips moved several times before he could speak. "A holy child," he said. "No, no, it cannot be." Slowly, unsteadily, he got to his feet. "A holy child!"

Hannah sprang up too. A new dismay rocked her. Not once had she anticipated this reaction. Romantic though he was beneath his brusque demeanor, mystic, innocent, dreamer, surely he could not accept this incredible thing. "It's blasphemy," she cried. "You must come home with me and help me to save her." She trotted frantically along beside him as he went wordlessly to unhitch the ox. "Poor child," she began to weep afresh, "poor baby. If she is truly in trouble through any man we must make her see that we will forgive her. We'll help her, see that no harm comes to her. But if this be blasphemy, then surely God himself will punish her."

"Blasphemy?" Joachim swallowed. The eyes that turned upon her were grave and mystifying, gazing through and beyond her. And Hannah's soul shriveled for she did not know him any more, this husband whom she had seen so often poring over his scrolls, heard so often discussing it with the more learned ones. She feared for him as she feared for her daughter. "Hannah, Hannah," he said, "have you no faith, either in our own child or your God?"

"You can't believe this thing! Surely you cannot believe it."

"How can I believe anything until I hear what Mary has to say? How can I dare to believe it? I am dumbfounded, Hannah, I am as shocked by what you tell me as you. Our daughter—that it might be even she!"

She stared at him aghast. "You're out of your mind to even consider such a thing. You too must be ill."

"It's lack of faith in God's word that bespeaks illness, Hannah. Have you never heard the words of the prophets? Every one of them from Samuel's time on has predicted the Messiah, to be born of a virgin, Isaiah said. And when has Israel ever needed a Saviour more?"

"I don't believe it," Hannah said flatly. She was angry now in her dismay. "Nor do you, not really. You've been out in the sun too long."

"The Lord himself promised us that the time would come—and the time is surely upon us. The scholars are convinced of it, all the sages and seers."

"People see what they want to see. Joachim, please, she has never needed a strong, straight-thinking father so much as she needs one now. I'm but a woman; our daughter's in serious trouble and I can't handle this alone. Nor can I handle it sanely if you too are carried away by visions that may only make her worse. Help me, my husband, please help me!"

Her cry broke through his soaring dream. A sound that was human and real, tearing asunder what must surely be only a fantasy of fulfillment, a hope pursued so passionately and long that it had become a kind of delusion.

"I'll try," he said. "I'll try to set aside my own convictions for your sake and listen without prejudice. Let's go to her now and see. But one thing I know—ill she may be, but never evil. Our Mary could not lie."

Mary was in the yard as they hastened up the path. She was at the fence, testing some of the clothes, turning them about, the better to receive the sun She too wore a skimpy washday garment and her feet were bare and a lock of hair fell into her eyes. She brushed it aside, lifting her face to greet them. And seeing her thus, so young, so normal about this everyday task, Joachim felt both a strange sharp disappointment and a glorious surge of relief. All was well. All was truly well with his daughter.

It was a grave thing to become involved with God. But now he saw that she had been spared. She hadn't been singled out, either for tragedy or an honor so enormous that it was beyond human comprehension. She and her mother must have had one of their differences, that was all, and Hannah always reacted in some fashion—a headache, a cleaning spree, or now possibly this fantastic account born surely of misunderstanding It might even be that Hannah herself was sick

"Come into the house, come in out of the sun," Hannah ordered as she made for the door. "I must see about the midday meal, we must talk, we must discuss this thing but first we must eat," she said incoherently. "The children will be back."

"They're here," Mary told her. "They came while you were away, they couldn't find the bees."

But her mother rushed on in, and she was glad. She was not afraid of her father; she always had had a dumb, consoled, fated feeling that he would believe. But to try to explain again in the presence of her mother—no, her voice would only shake, her ability to make it sound credible would be tried all over again.

"Mary, Mary . . . what is this thing that your mother tells me?"

"It's true, Father. Believe me—you must believe me. If you don't then surely all is lost."

"Come, now. Come, come. . . ." He led her to the selfsame bench under the dry dusty palm tree. His heart was sore within him at her tone. She seemed so little and lost, as she had often seemed to him when she turned to him after some bout with Hannah when she was small. So stricken at having done something, she knew not quite what, to estrange her from her mother. It was all he could do to refrain from putting his arms about her where she sat huddled into herself on the bench. "Have I ever failed to believe you, little Mary?"

"No. No, but I'm not a little girl any more. And this—this that has happened to me is an appalling thing. I am going to have a baby, Father, but I have not sinned. Joseph and I have not sinned."

"It would be no sin," he said almost too quickly, for he must give her that assurance, just in case. "It would be a grievous wrong to your mother and me, yes, but no sin in the eyes of God, Mary, since you and Joseph have publicly pledged each other and are betrothed."

"Don't make excuses for me, Father. They're not necessary. That is what I beg you to believe!"

She turned to him, her face grave. "The prophecies are about to be fulfilled, as you have always said. Father, I am the chosen one. Humble as I am, faulty, weak, wicked even—the Lord has chosen me."

"You're not faulty or weak or wicked!" he stormed, for he felt shaken now with his own dismay. It was an

effort to speak. "Mary, if this be true and not . . . not
. . ." he hesitated, "not just another dream—if God has
truly deemed that the time has come, then he has chosen
wisely. Surely he could find no purer or lovelier maid in
all Israel." He broke off, unable to continue. The divine
fate that he had sensed even in her infancy when he had
that strong impulse to give her to the Temple. Her whole
childhood, its queenliness, its touch of mystery. . . .

"*If* it be true, Father? If God has deemed the time
has come?" She gripped his great rough hand, her eyes
were wet. "Father, it is no dream. I am with child. A
child that can only be his child, since I have known no
man."

"How do you know?" he said sternly, almost impatiently. "Forgive me, but I'm your father and your mother
is right—I've got to deal with this sanely and wisely. I
must not let myself be carried away by my own tendency
to dream, or my long obsession with the hope of Israel."

"God's own angel came to tell me that this was to be,"
Mary whispered, eyes low. "And the Holy One invaded
my being—how, just how I cannot say. Only that I was
uplifted, I felt myself one with the infinite, one in a bliss
indescribable. . . ." Her voice broke, and through her
closed lids the tears glinted. "maybe somewhere, sometime
there will be an experience like that for all of us. Maybe
the grave is not the end, Father, maybe we are not doomed
to wander through Sheol forever. Maybe one day every
human being will know what it is like to be one with
God." She paused. There was only the dry clashing of
the palms, the sleepy mourning of doves in the nearby
meadows.

"I cannot tell you how it was," she went on, "I can't
even remember clearly, only that it was, it was! And now
—since then my very body has begun to change. There
are signs, purely human signs. It wouldn't be proper to
describe them to you, but I have told Mother what they
are and she—even she agrees that there can be no doubt.
I am to bear a child."

"Have you told Joseph?"

"No. I have been beside myself wondering what to do.
At first I wasn't sure myself. In my amazement I thought
perhaps I might be ill, or carried away by the intensity

of some childish dream. Then I knew, gradually I knew —and my body began to give proof. Until today I couldn't bring myself to tell Mother; and whenever I think of Joseph my heart dies."

"He loves you. Surely he, of all people, wouldn't turn against you." In great agitation, Joachim rose. "You must tell him at once. Tonight, if possible. Meanwhile we must try to think how best to handle this."

"Then you believe me? You do believe me, Father?"

"I have no choice save to believe. Like Joseph, I love you. And without faith love would be a mockery."

IX

JOSEPH was late that evening. He had wanted to finish off the batch of mortar he had made before it set. Then he could not resist gazing at the growing shape of his labors. It stood there, blowing with a soft and secret fire that his very ardor had blended into the clay. It had no roof as yet, but he had already begun the stairs that would lead to an upper chamber. It was going to be a good strong house, sturdy and graceful as it clung to the hillside, and it gave him satisfaction that it adjoined no other house.

In time it could be expanded so that their children could have more room. . . . Their children! His seed and Mary's. . . .

He turned abruptly, hurried down to his room to wash and draw on clean garments. His whole body was pulsing with love as he strode up the hill to be with Mary. He had never felt closer to Jahveh, whose sky arched above him, riddled with stars. It was as if his head and shoulders were crowding and thrusting among them, in a proud bright sharing of joy. He sang as he hastened toward her that night, he felt blessed above all men.

There was something arid and vacant about the house of Joachim; he sensed it as he approached. The family had come down from the roof, if indeed they had gone up at all. Hannah was putting the children to bed. When she came out and found Joseph there she gave him a curt, startled greeting and disappeared again. But there was no predicting Hannah. Joseph went into the garden where he found Joachim pacing, and Mary sitting in a strange attitude of quiet. Something was in the air. He could taste it, feel it, yet his earlier sense of elation was not to be denied. The life force was still throbbing within him, his manhood, his awareness of coming fulfillment.

Mary, sitting with her head bowed, had never seemed more beautiful, or her father's greeting more kind. "Peace be with you, Joseph. Mary, see who has come." Joachim's tone, hearty and rather anxious, sounded as if this were unusual. He turned then with a brief nod and left them alone. And this too seemed strange, yet in tune with Joseph's need. As if her father, in a burst of generosity and decency, had remembered what it was to be young.

Mary rose, gazing at him in a way that pierced him oddly. A direct and searching look, yet fraught with concern. "We must talk," she said, "let's go up onto the roof."

"Can't we walk down the path a little way, instead? It's a beautiful night." His voice was trembling. She must come. They had kissed in the olive grove a few precious times. "The flowers are so fragrant, let's walk down to the olive grove. Please."

She nodded almost absently. She moved ahead of him, her robes catching on the blooming oleander bushes, her sandals sounding like the scurrying of little animal feet along the stones. She moved swiftly as if in flight, yet she suffered him to catch her hand. How small it was, how cold.

"Wait," he cried out, laughing. "My darling, wait for me." She halted and he could restrain himself no longer, he swept her into his arms. He tried to find her lips and was the more aroused when she twisted her head away. "Mary, Mary, have you no idea how much I love you? How I think of you, nothing but you all day? Kiss me, Mary, in the way I want you to. Love me, Mary, love me in return. You've been so far away lately," he said, voicing what he had dimly sensed. "Come back, my beloved, come unto me." He was pleading in a way he had never pleaded before. His breath came hard. "Oh, Mary, my love, my sister, my child, my bride—hold me. Hold me close and suffer me to hold you. Let me love you as I long to, let me teach you what it is to know delight."

It was too much, it was folly, for she broke wildly away. "No! No." The concern he had sensed earlier had become an intense alarm. "You must not say such things, do such things. It isn't right!"

"But I love you and we are betrothed. We are husband and wife in the sight of God. Surely the one who made us did not give us these passions only to torture us. Surely a few more months can't matter, my dearest, when you are already my bride."

"We cannot, we must not, it isn't right."

"Right according to the cruel and foolish customs of Galilee, or right in the sight of God?"

But they were arguing now, and that was wrong. That was the only true wrong, to be separated from her in spirit, as indeed they had been separated these past weeks, he realized helplessly. What had come over her? What elusive yet insistent thing, changing her, making her so aloof, troubled, withdrawn? Had she tired of him? Was she ruing her bargain? Incredible. Such things might happen among heathen, but never among the decent women of Galilee. Never his Mary. She loved him. She could have no regrets—and certainly no other. She loved him!

Yet he stood shaken and baffled, searching himself for error. Desperately he regretted his outburst. He longed to cradle her against his breast, gently without passion; he longed only to know the touch of her once more. "Forgive me if I've spoken or acted rashly, Mary. I promise to bridle both my tongue and my desires. Only—don't look at me like that," he begged softly. "Don't draw so far away from me!"

She had backed up against the trunk of a tree. Her hands were behind her, clinging to it as if for support. Her face was a small white oval hung between the dark mists of her hair and the sheltering trees. "Don't come nearer," she whispered. "Joseph, I beg you—don't touch me! There is something I must tell you." Her lip trembled; it was a second before she could go on. But her eyes were unflinching.

"I am with child."

In the silence that followed he could hear her breathing,

or perhaps it was only his own blood pounding in his ears.
There was the incessant rattle and chirp of insects in the
grasses and the trees. Somewhere a pariah dog was yelping,
a wild and eerie sound. A bat dipped out of the star-
weighted skies, as if to mock him, then wheeled away.

Numb with astonishment, he could only gaze at her
for an eternity. Then he spoke one word. One alone,
which later seemed to him almost as unbelievable as the
thing she had told him.

"Whose?"

"I don't know."

"You don't *know?*" His hands, dangling at his sides,
felt wooden. A kind of paralysis had come over him. He
couldn't have moved nearer now if he had tried. "Mary,
are you mad? Or do you think I am?"

"Perhaps," she said. "Perhaps I am mad. At first I
thought so. How can it be? I asked myself that I am the
chosen one? How can it be? There are fairer girls in
Israel, and certainly purer ones. Girls whose only wish has
been to serve in the Temple, to fast and pray. No, there
had to be some mistake, I told myself. Yes, I have been
very close to God—especially in childhood; there were
times when I felt sure he spoke to me. But it is human
love that I have longed for as I grew older." She had been
staring into the darkness. Now she lifted her eyes to meet
his. "Flesh and blood love, Joseph. Your hands, your
arms, your lips, your body close to me even as it is close
to me now."

Again she paused, as if in a struggle to find the words
that would make it clear to him. Or to herself. At last,
drawing a deep painful breath, she went on. "So that
when it happened, when the angel of the Lord God came
unto me and told me that I was to be the one, the chosen
one—the one whose body was to carry the Christ Child
instead . . ." She made a little gesture of imploring. "I
could not believe it! I *dared* not believe it, Joseph. I was
dazed. I told myself it must surely have been a dream.
Or madness.

"But then gradually it came to pass, what the angel
had foretold. My body has been changing. It is not fitting
that I describe these changes but they are happening,
Joseph. They are real. Even my mother confirms them—

that I must surely be with child. And it can only be the child of—that other, the holy one himself, since I have known no other man. Not even you, Joseph, my husband. Not even *you*."

He stood frozen, uncomprehending. The lance had only stunned him as yet, it had not pierced his breast. He could thrust it almost impatiently aside. He said, in a voice that sounded puzzled and astonished, and yet somehow everyday: "The chosen one, my beloved? The Christ who has been expected so long? The Messiah whom so many people, good honest people, have believed themselves to be?"

"You don't believe," she gasped. Her eyes were stricken, she pressed one hand against her mouth to still its trembling. "For all your reading of the Scriptures, your voice in the synagogue, and those discussions you have with my father—you don't believe!"

"Mary, I do believe," he heard himself assuring her gravely. "God will keep his promise. The Christ will come to us one day."

"But not now? Not to us in our time, in our town, to us and our neighbors. Not to you and me. No, no, this great event is something that will happen far away, to other people. *That* will make it credible. And safe."

"Mary, you're right," he said quickly. "It isn't safe to trust ourselves too much to such beliefs. You've seen them yourself, the Zealots and false prophets being whipped down like dogs on the streets. You've heard them crying on the cross." His voice caught. "As for the women who've imagined themselves to be the chosen ones, as you say. . . ."

"I know. I know all too well. They're laughed to scorn, or become the butt of scandal. No, no, people won't have it—any evidence that God will keep his promise. Not if it's personal. Personal involvement in God's plan is too terrible, it costs too dearly." She took a step nearer him, her eyes were burning in the white leaf-shadowed oval of her face. "But isn't the test of faith suffering and sacrifice? A willingness to give up everything, if need be, Joseph, for what we claim to believe?"

Everything? To give up *everything?* He felt faint. His Mary, even his Mary—to deliver her unto this miracle that he, like all good Jews, had prayed for? The thought was staggering. He could not accept it. If it must happen let it happen elsewhere, as she said. Let this honor fall upon some other woman whose body was not already pledged to a man who loved her beyond all reason. Better even than life itself. Or yes, even more than God.

And now the shaft of the spear that had struck him down so unexpectedly out of the night plunged deep, deep, as if in punishment. . . . *I am with child* . . . the child of Jahveh, himself. Even he of Joseph's lifelong covenant. God the victor. God—he saw it now—the rival.

Rage smote him. And fear and a wild pleading rejection. He rebelled with all his being. He would not have it. Let it not be, let it not be! Yet, "I am with child," she had said. And if this were truly the case and not some fevered confusion of the mind, if this were a mortal child, then she had betrayed him. And the betrayal of God was more tolerable than the thought of her unfaithfulness.

It was too much. It was beyond his comprehension. He had worked hard that day and he realized suddenly that he was very tired. He said, his tongue feeling dry and heavy in his mouth, "What we believe, Mary, which of us knows what it is that he truly believes? Our land, our whole land is filled with sacrifice and suffering while it awaits this miracle it thinks it will accept and believe. Yet does Israel really want its own deliverance?" he demanded on a note of desperation. "Isn't it possible that we glory in our suffering? The suffering that binds us together as a people? Don't we rejoice in licking our wounds?"

He paused. Her eyes were intent upon him. When she did not answer he plunged on, diverting his desperation, focusing it upon this thing. "Maybe persecution has become dear to us—the whip of the Egyptians, the Babylonians, the yoke of Rome. So that we'd be lost without it. That's why, though we weep and beat our breasts at the scourgings and the crucifixions, how honest are we being? Isn't it possible that we're in league with them, privately relieved that once again our hopes are being put to death?"

"Oh, Joseph, Joseph," she said softly, out of her own desperation, "don't talk about Israel. Talk about us. I am going to bear a child! A child of flesh and blood. And if you cast me out. . . ."

"Cast you out?" A moan escaped him. For the shaft stirred in him deeply, bloodily now. *"Cast you out?"* he groaned again.

"Yes." She moved closer, young and small and pale with fear. "Divorce me for adultery. They will stone me in the streets, Joseph. You know the penalty."

He said, unable to keep out the bitterness, "Surely the God who has chosen you for such an honor would not let such a fate befall you."

"Joseph, have pity upon me!" Her hands were locked at her breasts in an attitude of unutterable supplication. She was at his mercy, this chosen child of God, this honored bride of the most holy enemy. And he was rocked by it, destroyed by the very power he had over her, her and the fruit of her outraged womb. He was unmanned, her tears dissolved him, so that his own eyes were dim as he folded her quietly against him, stroking her hair with his long work-scarred hands.

"Hush. Hush, hush little Mary, I love you. I love you! And so long as I live no harm shall come to you." Thus he gentled her, while his own soul threshed and strove against the invading spear. Presently, when she lay still against his heart he asked, "What does your mother say of this?"

"My mother is frantic. She can't believe that I'm without sin. She—forgive me my beloved, but she fears that it's Joseph's child I carry."

He moaned again, through clenched teeth. Would that it were! Would that he had taken her as his own weeks ago.

"She wants me to go away for a while. To visit my Aunt Elizabeth at a little town near Jerusalem. She thinks it may very well be a mistake, that I'm simply over-wrought. That perhaps if I rest there a while. . . ."

"And your father?"

"Joachim believes," she told him. "He doesn't question my story. To appease my mother he's agreed that I make the journey, but he knows that what I have said is true. The time is upon us. The Christ is surely coming.

And I, his daughter am to bear the holy child that is
to be our deliverer and saviour."

Joseph reeled through the darkness. He carried no
torch, and when an approaching light threw trees and
doorsteps into grotesque shapes, he turned and plunged
into the sheltering bowels of dark little alleys. Alleys
that would hide him in his blind agony.

He had been composed, parting with Mary. He had
walked erect, carefully, like a man determined not to
reveal his drunkenness. But once out of sight he staggered,
stumbled, not caring whether or not he fell. Longing to
fall and hurt himself in some manner so monstrous that
he could feel no other pain. For the spear now ripped
and bore viciously deeper, burning and tearing. *I can't
stand it;* he thought. Surely God would spare enough
mercy to lead him over a precipice, or to a well in
which to drown.

Mercy. The thought of a merciful God was so absurd
that he laughed aloud.

No, no, he was being a fool. He was not drunk but
perhaps he should be. He needed wine, strong wine to
soothe his shocked nerves, numb the agony a little, let
him sleep . . . sleep . . . and perhaps awake to discover
that it was only one of those nightmares wherein Mary,
his Mary, had just been carried, white and still, into a
burial cave. He ran wildly after the mourners, pleading
and weeping, but nobody turned even to allow him to
join the procession. Into the cave they carried her precious
body, and left her alone in the darkness and firmly
sealed the entrance with a rock.

"Mary!" He would sometimes waken himself with his
furious beating against it, or one of his brothers would
shake him back to consciousness.

Joseph. Joseph, you idiot, it's only a dream. But he
must have wine and there were no shops open and no
friends to whom he could turn in this state. *Cleophas.*
He came to a dead halt. Cleophas would be glad to share
a jug with him, to laugh, to boast. . . . What would it
reveal, that genial, arrogant face? Nothing. *Nothing.* Yet
he knew that he dared not risk it. That he was indeed

doomed if he went tracking down an evil that he feared so much he dared not even name it.

He did not trust himself. He knew that for the moment he was not quite sane.

But wine. Strong wine. Some of the wine his father kept hidden. Soft fat breasts of wine to suck on in secret, perhaps to ease the knowledge that he was but a sorry noisy little failure of a man upon whom other men, and sometimes even his wife, looked down.

Joseph groped into the dark little shop. Crouching, he fumbled around behind the boards, seeking the soft leathery touch of the skins. A loose plank came crashing down upon his foot and for an instant he sickened before the astounding physical pain.

"Joseph?" There was a stirring behind the drapery. He saw a small eye of light approaching. His mother stood in the doorway, her hair in a thick braid, a saucer of oil in hand. "Joseph, is that you?"

"Yes, Mother, it's only me. Go back to bed."

"Where have you been?" she said. "It's very late."

"Mother, am I a child that you should lie awake counting the hours till I come in?" He arose guiltily, trying not to wince at the excruciating hurting of the flesh.

"A child is a child to his mother until the day of his marriage," Timna said. "Surely you haven't been with Mary until this hour?"

"No, I've been walking." He turned his head aside as his mother drew nearer with her lifted lamp. He realized that he must be dirty and disheveled; he had crashed against bushes and trees in his wandering. "I didn't feel like sleeping, I've been walking in the hills."

"It's dangerous to go about so in the night." Her voice was troubled. "Joseph, is something wrong? Did you and Mary quarrel?"

"No! No, please—go back to bed."

"My son, I can see that there is something wrong. Is Mary angry with you? Is that it?"

"No, no," he said. "She's tired, that's all. She's going away for a little while." His own words startled him, as they also startled his mother. Until this moment he had scarcely comprehended this facet of all that Mary had told him.

"Going away?" Dazedly, Timna set down the lamp. "Within three months of her wedding?"

"Yes. Yes," he said hastily, "her parents think it best. She's going to visit an aunt in Judah, in the little town of Ain-Karem, I think she said. It's somewhere near Jerusalem."

"But why? With all the preparations, I should think she'd be needed here. Joseph, tell me. . . ." She came a step nearer and her gentle, frank blue eyes searched his. "You haven't done anything to offend her? As her betrothed husband surely you have treated her with respect?"

She regretted the words, so great was the anguish that came into her son's face. "Of course. How can you ask such a thing?"

"I'm sorry. Forgive me." She flung the braid back from her shoulder; quietly she wiped a bit of spilled oil from the base of the lamp. He was right, how could she? He was a man grown, he was not a child to be questioned by his mother. She was ashamed of her wakefulness and her lack of discretion. Yet his quick denial disturbed her. He had always loved Mary, and men were importunate. If he had overstepped the bounds of propriety he had been foolish, yes, but it was no sin. Certainly not enough to pack a child off on a journey that would keep her away from him.

That Hannah! The old antagonism flared up in Timna, the baffled knowledge that the house of Joachim considered itself a cut above her own. It was beyond her understanding, for she knew that the match was even. Lovely and desirable though Mary was, she was no finer than Joseph. And this trip, with its inference that she might not be safe much longer in the same city with him seemed to Timna cruelly unjust.

"I . . . it's just that I can't see why in the world Mary would want to leave at such a time. Or why her parents should let her go!"

"They think it's been too much for her," he said defensively. "All the preparations. They think she needs the rest." Then he said an astonishing thing. "You mustn't think evil of her."

"Think *evil*? Of Mary?" Timna gasped. "Oh, son, no. No, that's the last thing I'd think."

In her dismay she bade him goodnight and hastened back to her pallet. But now that he had planted the seed she could not rest. What was going on? What unspeakable mystery was stirring? Or was she only imagining things? Yet Joseph had been highly agitated. Something was indeed wrong or Mary would not even consider such a departure. A woman betrothed, within a few months of her wedding. The humiliation to her espoused husband, to all of them. It simply wasn't like Mary.

No, this must be Hannah's doing. But why? And then against her will, yet unable to deny it altogether, the question assaulted her: Mary, the pure, the exquisite, the pride of her parents—could it be that she was in the most serious trouble that could befall a girl?

Yet if it involved Joseph the problem could scarcely be considered that serious. In her confoundment Timna sat upright. But if, indeed, her son had had no part in it? What then?

X

HANNAH plunged into the work of preparing Mary for the journey. It seemed to her that by drowning herself in action she could somehow deny it, this madness that had come upon her child. The thing now was to get Mary out of the village, away from Joseph, away from prying eyes and busy tongues. In case. Just . . . in case. . . .

Not, truly, that there was cause for alarm. Hannah had reached a state where in sheer self-protection she was forced to reject the evidence that another part of herself, her pragmatic, common sense self, had witnessed. God would not do it to them! To her, maybe—she was only too bitterly aware of her grievous faults. But not to her husband Joachim. He had been punished enough. Wasn't it enough that their first son was twisted and doomed to walk in darkness? But not Joachim's daughter. Not Mary, their firstborn.

Mary was just overwrought with waiting, that was it. Hannah had had many dealings with midwives, often sat with them sucking a lusty pleasure from their tales. She knew that weird things happened to women sometimes when passion is denied. There was a girl who'd fancied herself pregnant by one of the high priests, and lo, her belly swelled, she had actual labor pains, and not until they showed her the newborn son of a neighbor did her straining subside.

Oh, but Hannah was tired, unutterably weary with

worry. She felt as if she had been carrying a bag of heavy stones up a mountain and now, somehow, she must drop it to rest before taking up again whatever burden lay in store.

Let Mary visit her Aunt Elizabeth for a while. Let Elizabeth shelter her and counsel her and nurse her, if need be, back to sanity. Elizabeth was older and wiser despite the fact that she'd never borne a child. Let her learn what it was like to worry about one; children were not an unmixed blessing!

Hannah had always felt close to her beautiful older sister, and when the priest Zachariah carried her off to Jerusalem she had begged to go along. Mingled with her awed respect for Elizabeth was a trace of envy for the more graceful life she led. Yet always there had been the consolation that it was Hannah's narrow loins that had found favor, and not Elizabeth's, in the sight of God.

Well now—Hannah's mouth tightened—how much favor she had actually found remained to be seen. In any case, Elizabeth would offer shelter for the poor confused Mary for a time, and a period of respite for the rest of them.

Meanwhile, Joachim set about finding a way to get Mary safely to Ain-Karem. It was a four days' journey at best—eight days away from the ripening crops if he were to go along. When he thought of all that could happen to them in his absence he shuddered. Marauders and thieves were so common that many men kept watch at night. If harm befell either his fields or his flock it would go hard with all the family; what's more, the prospect of a respectable wedding for Mary would be threatened. He still clung to that hope. Yet like Hannah he had moved into an area of numb withdrawal. What was to be would be, and the Lord would give them strength to bear it. As for now—Hannah's instincts were right; the thing they all needed was action, some definite step that would give them perspective on this astounding complication.

And so he made quiet inquiries in the village as to anyone who might be going to Jerusalem. It was a bad time of year, however, too close to the harvest and the ensuing Feast of Weeks when many of them would be making a pilgrimage to the Temple, for farmers even to think of leaving now. Then to his relief but somewhat to his consternation, Jacob came puffing up the hill one night to solve the problem.

"If it's true that Mary wants to go visiting," he beamed, as if this were a normal and joyous thing, the fool, "if she wants to go see her cousin and perhaps enjoy herself for a time in the city. . . ."

"Her aunt," Joachim said, "and it's no pleasure trip. . . ." though he hated his tongue for its harshness, for his galling need to reject and dominate this man at the very moment of his kindness.

"Yes, yes, well but whatever her reasons, I've learned there's a little company from Magdala who'll be passing this way tomorrow," he said eagerly, "and that if we had Mary at the fork in the road by noon, somewhere toward noon tomorrow she could join them and ride in safety to—wherever it is she's going," he finished lamely, albeit still smiling.

He reminded Joachim of a dog that comes trotting up with a bone. He was all but wagging his tail. "What sort of people?" demanded Joachim. "And how do you know?"

Jacob chuckled. "Oh, I hear lots of things from those travelers, it's not all time wasted, the time I spend visiting with those who pass our way. A man can learn a great deal." He ran a tongue around his puffy lips; his little gem-bright eyes glanced around hopefully.

Joachim rose and went to the cupboard for the cruet of wine. He poured some into a goblet and handed it to this man who was already practically his relative, trying not to wince at the way Jacob gulped it down.

He said, "Magdala's a city known for its wickedness. I'm not sure I'd trust my daughter with strangers from there."

"Oh, but these are good people. Several fishermen and their wives, a tradesman or two, the salt of the earth truly," he claimed. "They'd look after her and she'd have a fine jolly time besides."

He got to his feet, wiping his mouth on the back of his hand. Something in Joachim's pained silence penetrated at last. His eyes, in their purple pouches, were puzzled. "But if you don't want her to go. . . ."

"No, no. It's very short notice, I'll have to consult her mother." Joachim escorted him to the door. "Don't think we're not grateful," he said, forcing his voice to heartiness and clapping the pudgy shoulder. "But there's no hurry and—we'll see."

He stood, fists curling, watching the plump rather pitiful figure limp off down the hill on his never quite steady feet. He did not want to be beholden to the house of Jacob for anything, even so small a consideration as this . . . he wished . . . he wished. . . . But no, it was foolish to look back and try to trace what other course might have been taken. But he could not help wondering—if he had been stern, as Hannah had exhorted him to be, if he had held out against his daughter's imploring, given her to some other. . . . Joachim knew he was evading the real issue, the most oppressive and shocking of all . . . or if he had not been so quick to believe her! He in his long obsession with the coming of the Messiah. But it was too late to retreat now. Mary was already too ill and confused without letting her know what Hannah had finally made him realize: he could not, must not, accept her story.

Hannah did not go the crossroads with them. She awoke with a headache so severe she could scarcely raise her head. Mary had to tell her goodbye in the dim little room with its heavy odor of sleep, laced with the sharp taint of vinegar. Her heart broke at that tiny shape huddled on the mattress.

"Mother, it grieves me to leave you so." She knelt, helpless before this force that was sweeping them all before it so relentlessly. "I'll stay if you'll only say the word. I want to help you, I want to be near you always. . . . Mother?"

She remained so, gazing down, eyes moist. *Oh, embrace me, tell me you'll miss me, you're concerned for me.* There was no response. She stared forlornly out the window a minute as the enormity of it bore in on her.

Her voice was little and lost, saying, "I've never been away from home before."

Hannah forced herself to rise up on her elbows, though the fetid room rocked and her daughter's face, swathed in its veil, was a blur. "We've been through all that. Go now and don't keep your father waiting. If you should miss this meeting no telling when you could leave."

Mary rose, swallowing against the hurt in her throat. "You mustn't worry about me, Mother," she said from the door, fashioning the words for her own comfort. "I'll be quite safe, and I'll give your love to Elizabeth."

"Yes. You'll be better off there with her. She's wise. Sometimes women who don't have children are wiser about them than those who do," said Hannah. And her words compounded the irony. Mary stood torn. As yet she had not had the courage to tell anyone of that other revelation. Dare I? she wondered. But no, they would truly think her mad in claiming that Elizabeth too was to bear a child. Credulity had already been strained beyond the breaking point.

"Goodbye, Mother," she said softly, still hoping.

"Goodbye." Hannah's face was already to the wall.

Hannah lay still until Mary's footsteps had receded, until she could heard voices and the crunch of hooves and feet on the street below no more. Then when all was silent, Hannah gave way. She flung her tight-clenched limbs wide, she tossed her pain-lashed head. Her teeth were bared like those of an animal, and from her throat came a choked and bitter cry, its anguish the more awful because she must muffle its sounds so that the other children might not hear:

"Mary . . . Maaaary!"

They allowed Esau to walk along, leading the donkey, hobbling cheerfully through the darkness, feeling his way. As indeed they were all groping along, feeling their way no less than he. They kept to back streets as much as possible, but encountered a number of people even so. Among them Deborah.

"I've just heard," she exclaimed. "Oh, take me with you! What wouldn't I give to get away from all this hustle myself, sometimes I think I can't stand it, I keep telling my mother. . . ." She fell into step with them babbling enthusiastically, while her excited eyes and cool narrow nose seemed to sniff at the scent of the truth. She caught Mary's wrist, holding her a little back from her father. "I don't know whether to envy you or be angry wih you. You *will* be back in time for my wedding?" she demanded.

"Oh, yes. Yes, I wouldn't miss it."

"Or your own!" Joachim called curtly over his shoulder. "Come along now, hurry if we're going to make our rendezvous."

His tone signaled Deborah's dismissal; she had to stand watching them trudge on, with their strange and secret air of urgency. Certainly there was about them no air of holiday. Mad with curiosity, yet feeling that old bond of affection and loyalty for Mary, Deborah hurried home, debating whether or not to tell her parents.

Out in the open country they freed Esau's hand and let him bounce along leading the donkey and echoing the bird calls in the trees. He knew them all by name and could echo their cries so that sometimes they swooped down to inspect this otherwise solemn trio.

The day was bright and hot, with the rich sweet fragrance of lotus, flowering ginger, almond and lemon blossoms. For Mary every step was torment. She could hardly bear to think of her mother. Or Joseph . . . he had not returned to her since that night in the olive grove. And it was his father who had made these arrangements. Perhaps then his people, even his people, were anxious to be rid of her!

Thus when she saw Joseph waiting for them in the shade of the cypresses, she could not believe it. Such joy mingled with such anguish she could not speak, but only turn her wet eyes away.

Joachim too was startled. How dared he come, complicating things? He wanted to have these final moments alone with his daughter; perhaps to hear again her story, to restore and confirm that first blessed hour when he had been rocked to his soul by her words. When, awed, stunned but unquestioning, he had believed.

Perhaps fortunately, there was time for only the briefest of greetings. "They're coming, they're coming!" Esau announced, though it was a moment before the rest of them could see the film of dust that began to hover over the burning hill. He had heard the creak of harness and plod of hooves, and he hopped excitedly on his crooked legs predicting accurately, "There are horses among them along with the asses, I can tell. When they arrive will you lift me onto the back of a horse, Father, that I may know how it feels?"

"We'll see, we'll see," Joachim told him indulgently.

Frozen, in a kind of dumb fascination, they stood watching the figures in the distance grow larger, until Joachim stepped into the road to wave them down. Then, only then did Joseph turn to Mary. "Don't go," he said grimly, without warning. "Mary, I can't bear it. Don't go, even now. Stay here with me."

"I can't," she gasped. "I must go. I've already caused our parents enough grief." Her heart was hammering. The company of strangers was drawing nearer. She could hear their voices, and the fated rattle of stones beneath the hooves of the beasts they led or rode. She had never seen any of them before—alien faces, dusky, laughing or grave—a mass of indifferent unknown faces behind the veils or under the soft round hats. She was frightened, she had never been away from her mother, and she wanted desperately to go home.

"I must go!" she cried and forced herself to hasten forward, clutch at her father's sleeve.

He was conferring with a tall swarthy man in striped garments who was leading a horse, as Esau had predicted. He was delivering it to its owner in Jericho, he explained. He seemed proud of having it in charge but was afraid of mounting it and advised against Esau's trying. They listened nervously to his friendly tale, diverted but preoccupied. The man told Joachim they'd be glad to have Mary accompany them. They had decided to avoid the Samarian towns that lay along the Sichem-Ephraim highway; they felt it would be safer to take the longer more rigorous Jordon mountain route, but if that was acceptable she was welcome. He waved aside Joachim's offer of money.

Thus her fate was settled. She kissed Esau, who now began to cry and cling to her, and the rough grizzled face of her father. He would have lifted her onto the donkey, but Joseph reached for her first—between them she almost fell. Then she was on its back, the paniers at its sides bumping, and Joseph's face was tormentingly near, moving along beside her. "Don't stay long, Mary," he pleaded. "We've got so much to talk about, there's so much I must know. . . ." But the others were crowding in upon them, the animals and the people who wanted to continue on their way. "Oh, Mary . . . Mary!"

The donkey rocked and jarred along beneath her. She turned for one last forlorn, near panicky look at the three who stood shielding their eyes. They lifted their hands stiffly to wave at her and she made a wistful little gesture of waving back before grabbing the reins once more.

Thus she left behind her all that she loved in Galilee.

On they moved, on and on forever. The muscles of the sturdy little beast had become her muscles, nerveless, insensate, a part of the endless winding road. Across the boggy plains of Esdraelon they plodded, then east across the Jordan and up into the mountains where she must clutch the reins tighter, though they were already cutting her wrists where she had wound them lest she fall asleep and pitch headlong off into one of the steep gorges where the tiny hooves picked their way so gingerly.

At night she lay shivering in her heavy wool cloak, wrapping it closer around her, trying to rest upon the hard ground. The campfire was a core of comfort in the darkness; figures huddled around it, some sitting, some sprawled. Fear lurked in the shadows. Once there was a bloodcurdling cry. She sat up, dry with terror. But she heard the shouts of the watchers, and their beating staves. Hagar, the wife of the leader, lying near, reached out a motherly hand. "Lie still, child, they will drive the lion away." Trembling, Mary crept nearer to her, this large rawboned woman, who had taken her under her wing. Except for several small children Mary was the youngest of the group.

One night when they had reached the stony wilderness of Judeah they took refuge in a cave. Perhaps one of those that had given David shelter from the pursuing Saul, the men remarked as they built the fire at its mouth. Or where he had taken his child bride of the wastelands on their wedding night, Mary thought as she lay down. She could not sleep, she lay stiff with weariness and homesickness and longing, she lay thinking of Joseph. His last words, his bewildered and tormented eyes. She ached with a hunger which she fought to set aside . . . it was not right, it must not be. A different fate awaited them.

But oh, Joseph, my Joseph—believe in me. You must believe.

Toward evening of the fourth day, tired as they all were, a sense of excitement gripped everyone. They were nearing their destination. Some of the families had already dropped off at small mountain towns. The others were proceeding on to Jerusalem. Mary's anticipation was surpassed by her anxiety. Only twice before, with her parents, had she been in the teeming city of Jerusalem. Already exhausted, half-sick from the journey, now she was sick with dread lest she fail to find her way to Ain-Karem. But Hagar put her mind at ease; she and her husband would not think of abandoning her, they would ride on with her to make sure she found the home of her aunt.

Elizabeth had been restless all night.

The child was now so big she found it difficult to adjust its crowding weight to the couch. She flung off the coverlet and walked about to ease herself, her bare feet noiseless on the marble floors or the soft Persian carpets of her house. She could not leave off touching it, this precious bulge that she carried, for to do so eased a constant concern. It was there, daily growing heavier, and so surely it lived, this belated gift from God. Yet thus far she had not felt it move.

Was it in the fourth month or the fifth that women said the mysterious stirring began? She was nearly six months now. Six proud, anxious, enthralled months since her husband had come home from the Temple, white and shaken, struck dumb by some experience there too awesome to reveal. And that night when she had lain down with him to comfort him he had come into her with a power and strength amazing in a man of his years. And when she arose from his side she had wept for the joy that had been so long denied them. Her seed had been quickened at last—she knew at once, she knew! And for

days she too had been almost too overcome with thanks-
giving to speak.

The moon laid a tracery of silver on all the finely
wrought furnishings of the house, and the broad balcony
that overlooked the town. Elizabeth made her way there
and stood gazing out. The moon was a half-man lying on
its back, laughing down. "You are too old to bear a child,"
the shadowy mouth taunted. But she tipped her black
head proudly back; the two white wings at her temples
were all that revealed her age. She had a glad sweet
noble face that pregnancy had enhanced. Yet alarm
touched her, unconsciously she stroked her sides, as if
to force some signal from them.

What if it were true, what if she were actually too
old? What if Zachariah's muteness was not from wonder
but from fear for the greater disappointment that awaited
them? God's miracle would prove only a mockery if she
delivered a stillborn child.

She clasped her bare arms against the chill of the summer night. Fireflies winked like little fallen stars over the
rooftops that fell away and away, down the hillside, at
the foot of which ran the narrow road to Jerusalem. The
city too glimmered with a few late-burning lights, while
beyond, swathed in pearly clouds, mighty and eternal,
rose the Mount of Olives.

A sense of anticipation began to mount in Elizabeth.
A strong conviction of some important thing impending.
She could hear the crickets singing, the beat of a night
hawk's wings. And quite clearly, far below, the rhythmic
pluck and plod of hooves as some late traveler persevered
along the winding road.

She had settled down on her couch once more, and
was half-asleep, dreaming, dreaming . . . when she heard
the insistent pounding on the thick oak door. Alarm
tightened her skin. Twice robbers had crept up the steep
stone steps and forced their way boldly into the home of
the pious unarmed priest. But it wasn't of her remaining
silver she was thinking, only the safety of the child.

Then the voice came to her. The sweet young voice
that sounded so familiar and yet so startling. "Aunt
Elizabeth. Don't be afraid, it's Mary, your sister's daughter. It's only me."

"Mary!" Fumbling for robes, Elizabeth caught up the night lamp. "How can this be?" She hurried to the door, flung it wide. In the added glow of a sputtering torch two figures were revealed.

"Forgive us for disturbing you so late," Mary said. "We took the wrong fork in the road." She turned to the heavy dark man in the striped robe. "Thank you, Seth—you and dear, dear Hagar. I'll never forget your kindness in coming with me."

"Yes, yes," Elizabeth cried. "Bless you for bringing her safely to me. But why? How? No, time for explanations later, when you have come in and refreshed yourself. Let me call my husband."

No, no, the man said, his wife was waiting below with the beasts, they must be on. He hesitated. "However, if you could send someone to stable the ass."

"Yes, I'll send a servant," Elizabeth said. "If you're sure you won't summon your wife and honor us by your presence?"

No. No, they must be on, he insisted. He was a bluff and hearty man, vigorous and talkative on the trip. But now a great shyness had come upon him. He lingered, his eyes fixed upon Mary, his large jaw thrust outward. It was plain that something within him was struggling to be said.

"Farewell," he blurted finally, and had started awkwardly down the steps when suddenly he halted, jerked back his head. "Forgive me, but I—I feel that some strange honor has already befallen me this night!"

The two women gazed at each other in wonder a second after they had embraced. "Is it really you, little Mary?" Elizabeth asked. She lifted her lamp to the young face, so sunburned and dusty from the road.

"Yes. Though I can hardly believe I'm here. Never has a journey seemed so long, never has the distance from Nazareth seemed so great." Her voice broke. "And I—I'm not little Mary any more, my aunt. I am a woman grown."

"It becomes you," her aunt said softly. "You are even more beautiful as a woman than I would have believed."

"I had to come," Mary said. "My parents wanted it,

and though I dreaded leaving them I realize now that I wanted it even more. I had to come," she said again. "Seeing how it is with my aunt. That God has finally favored her with seed that is likewise fated to be holy seed. I realize now that my aunt, and only my aunt, will understand."

"Mary!" Elizabeth's face was contorted with a joy that was akin to pain. "Oh—*Mary!*" Again her hands flew to her bulging body, but this time to know and savor the sweet throbbing. "It moves, it moves! My little one moves. Zachariah!" She turned to the slight figure that had appeared blinking in the arched doorway, bearing another lamp. "Oh, my husband, our baby lives and breathes and twists its little body within me. Our baby moves!"

She was crying. The tears ran unchecked down her cheeks; they mingled with the kisses that fell on Mary's face, her hair, her hands. "Blessed are you among women," she cried. "And blessed is the fruit of your womb." Still weeping, she knelt and kissed the girl's grubby feet.

"Then you know? You already know how it is with me, my aunt?"

"I know. I knew it on the instant that my own child leapt. How is it that I have deserved to be thus visited by the mother of my Lord?"

His mother. . . . The mother of their Lord.

Mary stood shaken and dazed. It was true then, true. Her aunt bore witness. This, then, was the reason for the long arduous journey. This confirmation.

But she was so tired, so tired, rocking back and forth on the small beast still, making her way forever to this place of light, high on a mountainside. This pure and quiet place of peace and confirmation and holy refuge. And the voice of her gratefulness rose up in her, it poured forth from her in joy and wonder:

"My soul doth magnify the Lord! . . . My heart rejoiceth, for in him is my succor!" she cried. "He hath seen the lowliness of his handmaid, and behold, from this day all generations shall call me blessed, for the mighty one hath done great things in me. . . ."

And as her song of bliss and prophecy continued,

Elizabeth could not leave off kissing her dusty feet and washing them with her tears. And Zachariah, Elizabeth's husband, wept too in exaltation for this thing that had come to pass.

XI

Now in new ways she heard the voice of God. It roused her at dawn when his seven silver trumpets at the Temple heralded the day's first sacrifice. And every few hours the hills were pierced again by these wild and holy signals for songs and psalms. Each time Mary trembled; it was as if the thrill of his presence rang through her, rousing her from her dreamy meditations that were a strange blend of homesickness, bliss and awe.

How had she ever lived otherwise than in this place of gentle elegance that was itself a kind of temple, spare and sanctified like the aged priest who dwelled here, yet rich with the warmth and color of his wife? The walls and floors and draperies were purest white; not the flaking gray-white of the little houses of Nazareth, but radiant with the sunshine that spilled from the sky by day, and the brilliance of the huge Judean stars at night. White and shining like Zachariah's hair and beard and robes. He almost glistened as he moved about, his hands, so curiously massive compared to the rest of him, clasped across his breast.

Or the hands would gracefully beckon, direct—communicating as clearly as the prominent eyes that shone in his pale and shrunken face. Before him Mary felt a kind of stricken adoration. She flew about waiting on him, smoothing his bed, bringing him sweets from the table, sometimes washing his parchment-yellow feet. These duties

were like devotions, or supplications. He seemed, in his
shadowy rustling radiance like some emanation of God's
very breath. Surely he had the ear of the almighty, for
in his power and purity he flowed into God like some
undefiled stream. Let him then persuade the Lord to
absolve her of her unworthiness. The anxieties that still
plagued her, the purely human concerns. For she still
longed desperately for Joseph; consciousness of him was
with her always, despite this life so different from the
one they had known. What was he thinking? What were
his plans? Would he ever truly believe her? Would her
mother? Or the people of Nazareth? Did even Joachim
believe any more?

Oh, my uncle, she thought as she dipped the sponge into
the basin and cleansed the precious feet. Let me be like
you, utterly trusting, even transported by what the Lord
has decreed. Ask my Lord and my God to forgive me
for being so troubled when he has surely brought me
here to rest and put my soul in readiness. Ask that I
be given the peace and the will to be worthy of the honor
of bearing his son!

She was more at ease with her aunt, who had a joyous consoling reasonableness; without detracting from the
mystery, Elizabeth could reduce Zachariah to human
terms. He had served in the innermost sanctuary, she
told Mary, where the altar of incense stood. "Only once
in his lifetime does it fall the lot of a priest to burn the
incense. And it was on this day, behind the curtain in
that secret sanctum, that my husband had an experience
so profound that it robbed him of speech. When he finally
emerged before the multitude who were praying outside,
he couldn't address them."

She went on working on the mosaics as they sat in the
garden. She was teaching Mary the art as she taught the
Temple virgins. "A priest works very hard. He draws
his duties by lot, and often they're exhausting. They
have to lift the heavy carcasses onto marble tables and
flay and scrape them, and drain their blood and carve
them for the offerings. This can be quite a strain on the
older men." There was a look of tender wifely speculation
on her slender, always faintly smiling face. "Maybe

God saw that he needed the rest. That too may be a reason for striking him dumb. Maybe the Lord in his wisdom realized what a comfort it would be to me to have my husband with me while we await the coming of this long-delayed little one."

Her aunt's rich throaty tones—how was it that they came from a woman born in the selfsame house as Hannah? She was like a highborn lady. And she knew how to do everything. Embroider, play the lute, make beautiful arrangements of fruits and flowers. She was partial to poppies; she had coaxed them out of the arid soil so that their scarlet banners flowed down the long white flights of steps. Her food was exquisite, served on dishes as delicate, pale and old as Zachariah. There was meat almost every night, and from it Elizabeth would carve the choicest pieces for her niece.

The maidservant cleared away each course and brought them heated wine. The couches were covered with a silken stuff threaded with gold. The glow from a hanging alabaster lamp fell on their faces. Zachariah, helpless to pronounce the prayers, would sit lost in his private rapture, yet alert, while his vibrant wife spoke of their gratefulness to God. How close to God they all seemed, here in the very shadow of his Temple. How different all this from the noisy clash and confusion at home, the earthier manners.

Mary's head swam. Who was she really, and where did she belong? This graciousness, this rustling quiet with the gently burning lamps, making her feel cherished, surrounded by a love that was almost sublime. Yet making her feel her awkwardness as well, a bumbling country girl. She felt curiously shamed before the servant, and akin to her. As if she too should be in the kitchen or scurrying the dishes away.

Why then had God brought her here to merge with this rare and dazzling household? Was there another reason? Was it perhaps to rouse up such royal blood as flowed in her veins; to make her aware of what responsibilities she must be ready for? Her fingers tightened around the silver goblet. She must strive to be equal to them, to learn these aristocratic ways.

She must remember that she carried a king!

Jerusalem itself was a part of the thrall. Jerusalem, City of David. City of God. For had he not fashioned it, had he not named it? Was it not toward Jerusalem that one turned to pray, however far away he lived? Was it not to Jerusalem that every good Jew made his pilgrimage? And always the pilgrims sang as they approached: "Within thy gates, Jerusalem, our feet stand at last. . . ." It was their favourite song of ascent. Mary had sung it with her parents as a little girl. And it rang in her blood now, gazing toward it from a balcony in the terraced garden one evening at sunset.

From this distance it looked rather like a tawny old lion lying among the golden limestone hills. The intense light fell upon its rosy flanks, working patterns of shadow. She could see its mighty gates, its historied walls, the rooftops and spires and towers, and soaring above all in the east the blazing glory of its Temple, where dwelt the very being of the Most High.

"It's so beautiful here," she said, moved and lost. "Everything is. No wonder you are so beautiful, Aunt Elizabeth."

Her aunt laughed. "Oh, but I'm not. And Jerusalem— you'll find much there that is anything but beautiful, Mary. But right now, with the miracle that has befallen you, everything you behold must seem incredibly beautiful."

Elizabeth eased her body down upon a marble bench. The child had crowded up against her lungs, she pressed her hands against it. "How strong is my little occupant, he is making up for his long sleep."

Lightly Mary's fingers brushed her own body. Nothing as yet, no further sign. She had a startled sense of vacancy and loss, followed by a shock of rejoicing. What if she had been dreaming? Or only deluded, as her mother said, overwrought? What if all she had needed was a change— to get away from Joseph. Joseph, her love! What if she could go back to him now, even now, as his wife and not the cradle of the hope of Israel?

She clung to the parapet, shaken by her own thoughts. Elizabeth was saying, "What passes for beauty isn't important, Mary. My sister's house will always be more rich than mine; its children are its treasures."

"God has favored you too at last, my aunt."

"Yes, oh yes, and all the more because like Sarah, mother of Isaac, nor like Isaac's own wife Rebekah—like these great ancestors I too was forced to wait." She reached for a little box of tiles they had left from a mosaic table on which they were working. It was to be a wedding gift for one of the Temple maids. They made a musical clicking in her fingers as she mused. "Of course serving at the Temple helped ease my spirit and my shame. And to work with my little virgins—mothering them has been my compensation. They all need mothering so much, especially when they first come. Take Phora." She gestured toward the table. "Such a shy little thing when her parents brought her to us. I'll never forget how she cried when they left."

"How can they do it?" Mary gasped. "I mean—your own baby. How could you give up your own child even to God?"

"These people were very poor and there were many other children. But yes. . . ." Elizabeth made a little cradling gesture across her womb, "it seems inconceivable, doesn't it? Even that other Hannah, another one barren so long—it may sound wicked, but I sometime wonder how she could bear to give back little Samuel to God, despite her vow?" The dusk was falling, but Elizabeth fitted a few more tiles into the small table. "With daughters it's usually not so much devotion as advantages," she said. "Girls who've been trained in the Temple make excellent marriages."

"I too am going to make a good marriage," Mary said. "I'm betrothed, Aunt Elizabeth. To a man named Joseph. A man I love and persuaded my parents to give me to. A—a carpenter," she rushed on, as her aunt regarded her with surprised and troubled eyes. "We're to be married when I return home." She said it for the joy of saying it; she said it to make it so.

Elizabeth put down the tiles. "Oh, Mary, are you sure of this?"

"Yes. Yes, he knows what's happened."

"And he accepts it? He understands?"

"He will. He loves me. Oh, I know he will!"

"I hope so. For your sake, Mary, I hope so." The older woman halted before the look in her niece's eyes.

She said carefully, trying to hide her concern, "But if—it should turn out otherwise, you must stay here with us. Here you'll be safe, you and your little one. And who knows?" she said cheerfully, soothingly, "That too might be part of God's plan. To send you here to be near Jerusalem when the child is born. To have him grow up here with his cousin."

"Oh, no," Mary said quickly. "That's very kind of you, but I don't believe Joseph would have it. His love for me—it's so intense it frightens me at times. He would never give me up, not for any reason."

Saying it eased her heart about him, made it so. Surely these things she claimed were true. He would tell her so himself when he came up for the Feast of the First Fruits. As he would come, as he would surely come. She began to count the weeks until that day.

When Mary was sufficiently rested from her journey, they walked to Jerusalem. Flinging her veils about her, Elizabeth strode along head high. It was good for a woman with child to walk, she said. "I hid myself for five months lest the Lord see fit to dash my baby from me after all. But now that you're here, Mary, you who caused my child to leap within me, I have nothing to fear."

Nothing to fear . . . Mary hastened to keep step with this proud and joyous woman with the high cheekbones, the gay little wings of hair. She tried to draw courage from her aunt, to hold fast to her own conviction. But Elizabeth's coming child was flesh as well as spirit, flesh of her husband's flesh so that they two were united. While my son, Mary thought shakenly—my blessed son. Whom shall he call father if Joseph should put me away?

But Jerusalem. Ah, Jerusalem! As her aunt had warned, it was not all beauty. It had its palaces yes, its rich houses whose tile roofs gleamed. The most fabulous palace of all was that of the hated Herod, built on the very site where David had sung his psalms. But it also had its hovels, its dirt and its stench. They passed through massive gates where Roman soldiers stood guard in watchtowers overhead. Men who looked mostly bored, hot and uncomfortable in their heavy metal helmets and vests. Some were mere boys. One of them caught Mary's eye one day and she was torn by the frank pleading girl-hunger and homesickness in his eyes. Shaken, she hurried on beside her aunt.

The streets and shops swarmed. All was vivid, exciting, reeking with the scent of hot grease and a frantic din of shouting and haggling. Bland, insolent camels were maneuvered through the crowds, and donkeys whose backs and sides bulged with so many crates and bundles people must press back against the walls to give them passage. Drivers cursed and yelled and brandished sticks. The narrow streets, tented against the fiercely burning sun, or tunneling through the dark rocks, were a series of steep cobbled steps. In the bazaars and marketplace all the treasures of the world seemed on display. Cashmeres and tapestries and silks, spices and ivory and jewels, perfumes, carpets, lamps, exotic toys. Their colors assaulted her senses, rousing up visions of the lands from which they had been brought in ships and caravans. She ached at their wonders, for she longed to buy gifts for those at home.

But the true gem of Jerusalem was the Temple. Eastward it soared in all its splendor, stirring in Mary emotions so profound they were like travail. She divined how it must have been for David when at last he beheld the sacred ark being brought up from the desert, ransomed from the Philistines, to be safely housed here forever. How in a passion of exaltation he had stripped his garments from him and sung and danced before his subjects in the palm-lined streets.

Gone now, that celestial vessel that had been carried by the sons of Levi through all the wanderings in the wilderness. Vanished, destroyed along with the magnificence of the Temple that had been built by Solomon. So that now the Holy of Holies was empty of all save the presence of the invisible God. Yet the rapture remained. And Jahveh's will prevailed. For twice more after violation and vanquishment the Temple had been restored. Ironically, this time by the despised oppressor Herod, who sought to appease the Jews. And though a thousand priests and ten thousand workmen had labored on it for more than forty years, its vast complex of walls

and courts and gilded columns were not finished even yet.
And to pass through the high wall surmounted with its
twinkling spikes was to feel such anticipation that it was
scarcely to be borne:

> How amiable are thy tabernacles,
>   O Lord of hosts!
> My soul longeth, yea, even fainteth
>   for the courts of the Lord. . . .

Through the Gate Beautiful into the Court of Women,
which was as far as they could go. . . . The trumpet
blasts were enough to rip the skin from flesh. Ranged on
the marble stairs, in garments of purest white, stood the
young Levites, harps in hand. Their music was like something straight from heaven as they played and sang. A bliss
of adoration swept her . . . at first.

At first.

Then gradually the suffering intruded. Wherever she
went she heard it, smelled it, tasted it and could not cast
it out—the piteous anguish of the sacrifice. How plaintively they cried, the beasts and fowls being brought up
for the offering. Her soul shriveled at the sound of it, she
could hear the music no more—only the deep and awful
crying that seemed to come from somewhere in the pit
of herself.

Why? Why? What did God want of all this? Why
should the creator of life wish his creatures slain? The
gentle, snub-nosed sheep, the awkward cattle pulling back,
the soft white doves fluttering in their cages. Why?

Revulsion assailed her. This was not the joyous communion with that one who had seemed to speak to her
from the stars. This was wild and strange. Her uncle,
the pure white priest—she saw now what he was actually
about when he served at the altar. The hot blood spurt-
ing, the sticky feathers, the tough hide scraped, the
hacking and plucking and the carving of the raw red
meat. Those hands, those holy hands. She realized now,
appalled, why they were so large. They were the hands
of a butcher!

Mary swayed. People pressed close in the heat. There
was the heavy odor of the beasts, musky, nostalgic and

of the farm, those that were still living; there was the
sickening succulence of those already roasting. Smoke
poured down, mingling with a sweaty woman-smell and
the dizzying aroma of incense. The doves crooned and
cried. Cattle bellowed. And rhythmically behind it all, like
the sound of tambourines, was the tinkling of coins being
dropped into the money boxes.

The world began to rock as it had on the journey.
Frantically, like one of the frightened doves, Mary struggled to hang onto consciousness. She could feel her aunt
looking at her anxiously. "Are you all right?" She nodded,
it would be an offense to leave. And the other girls,
Elizabeth's charges, all so poised, she could not suffer
them to see her disgrace. Yet as she prostrated herself
and prayed, she had a vision of a greedy, bloodstained
mouth laughing at his victims—those who enriched the
money-changers, trying to buy favor with their gifts and
sacrifices. And the leashed and terrified creatures—and
all the terrified people on their faces or their knees.

Jahveh, forgive me! she prayed in new horror at her
thoughts. But it seemed to her something was wrong. Such
was not the father of her spirit, the voice that had spoken
to her in childhood, the love, the bliss that had invaded
and quickened her womb.

In the fields and orchards the grains and fruits ripened
and swelled, like the bodies of the two women. Mary's
now, as well. And remembering her earlier misgivings,
she was ashamed. Why could she not have been like her
aunt, swept utterly into the marvel, beyond questioning
or human concerns? Then one night she learned that despite Elizabeth's continual rejoicing, she too had misgivings.

"I feel sure it will be a son," she said as she walked
about in the garden, to relieve her discomfort, after Zachariah was in bed. "I doubt if such a miracle would have
been vouchsafed me if it were not to be a man-child."

"It will be a son," said Mary.

"Yes, a son, who will be a man of destiny." Elizabeth
caught her breath, stood silent a moment, pulling some dry
leaves from the ivy. "With all the penalties that implies."

"Penalties? What do you mean?"

"It's a serious thing to be a leader sent from God. It's a grave thing even to be a priest. There are responsibilities, such terrible responsibilities. And if this be true of priests, how much more so to be a prophet or a king. The mother of such a man pays dearly for the honor."

Mary couldn't answer. The Zealots . . . she remembered, she remembered. Yes, hideous things happened to them. And often the foaming prophets. They were not men to be envied. But that the king should suffer? The very king?

Seeing how white and still she was, Elizabeth turned and came to embrace her. "Forgive me, Mary, for going on so about myself. Or for causing you to worry." She lifted the small set chin, gazed into the troubled eyes. "My son—greatly as I love him already," she said, "I know that he will be as nothing compared to the child you are going to give the world. And we must trust in the Lord who will bring all this about. We have no right to be afraid."

"But what will he be like, this child that I carry?" Mary begged. "This baby I have been told is to be the Messiah? The Messiah—I've heard of his coming all my life, at home, and in the synagogue, but I'm confused. Will he come as a king to reign over Israel only, or over all the world? Tell me, my aunt, you are married to a priest and you have studied. Will he have to go out and do battle with our enemies to bring that kingdom about? And is he going to bring an end to Israel's suffering as a nation, or an end simply to suffering? All suffering. To the lepers and the beggars and the slaves, suffering such as I've seen on this very journey, in Jerusalem. And in Nazareth— suffering such as my brother's blindness."

"We don't know," Elizabeth said. "God reveals to us only as much as we're able to accept. We don't know, Mary. And the prophets themselves didn't know. They disagreed in so many ways. Some said the redeemer will be a king descending in triumph even as you describe; some said he will be a very poor man riding on an ass." Her eyes were shining now, her long lips parted so that her white teeth flashed. "Only on one thing they all agreed—he's coming, he's truly coming! And there will be another before him who will help to pave the way.

"And the time is upon us," she went on. "That much we do know, Mary. And we're a part of it, you and I. Exactly what our roles are to be isn't clear as yet. We can only wait and see. But that's part of the wonder of it too, the mystery. To wait patiently, not knowing, only trusting—and to try to be worthy of whatever is to be. To know, to have a conviction deep in the heart," she cried softly, "and yet really not know at all. That's life, Mary, and it's also religion. God—who can really know God even after revelation?" she asked. "And who can convey to another the essence of the revelation he has had? He can't, he can't. We can only wait and find out his meaning, each of us for himself, slowly, gradually."

Mary was staring at her as if transfixed. And Joseph? She was thinking. What of my beloved? What is to be his role in all this? A sweet anticipation smote her, almost too intense to endure. The Feast of the First Fruits was almost upon them. Already pilgrims were on the road. Perhaps even now he was heading for Jerusalem!

The day before the festival Mary and Elizabeth went to the city. They set off early in the day, hoping to avoid the crowds. But the roads were already thronged, they were a long time even getting through the gates; and within was a teeming chaos of singing, shouting, laughing people, laden with their offerings. Men carried kids or lambs across their shoulders, women bore jugs of precious oil, children lugged bags of grain. Asses were everywhere, so loaded they sometimes stumbled. The water carriers did a tremendous business, for the heat of the day coupled with the press of sweating, straining humanity created a violent thirst. "Water, fresh sweet water! Wait your turn —" In the marketplace it was almost impossible to reach the counters piled high with sheaves of yellow wheat, pyramids of fruit, and garlands for the procession.

"Wait here," Elizabeth said, "I'll buy the pomegranates and make my way back. No use both of us being crushed."

"Let me go," said Mary, for her aunt was so much nearer her time. But Elizabeth was already lost in the crowd. She stood waiting, listening to some musicians who were playing in an alley where children were dancing. An atmosphere of adulation and celebration prevailed. As one of the spectators drew away she caught sight of a familiar long-jawed face. "Uncle Nathan!"

He spied her, too, and waving one hand, struggled toward her. "How is it with you, Mary?" he cried as they embraced. He was a homely man, heavily pock-marked, but his eyes were tender and pleasant. "We miss you at home, all of us. Let me look at you," he exclaimed in innocent appraisal, "see if you've changed. . . ." His voice broke off in acute embarrassment, he looked quickly away.

Mary could feel the color sweep her cheeks. "I'm fine, fine," she claimed. "And you? And Deborah? Did she come with you? Did any of your family come along?"

"No, all of them are too busy with the wedding—except for your cousin Isaac, who was with me a moment ago. I seem to have lost him, I'd better go look for him." He was obviously anxious to get away. "I'll tell your parents I saw you and that—that you are well?"

"Oh, yes, yes, very well. Only, wait!" She must cling to him a moment more, this dear homely relative who seemed to bring that long-lost country of home suddenly near. "Didn't my family come then, not any of them?"

"None that I know of, at least not with our party. Your father may have joined others. We left early, Mary, he may very well be on his way." Again that flick of a glance, startled, unwilling, as if to confirm or deny what he could not believe he had seen. "Goodbye, Mary, there's Isaac. I'll give everyone greetings for you."

Elizabeth reappeared with her bag of bright red fruit. Her hair had become disheveled and there was perspiration along her ever-smiling lips. "This crowd! I fear we were foolish to get into it, we'd better go home."

"But if my father has come for the festival?"

"Then he'd scarcely look for you here. Surely he'd go first to Ain-Karem."

It was a relief to reach the comparative coolness and quiet of the hillside house; but a terrible tension had begun to mount in Mary. Certainly she could not lie down and rest, as Elizabeth urged. Instead, she went up onto the roof to watch the road. She flinched each time she remembered that chance meeting with her uncle. What must he be thinking, and what would he surely report at

home? But no matter, no matter any of it if her father
and Joseph came. She could see them now, toiling along
the great highways together, or entering the city or approaching along the road. She crouched by the parapet,
shielding her eyes. Somewhere among that stream of pilgrims two people, please Lord, just two people. The two
she loved. Please. Or even—only one.

All afternoon she waited, until her bones were stiff until
finally as the sun was setting, she dozed. And it was then,
when her eyes could watch no more, that Joachim came
stomping up the steps.

The servant roused her. "There is someone below who
asks for you. There is a man."

She sprang up, flinging back her dark hair. A man! *Joseph*. All her senses leaped toward him, all her blind singing hope and need. For an instant she had forgotten she
expected any other. Joseph waited below, Joseph had
come!

The blow of seeing that it was Joachim who stood there
was almost too stunning. She stumbled and would have
fallen except for his quickly outstretched arms. Then she
was cradled against him, comforted by his rough burly
tenderness in his robes that smelled sweaty and travel-
stained. And as she sobbed, "Father, Father," he thought
it was only tears of joy that she shed at seeing him.

"Are you alone?" she begged. "Hasn't anyone else
come?"

No, Hannah hadn't felt up to it, he said, and the
children had remained behind to help her, but she had
sent a few things. Eyes low, he began to fumble with
the hamper, to bring forth gifts—a jar of the wild honey
that Elizabeth had always loved, the raisin cakes and
barley loaves and some of Mary's favorite cheeses. He
did not trust himself to look at his daughter just yet. He
had a strange fated feeling that so long as he postponed
that moment he would be safe, spared some vital and
intolerable acknowledgment.

He was tired and still worried, despite the prayers that
he said day and night for her, for Joseph, for all of them.
His confoundment had not abated during these past weeks;
if anything it had grown more intense. He didn't know, he
simply didn't know. And he was here now in his darling's

presence, but he could not bring himself to confirm or deny this wild complex of fears and hopes by whatever truth, or lack of truth, might be revealed in one frank searching appraisal.

Elizabeth had heard and came to join them, walking with a heavy yet graceful dignity, her ringed hands outstretched. "Joachim!" No one had warned him of her condition. Now the shock of seeing her thus was so great that he looked dazedly about for a place to sit . . . *Elizabeth* . . . sweat poured from him. He knew that his mouth hung foolishly open, and how awkwardly he perched on the slender Grecian chair, afraid that it might not support his weight, either of flesh or sheer astonishment. He sat stiff and absurd, with his legs apart. Elizabeth—at her age! If a man had come seeking miracles. . . .

He could think of nothing to say to her. He turned to Mary. "Have you a message for your mother? When do you want to come home?"

"Oh, not yet a while, please," Elizabeth said. "You can see how it is with me, my sister's husband. The Lord has finally seen fit to bless us too, even his servants Elizabeth and Zachariah. And the presence of your child at this time is a great delight to us." She smiled toward Mary, "We're a comfort to each other in our time of waiting, Mary and I."

"Blessed be the house of Zachariah, may it be thrice blessed and know only rejoicing in the fruit of my sister's womb." So it was true then, he was thinking. This other dread complication was still upon them. It had not departed with the departure of Mary, but had only grown within her. Slowly Joachim forced himself to raise his eyes and gaze upon his daughter. How little she seemed still, how slender and unformed; why she was but a child herself. Thus he strove to dissuade himself from what he too saw before him. From this other, this second discovery that somehow, some way he must manage to convey to his wife.

"But if Mother isn't well," Mary said, "if she needs me more. . . ."

No, no. Joachim lifted a bluntly restraining hand. Hannah had given specific instructions that Mary was to stay as long as she wanted, or was welcome. He glanced about seeking an excuse to be gone. He had always felt himself uncouth in this splendid house; now in his distress and bewilderment, an old antagonism rose up as if to divert his senses from larger issues. These priests lived well on other people's tithes and offerings. This chair with its silken cushion, these hanging lamps and brocades, was it for this a man fought beast and insect and hail and drought to wrest the crops from the soil? Of a sudden he recoiled at the thought of the procession of goods into the Temple tomorrow. Gladly a man gave up a portion of his products unto God and the servants of his God, yet it was hard at times not to be galled at how handsomely the servants also served themselves.

Enough. He was ashamed. He wrenched his thoughts back to the present. How could he get away before the evening meal? The strain of watching his manners would be too much after this. And he couldn't bear the look in Mary's eyes—their silent pleading. She'd be asking about Joseph, and what could he tell her? That there had been no more dealings between the two households, that he'd scarcely seen him. And that gradually, intolerably, the fear had taken root in him: Joseph might be preparing to divorce her. No. No, he must get out of here. If he remained she might wring it from him—he had never been any match for her.

But he was forced to stay, there was no help for it, not when Zachariah appeared and Elizabeth explained why he couldn't voice his welcome. Evidently the thought of reproducing himself at his age had proved too much for the old fellow, he'd been struck dumb! An irreverent, vaguely horrified amusement shook Joachim. He could hardly blame him; he was dumbfounded himself by these happenings. Thus he too could only sit pretty well speechless throughout the long meal and the prayers and the washings to which he was unaccustomed, suffering, praying mostly for escape.

Afterward, claiming that he already had a room at the inn and had many things to do to see about tomorrow's offerings, he made haste to leave. Then it happened as he had feared. Mary accosted him on the steps. But she seemed so small and lost and far from home, and her little white face was so eager as she lifted it to his, her eyes so large with hope, that he couldn't do it, he was forced to lie.

"Joseph is fine," he assured her heartily. "He couldn't make the journey, at least I didn't see him among those who came up from Nazareth. But he sends you greetings." Then he made off fiercely down the hill.

XII

To work, to keep building, that was the main thing. For when we cease building, hope dies. And so each evening Joseph plunged doggedly up the path to his unfinished house.

How had it ever seemed beautiful to him? he wondered, gazing at the dull stone walls. They were dead now, no longer suffused with light. They were as a tomb.

> My heart throbs, my strength fails me;
> and the light of my eyes—it also has gone from me.
> My friends and companions stand aloof from my plague,
> and my kinsmen stand afar off. . . .

Then he told himself that he must not wallow in such depths. Psalms didn't help, there was no comfort in psalms. And to embrace despair would be to confess his betrayal before the world. No—no, the thing was to work, to mix the corpse-gray mortar and fit the brutal rocks. And the roof—it was essential to get the roof on. So long as these poor walls stood roofless he had a queer feeling of exposure. It seemed to him that once the house were firmly roofed, then Nazareth's mouth would be shut as well.

For there had been talk, much talk. At first a half-merry astonishment that his betrothed, who should be firmly in his charge these months before their marriage, had taken herself off. That had been hard enough to bear, the jests,

the thoughtless teasing, but he had managed to grin and
return them in kind. Yet as the buds of spring gave way
to green burning summer, a new tone came into the questioning, as if scandal-hungry tongues were already beginning to lick their chops.

"Where's Mary? When is she coming back?"

"Oh, any day now," he lied cheerfully, over the coals
in his throat. "Soon."

He had not gone up for the Feast of the First Fruits.
He had looked forward to it wildly—to see her again,
discover that all she had told him was but a fantastic
dream, and since she was recovered in mind and body to
bring her rejoicing home. But Jacob had fallen ill. He
had been given more and more to the hidden wineskins
and when they were empty and he was too bloated and
breathless to get more, he had begged Joseph in secret
to obtain them for him. Timna had been beside herself.
"You must stay with us, Joseph, you're the only one
who can handle him."

So then he had thought of sending a message to Mary.
But there was no money for papyrus or parchment which
could be rolled up to keep his words private, and he was
ashamed to set them down on ostraka, those broken pieces
of pottery that the poor used. His thoughts were too
precious, his torment of longings, and the way it was
between him and her family—how Hannah scorned to
speak to him at the synagogue, and Joachim's look was
one of dark reproach. No, there was not room for all
this on fragments of clay, nor could he have brought
himself to write it. This was his private hell, and until
he could be with her again he would have to endure it
alone.

Then he began to count the hours until Joachim should
return. Perhaps bringing Mary! Or at least a message for
him. In his mind he began to fashion it, this letter of love
and consolation and explanation that Mary would surely
write him, if indeed she didn't come.

Then the spear out of the darkness. The shock of the
unprovoked assault, plunging, plunging . . . *I am with
child*. . . . he would rise up from his labors, clutching at
his back as if to tear it free. The perspiration stood out on
his face . . . *I am with child*. . . . yet no. No! The letter

would eradicate all that. Or she would give the lie to it herself with her lips pressed against his.

Thus he lived in an agony of suspense until Joachim's return.

Then his mother remarked one evening that Joachim had been home for several days. "Your brothers tell me they saw him in the fields."

Joseph gasped. "Why didn't someone tell me?"

"Your brothers probably wanted to spare you embarrassment."

"And Mary?" Bitterly—though it shamed and sickened him to inquire thus of his own betrothed—"Do my brothers, who are so anxious to spare me, are they also whispering behind my back that they have seen her too?"

"Son, son." His mother's tone was weary; she went on setting food away in the chest. "I'm sure that if Mary were home she'd have been seen at the well. I'm sure all Nazareth would know."

"Haven't the tongues of Nazareth anything better to wag about than the comings and goings of a young girl?"

"Why should you sound so offended?" Again that patient, unutterably weary tone. "There's always interest in such things, it's only natural." Timna continued to arrange the bowls upon the shelves, with a calm so dignified, bland and still it was almost threatening. "Mary's been gone over two months now, it's natural that people wonder."

As Joseph's brow darkened, she turned, and he saw that his mother's composure was breaking. The placid face was struggling against tears, her mouth worked. She who was usually so gallant became pitiably grotesque. "Haven't I enough to worry about with your father? This sickness of his, this shameful sickness that causes him to stumble and fall in the street, isn't that enough?" she demanded. "That he can't drink wine openly with other people but only secretly, to become besotted, so that he's a joke and a spectacle to the public and a grief to his family—and ill, so ill from it too. . . ." She broke off, shaking with soundless sobs. "Must I endure all that and this—this other? This shame and disgrace to my son as well?"

Helpless, Joseph regarded her, her tears scalding his soul.

Abruptly she went to the pitcher and poured a gourd of water to calm herself. She took a towel and wiped her eyes. When she faced him once more where he sat at the table, her eyes, though red, were stern.

"You don't sleep nights," she said. "We hear you prowling around to all hours. You're working yourself into the grave. For what? For a maid who may or may not return."

"Mother, I beg you, don't say such things!"

"Well, what is your understanding with Joachim? You have some rights in this matter. A bargain was made between us. Is that bargain to be fulfilled?" And when he didn't answer, "Forgive me for speaking bluntly, but your father and I—all our lives it seems we've seen you waiting for this one girl. And though it would have pleased us to see you take another and give us grandchildren long before—no, no, you would not. And so, knowing that they are stiff-necked people—they *are*," she insisted— "even so, I persuaded your father to humble himself by going to them on your behalf.

"And though they accepted," she went on, "even so your father and I have still been humbled by the family of Mary. He's so cheerful, he pretends not to notice, but he has been hurt by them, nonetheless. But there are some forms of humiliation we should not be called upon to bear," she said indignantly. "This long absence. If there is any reason for her to absent herself from her home and her betrothed husband, let it be known. And let it be known as well what you are going to do about it."

Joseph stood frozen. "Mother, what are you inferring? What are you suggesting?"

"Only that you face up to your own sense of honor, and the honor of your father's house. Jacob deserves that much of you. That much at least. A man who has been misused in a marriage contract can set that woman aside. I know it seems harsh, but sometimes there is no other way when a man has just cause."

"I have no such cause!"

Then because he had shouted and his mother seemed so shattered, he embraced her with a blind desperate tenderness. "Please don't worry," he said gently. "I'm sorry if I've failed you or caused your further grief when you are already so burdened. But God will surely send Mary back to me in order that our marriage contract may be fulfilled. Meanwhile . . ." He hesitated. "Meanwhile, I'll go to Joachim."

The confrontation came about unexpectedly the following day. Looking up from his work, he saw Joachim walking across the street. Sight of that stolid, impregnable and somehow haughty figure tore Joseph from his bench, his dreaded arguments unformed. He found himself standing breathless before him, half-angry, half-imploring.

"Joachim, tell me. *Tell* me. Did you see Mary?"

Joachim halted. Slowly, ponderously, he turned his whole body to regard him. His expression was inscrutable. "Yes," he said. "I saw her."

"And how is she?" Joseph begged. He glanced about and lowered his voice. "In the name of human pity tell me how she is and when she is coming back to Nazareth."

Joachim stood rooted, heavy with his own overpowering dread. And with his bitterness that was not a clean, clear-cut bitterness, because he remembered so vividly the desires of his own youth. And because he blamed himself for so much. Hannah had been right, this was what happened when a family stepped down. And yet he did not hate this comely and fervent youth. What he had done, if he had done it, was foolish but not evil. Resent him, yes, but he was ridden by a sad compassion for him too. Joachim realized how cruel he had been in not seeking Joseph out at once.

"This is no place to discuss such a matter." He gestured toward the shop. "Is anyone there?"

"No, we can talk there."

Inside, Joachim sat down on a bench. He looked tired, dull and stricken, rustic and yet cloaked in his peculiar superiority.

"Mary is well, considering. . . ." he said. He set his teeth. "She is several months with child."

I am with child . . . I am with child. . . . The words only confirmed the festering spear. It hurt when Joseph moved in certain ways, or when someone struck it as now, and yet even now he need not clutch himself or cry out. He only sat staring at Joachim.

Joachim returned the steady gaze. He leaned a little forward. "Tell me," he demanded grimly, "Joseph, tell me what you know of this. Have you brought dishonor to my house?"

Joseph could feel his heart's mad hammering. The swift hot stinging that spread across his face. A sense of peril came over him, every nerve jangled warning.

He could lose her. *Through his denial he could lose her*. And no matter what he owed to the honor of any house, his father's or that of this man before him, yet the prospect of losing her was to feel the clammy breath of sheol and the grave.

He must proceed with caution. He said, "I love Mary. The last thing I'd wish to do would be to bring dishonor upon either her or her people." Yet his blood continued to throb so painfully it must be heard, and he knew that it burned his cheeks. He was guilty even so. Joachim must surely see that he was guilty. That night among the olive trees he had wanted her as his wife, would have taken her as his wife if she hadn't resisted. Told him . . . *I am with child . . . I am already with child. . . .* The pain was not to be concealed; he knew that his face was contorted with it. And yet he must not flinch before the fierce searching of her father's eyes.

He said, "Waiting can be torture for a man in love and entrusted with his bride. Waiting is sometimes beyond endurance."

Evasion though it was it was also the truth. He would have sinned against Mary and her father's house, only God had stepped in triumphant. God with this punishment that he was never to escape.

He went on, "And is it truly so great a dishonor that a man finds his own bride too fair to wait for the wedding feast? Might there not be more happiness in Israel if more couples loved each other in the manner of some of our great ancestors? Isaac and Rebekah, Jacob and Rachel."

He would have said more but Joachim stopped him with a little growl. He's protesting too much, the older man thought, he's seeking to divert me. And the sense of injury he had nursed so long that it had become almost essential to his self-respect, gave way to that which he abhorred to face. He arose and went to lean in the doorway. "Enough. There's a great deal I don't understand, but I'm not stupid, Joseph. I think I know the truth when I hear it. But I too have my honor," he said curtly, "and if it is my house, instead, that is threatening disgrace to that of your father Jacob, then I can only say. . . ." It was a second before he could go on. "Do what you must."

He squared his shoulders, forced his voice to be steady. "I ask only that you deal with her kindly. Perhaps if you were to go to the elders quietly, while she is yet in Jerusalem. . . ."

Joseph was stunned. He took a step nearer. "What are you saying?" he gasped. "You—her own father. Are you proposing that she stay there? That Mary never come *home?*"

"In time she could return. Perhaps in time, when the danger has passed."

"Danger!" It was impossible not to scoff. "It would never come to that. You're an elder yourself, you're respected in this town. And Mary. Everyone loves Mary. Surely everyone knows. . . ."

"God forbid that a hand should be raised against her." Joachim's face was ashen but he did not falter. "But the Law is the Law. And there are those—always those who are jealous, suspicious, who could actually think. . . ." He broke off, in his confusion. What did parents know of the wakening rivers of life within their children? You guarded them, taught them, arranged suitable marriages for them, but devious and sly are the rivers once aroused.

What did he think? What did he himself actually think? That his own daughter was an adulteress? It was inconceivable. Yet again the question taunted—what did a father ever know of his own child? He thought of heady afternoons on the shimmering meadows when youths might waylay a maiden tending her sheep. He thought of the dancing at betrothal and wedding feasts. He thought of the sheep shearing and grape trading, the flashing eyes, the tasting of the wine. He thought of the kisses he had exchanged with the passionate, unobtainable Abigail.

Joseph's words broke in upon his reverie. "So long as I live no harm shall come to her. No matter what other people say."

That old protectiveness which Joachim had always felt in him. It was consoling now. And Joachim wondered how Mary might have fared with one of the others? He had been right in overriding Hannah in at least that much. Right in trusting this man then, as he trusted him now.

"But aren't we forgetting one thing?" Joseph asked. "Or are we perhaps avoiding it?—this story that she told us before she went to Jerusalem."

Joachim had been clutching the doorframe. Now he swung around. "I dare not believe it," he said. "At first, yes, I was carried away by it. My own dreams, my own wish to believe. The Messiah! I've expected his coming so long, it seemed a certainty—related somehow to all of us, even me. And my child, our Mary," he said brokenly. "So beautiful, and in my eyes at least, so perfect. No—no, it did not seem impossible to me then that she could be the one.

"But once she was gone I began to see my folly. Hannah made me realize, and she is right—we dare not imagine such a thing. Either our daughter is ill, or she's sinned, or been betrayed. And to charge human error up to God. . . ." he said, appalled. He shook his head.

"He'll come," Joachim went on. "Nothing will ever change my faith in that. In this time of trial I need to believe that more than ever. But we are humble people in a remote village. When the Lord sees fit to send us a deliverer he will surely find better soil than ours and worthier people than such as we."

A bell rang in Joseph's blood, for he was remembering Mary's impassioned words: "Why do you think miracles can happen only to others?" He said, troubled, "And yet, how can we know? The ways of God are strange. And fearful—even if it were true as she claimed, it would be a fearful thing."

"No, no, we must not delude ourselves by toying with ideas for which we too might deserve to be punished. This is surely a matter of human trouble and human

decisions. A matter that involves your honor as her
espoused husband." Joachim had recovered his dignity.
He spoke almost imperiously. "As such, you must do whatever seems to you just right." He swallowed. "I only
pray that you will deal with her as mercifully as you
can."

"Deal with her mercifully. . . ."
The words had joined those others to torment Joseph
as he beat away at his small house. They clamped him
in a vise from which there was no respite save to lose
himself in that fierce and stubborn labor which had become itself a mockery. And yet he must go on despite
the now frankly gossiping tongues. Mary had been seen
in the streets of Jerusalem. So now all Nazareth knew
that Mary, daughter of Hannah who had always been so
proud, the espoused of Joseph whose patient wait and
ultimate triumph had been the delight of the town—that
she had fled only to hide her shame.
His mother had been right. And Joachim. A man's
honor and the honor of his family was involved. But
neither Joachim nor Timna nor any other who spoke of
honor—could conceive that there was a value even greater
than honor—a man's love. However forsaken, bereaved,
humiliated, a man's hopelessly abiding love.
He wanted her back, no matter what. Perversely, he
wanted her back even more the more people talked. Yet
it was so much greater than that, it went so far back
and so far beyond. She was his life's purpose, his hope;
she was his Messiah. And even as Joachim could not
suffer the thought of giving up his dream even now, how
much less could Joseph forego his so-nearly-realized
dream of Mary.
As mercifully as you can. . . .
Yet what was truly mercy? In his determination not to
lose her, was he only being merciful to *himself?* He
paused one night as he crawled about the rafters. The
thought had gnawed at him before, but only as a half-
smothered fear. Now it stabbed him with the sudden
clarity of the lightning that forked the sky after the
day's heat. Joseph jerked upright before it, his hammer

clenched in his hand. For the first time he was forced
to face the shattering possibility: Mary might not want
to come back! Whatever the circumstances that had taken
her to Jerusalem, she had been there three months now.
She must be heavy with child.

Whose child? *Whose child?*

The agony smote him again, racking his sweaty body.
He hurled his hammer savagely into a corner and covered his face with his hands. He crouched there under
the lightning that splayed in daggered leaps across the
rumbling sky. He felt the absurd and abject spectacle
God must be making of him as he sat thus on his heels.
"Pray!" the thunder seemed to growl. "Pray, you pitiful
fool."

Yet he could not pray, for God had tricked him. For
whether the child she carried were human or what she
claimed—a child of mystery, of something too awesome
for his poor sinful being to comprehend—the fact of
the child shut him out. If it were the child of some
earthly rival then in all decency he ought to set her free to
marry him. But if it were indeed divine then how
much less she belonged to him and his rude house in
Nazareth. Her home would surely be the holy city, her
domain the very Temple. He was building a home for a
ghost bride who no longer belonged to him.

It had begun to rain, a few bright drops that spattered
coldly on his hot tormented face. From force of habit he
wished dully that the roof were complete to protect it, as
the rain fell harder, though he knew that the shower, so
rare in mid summer, would not last long. He walked
about picking up tools, forcing himself to think of this
so as to postpone the larger decision that was upon him at
last. He felt dazed and shaken, yet curiously relieved that
it was no longer to be escaped.

There was a bench in a protected corner. His mother
had left an old moth-ridden shawl there; he drew it up
about him to warm and quiet his trembling limbs. He
was very tired, he realized, quaking from both his fatigue
and the chill of his damp clothes. Yet he felt oddly calm,
too, in another area of himself, a severely vacant place
where no emotion could invade. He lay gathering all his

suffering self into a whole that could be plunged into that blankness and be safe.

In an access of weariness he lay listening to the cold beating fists of the rain, which finally trailed off until there was but a rhythmic dripping from the beams and the scolding of birds that had been disturbed in the trees. He lay staring into the darkness of his house, and gradually facing the bare truth of his position.

Three courses were open to him. The first unthinkable —public denunciation with its possibility of public infamy and even capital punishment. The second, to assert his rights as her espoused, demand that she be brought back to consummate the marriage by living with him, and assume the legal paternity of her child. But that he dared not linger over; that he had just foresworn. The third, to go quietly to the authorities and divorce her without scandal. The elders were just men, they knew and respected everyone involved. Perhaps they would not insist that he specify adultery as his grounds. They would accept what was only too evident, desertion. He fought off the despair that threatened once more to overwhelm him. He turned over on the narrow bench, pulling the cover to his eyes.

Suddenly he could not bear it, to be here with his decision in the house so nearly completed, the place that was to have been their own. Yet he could not face the people he was likely to meet on the streets, and he could not bring himself to go home. He lay there like a wounded thing, enduring his suffering. All night long he lay awake with it, or so it seemed, trudging the same bitter paths and always arriving at the same terrible conclusion. But now and then he dropped off, for now and then he dreamed. Figures scurried along the paths with him, arguing among themselves and pushing him this way and that. Sometimes he stumbled as he had that first night of Mary's announcement, but always he would rise up bruised and bloody and plunge on. *Put her away. Give her up.* Yes, yes, you've reached that end, now go to sleep. But I *am* asleep. . . . I'm dead and in a coffin, I am in a cold rock cave. . . .

He clawed about for the ragged shawl that had fallen

to the floor. A chill breeze blew through the open door, though a great moon seemed to have risen. A moon whose light was so intense that he must shield his eyes. He half-roused, blinking, his blood racing. For it seemed to him that he was not alone.

"Who is it?" he demanded. "Where are you and what do you want?"

His own voice startled him. He realized that he must be talking in his troubled sleep. And yet his fear did not abate. He was ashamed of it and yet he couldn't help it. It was like a familiar nightmare where there was great danger or great ecstasy forthcoming and he was powerless either to rise and flee or to lie in quiet expectation.

Then he heard the voice from the half-sensed presence at his feet. *It's all right, Joseph, Fear not. Be calm.* And as he waited, still only half-awake the voice came again: *I am a messenger sent from God. I am sent to tell you that you must not fear to take Mary your wife, for that which is conceived in her is indeed of the Holy Spirit, as she has said.*

Joseph opened his mouth but he could not speak. His elbows bit into the hard bench where he lay, half-sitting, yet powerless to rise. The light was a blinding flame.

She will bear a son, the voice continued, *and you shall call his name Jesus, for he will save his people from their sins.*

"Don't mock me," Joseph whispered. "Whoever you are, whether from God or the devil, in God's name don't torment me further!"

But it is true, Joseph, even as she has told you. Remember the prophecy: 'Behold, a virgin shall conceive and bear a son, and his name shall be called Emmanuel.' That prophecy is to be fulfilled, Joseph, son of David. So delay no longer in taking her as your wife. But know her not until she has borne this holy one.

What happened after that Joseph was never quite sure. He only knew that suddenly it was dawn, gray and misty in the shell of his house, a cock was crowing, and rough hands were shaking him. He found himself blinking into the face of his brother Samuel. The usually merry mouth was grim now, taut with disapproval and concern.

"I told our mother I'd probably find you here. She was upset when she got up to attend our father and found you hadn't come home."

"I'm sorry. I lay down to rest and fell asleep." Joseph stretched his cramped body, and as he did so the dream began to bloom within him, burst all its brilliance upon his consciousness. The astounding dream! Striving to re-create it fully, he turned his dazed face toward Samuel's scowling one.

He realized that his brother was berating him. About the house, about being laughing stocks in Nazareth. About how difficult it would be for the rest of them to make decent marriages, "until this thing between you and Mary is settled. As for our father—he's dying. Are you too selfish and blind to see it? You owe it to him to take the step that will let him die in peace."

Dying? Joseph had been fastening his leather girdle around his waist. He looked up, startled. This was no idle threat meant to bestir him. Guilt smote him. He had known it, must have known it for a long time, but even that had been secondary to this other all-absorbing anguish. He said, "Forgive me. I'll do everything in my power to make amends." He strode toward the door. "I know now what I must do, and I promise you there will be no delay."

Samuel followed him. "I knew you'd finally see it. It won't be easy, but it's for the best, and you'll feel better for getting it over with."

"I'll have to ask you to look after the shop while I'm gone."

"Gone?" Samuel halted. "You don't mean to say you plan to journey clear to Jerusalem to fetch her back?"

"Even so," said Joseph. "If I hurry I may be able to set forth before this day is past."

"But I thought—I thought surely you'd take care of it quietly here without exposing her!"

"Expose her?" Joseph gasped. "How can you ask such a thing? Hurt Mary? I'd sooner be crucified. I'm only going to Jerusalem to claim her as my bride. To bring her home to our house."

He turned to take one last look about. The pink light

was falling through the rafters now; again it was shining, shining.

"Work on the roof for me will you, Samuel? Finish it as swiftly as possible. For she'll live with me here and bear our son here. And if God is merciful our father Jacob will live to hold his grandson on his knees."

XIII

JOSEPH was destined to take a different journey, however, before the day was over.

He sensed an unnatural stillness in his father's house. And seeking out his mother, found her sitting, already dressed, beside her husband's bed. She sat quite erect, in an immense and terrible composure, holding Jacob's hand. One glance at the remote face on the pillow told him that his father was dead.

Suddenly the whole household was awake and wild with knowing. Cries rang out, there was the scurry of feet. Grave faces appeared, the doctor, the rabbi, neighbors. The day was only beginning to assert itself, yet half of Nazareth had roused and come running, with lamentations on its lips. Joseph was swept up in it, the macabre and insistent regimen of death.

Kneeling before the as yet unwashed body, rending his garments and pouring ashes on his head, he begged its forgiveness that he had not loved it more, nor been more understanding of the craving that drove it to its solace. . . . Father, Father! . . . Jacob lay detached, the coins glinting upon his eyes in the early light. And Joseph had a strong feeling that his father was rather delighted at all the commotion and arrangements on his behalf. For the dead did not immediately depart for Sheol, but hovered watching as was their due.

So there was time. Time to tell him how it was with

Mary. "Listen and hear me, Father, it isn't shame that she brings us, but glory. The fulfillment of the prophecies, the Saviour, the holy child itself. And your son is involved. She has been given into my keeping that this wondrous thing may come to pass. Father, hear me—the family of Jacob is to be honored above all men!"

Surely it was not too late. It seemed too cruel that Jacob, whose pride had had so little to feed upon, should not be reassured before slipping away into the lonely darkness. Surely God would grant him this much comfort before snuffing out forever his own peculiarly gay and pathetic little light.

Joseph stumbled to his feet, for there was a clicking of basins in the doorway, a strong smell of aloes and myrtle. The women had arrived to prepare the body. He was astonished to see that Hannah was at their head. "Joseph!" She broke into a wail at sight of him and clasped him to her breast. She screamed likewise at sight of Timna, and Timna rose slowly, gravely, and held the small weeping woman, as if it were Hannah who was bereaved. And Joseph knew, grateful and amazed, that in this drama of death and family Hannah must be involved, she simply could not bear to be left out. Then the other women led the rigid, vacant-eyed Timna from the room.

One of Joseph's sisters found Jacob's best Sabbath garment and washed it and mended a tear in it. Joseph and his brothers set about building a coffin. No mere frame for their father's body, he would be buried as if he were a king. In a fierce recklessness they chose the finest planks, some of the wood that Joseph had meant for the sills of his house. Their hammers rang above the sounds of practiced agony that were coming from the yard, for the professional mourners had arrived.

In the shop the sweat ran down the faces of the brothers as they labored at the box in which to bear their jocund little father away. Before noon the thing was done, and they lifted him into it, where he lay serene. He was inviolate now. Nothing could hurt him any more, nor make him laugh. In death he had gained a dignity unknown to him in life. And all the town came to pay him homage, and the trumpets blew and the cymbals clashed. And when the day was well advanced they lifted him onto their shoulders and carried him, sharing the burden by turns, up into the hills to the family burial cave. "Farewell, depart in peace," each of them bade him. And then the heavy rock to keep the animals away, was rolled before the door.

This was the journey that Joseph made that day instead of setting off for Jerusalem.

"Don't delay," the angel had said. Yet in common decency he could not leave until after the period of mourning. To do so would be too cruel to his mother, and only make things harder for Mary. But he made his plans for the journey even as he grieved for Jacob.

Then on the final day of mourning Joseph saw her. He felt at first that it must be an illusion. His head was light from fasting, the hot day tricked the eyes. He thought it must be only a mirage, the donkey plodding along with the likeness of the beloved upon its back.

Then the beast drew nearer, he could hear the clop of hooves, its labored breathing. And the girl who rode the donkey ordered it to halt. She was Mary and yet not Mary, for she had been gone so long. He was afraid that he was dreaming, he was too weak and shaken to acknowledge the reality of her just yet.

She slid down, took a step toward him where he stood in the yard. But he lifted a hand to keep her away, for he was unclean, he had touched his father's corpse.

"Joseph?" She stood trembling, all her anticipation draining away. "Joseph! Aren't you happy to see me?"

He dared to look at her then, desperately recreating the shape of her beauty—the dusky hair damp and curling, the full sweet mouth, the luminous eyes. She was different. He felt the aura of the city about her, the fine house of her aunt, the magnificence of the Temple. She had pushed her veil back and he saw that her hair was brushed in a new way, she wore gold circlets in her ears. Her gown was too fine for Nazareth, there was a mantle of blue shimmering stuff across her shoulders.

He stood dazed and rocked and afraid of her, this angel so suddenly descended, this woman whose body bulged with the fruit of God. He was aware of his garment of sackcloth, the cruel lacerations upon his face and arms. And now, startled, she too became aware of all this.

"Joseph," she gasped, "you're in mourning! Who?" she whispered, at the sound of wailing from the house.

"My father Jacob."

"Oh, no." Her eyes went dim. "He was such a joyful man, I had looked forward to having his laughter in our house. Oh, Joseph, I too grieve for the father of my beloved."

He could not answer for the longing that assaulted him—to touch her, hold her, and the sheer relief. He must wait until his knees had steadied, until he had overcome this terrible desire to throw himself at her feet and weep. Weep as he had not wept even for his father. He turned his face aside. "What brings you back to Nazareth?"

"My need for you, Joseph," she said simply. "We learned of a caravan that was coming up from Hebron and I was allowed to join them. Also, my aunt is also expecting a child and her time is upon her. It isn't fitting that a virgin remain in the house of birth." She glanced down at the curve of her waist, a smile touched her lips. "Even such a virgin as I."

"Mary, blessed Mary. My blessed, my beloved. Forgive me for ever doubting. I know now, I know!" He did crouch then at her feet, he could not help it, and he kissed the hem of her gown.

Salome spied her first. "Here comes Mary leading the donkey," she shouted to her mother on the rooftop. "Mary's come home!"

She set down the lamp she'd been cleaning and rushed to meet her, skirts flying, little Micah and Judith close behind. They flung themselves into her arms, laughing and asking questions and demanding to know what she'd brought them from Jerusalem. "Hush, wait a minute," Mary begged, putting them aside as gently as she could. She was unutterably tired, and anxiety warred with her joy at being home.

"Here." She fumbled in the panier and brought forth a parcel of presents. "The tops are for you two. I brought you an Egyptian doll, Salome, I hope you're not too old for it." She glanced about eagerly, nervously, for she had so much to tell before Joseph came to fetch her. "Where are the others?"

"Mother's flailing barley. Oh, she's coming, she heard us. And Father's in the stable with Esau."

"Mother!" The word was a choked little cry as Hannah came hastening down the steps. "Mother, Mother, I'm home." They clung together, weeping and exclaiming, touching each other awkwardly because of the embarrassing burden between them. Hannah was aware of Salome's troubled eyes. The boys had darted off to try out their tops.

"Go fetch your father," Hannah ordered, still gazing avidly upon her firstborn. She wiped her dusty hands on her tunic of rough homespun. Bits of chaff clung to it, and there was a jaunty, rather pathetic tuft of the bearded barley in her gray hair.

She clenched her small red fists, regathering herself. It was needful to resist these tides of love; if you did not you were lost. For her heart's darling was back, no longer safely in the keeping of her aunt, even though that separation had been agony. And although Hannah was near to swooning in her joy, a part of her recoiled. For she also beheld that it was true, what the cousins were whispering, and half the town. And what Joachim himself had seen. And although he had told her, and Mary herself had forewarned them long ago, until this moment it had simply not been true.

"I've been counting the hours until we reached Nazareth," Mary was saying.

"To see me or to see Joseph? I should think you'd do well to be counting the hours until you could reach the husband who might be willing to hide your shame."

Mary winced. Her face paled. "Must you speak so to me, Mother, when I am so weary and so glad to be home?"

"I speak out of my terrible concern. You must forgive me, I speak out of my own weariness." Hannah turned on her heel. "Come into the house and rest. Let me bathe your feet, let me take off your fine clothes. Why did you wear them on the road?" she scolded with her old inconsistency and petulance. "Such beautiful garments don't seem practical for traveling."

"I put them on only a little while ago when the caravan stopped to rest. I wanted to look nice when I first saw my dear ones after so long."

"I suppose we can thank Elizabeth for them."

"Yes. My aunt was very kind to me and very generous."

"She can afford to be."

"She sends her love, Mother, her dearest love, and there are gifts in my knapsack. She too is soon to deliver, her time was upon her even as I left. By now your sister surely holds in her arms the baby she's prayed for so long. Surely you can spare your sister and my aunt a moment of rejoicing and tenderness."

Hannah's hands were trembling as she squatted to pull her daughter's sandals off. "I'm sorry. All week I have sat with the mourners, so that my whole outlook is surely forlorn." She dipped a gourd into the stone jug that stood by the doorstep and began to sponge Mary's swollen feet. "Jacob ben Ezra died, did you know?"

"Joseph told me only a little while ago."

"Then you've seen him?"

"Yes, I've seen him. And he's coming for me, Mother. He'll be here to get me within the hour."

"No, oh, no!" Hannah cried out, and there was a great tearing asunder within her. "Wait, come inside, let's say no more of this until your father appears. Joachim!" she called shrilly.

Her husband heard her in the stable where he was fumbling with a broken plow handle. There was such urgency in her voice that he flung it from him and started up the path, knowing that it had something to do with Mary.

"Now? This night?" For some reason Joachim was dismayed. Like Hannah, he had risen to the occasion of death, even felt a certain sense of connection, as if some force beyond themselves were thrusting the families into the mesh of each other, whether they willed it or not. But he recognized with remorse that there had also been a certain expedience in his daily going down to tend their stock and bring them food or wine. He needed Joseph's good will. It had been weeks since their conversation, and Joseph had not made his intentions known. But now that salvation had been offered them, his relief was less than his sense of loss. "But you can't go, Mary, you've been away three months and you're only just now home."

"I must go to be with my husband, Father. Surely you see how it is with me. Even the children have noticed." Mary knelt by her dowry chest, sorting out the things she would need soonest, sheets, napkins, a pair of goat's hair pillows. Linens that she and her mother had worked on so peacefully when it seemed that her marriage would be consummated not in haste but in celebration. "I'd love to stay longer, I've missed you and I've so much to tell you." The wonders of Jerusalem, she thought. The Temple, the gracious ways of Elizabeth's house. "But surely you will agree that the sooner I go to live with my husband the better."

Hannah's eyes arraigned her. "Then you know what people are saying?"

"Yes. And I know how much it must have hurt you, which is all the more reason I must hurry to go to my husband's house."

"His house? His house is not yet finished, and his mother's house is a house of mourning."

"He has sent the mourners home," Mary told them, rising with the linens in her arms. "He's washing himself even now and changing to other clothes. He's bade his mother and sisters to prepare the evening meal. And if you're willing, if you and my father will come to share it," she said wistfully, "it would add to our happiness."

The children came bursting in, quarreling over their tops. And hobbling behind them was Esau, who'd been watering the ox. "Mary!" His sightless face was shining, his arms were outstretched. "You're here, you've come home for your wedding!"

His mother snatched him from the embrace before his hands could discover what his eyes could not. "Hush, there will be no wedding."

"No wedding?" he said, bewildered. Then in a rush of understanding, "Well, but our cousin Deborah is to be married next week, that will be wedding enough."

"Hush, don't speak of weddings." Hannah made a grimace of pain. "Go away all of you, we have things to discuss." Abstractedly she went to the chest and began to finger its contents. "No wedding," she said piteously. "No happy procession, no torches, no music, no feast. After all our plans—that our daughter should only be led off with bowed head into a small crowded cave of a house where the dead have lain."

Joachim spoke up. "Let's not bemoan the matter of a wedding, rather let's be thankful that Joseph is willing to take our daughter as his wife."

"Father's right. What if I had been betrothed to someone else? Is it likely that another man would accept my story and have me as I am?"

"He's always loved you beyond all reason." On Hannah's lips it was an accusation. "He's simply unwilling to give you up."

"Surely you aren't saying that it would be better if Joseph were the kind of man who'd abandon me?"

"Listen to Mary," said Joachim. "Knowing that the child she carries is not his, then Joseph is indeed doing a noble thing."

"But Joseph believes!" The wonder of it rose up in Mary, lending a new radiance to her tense face. "He believes. He is not taking me out of kindness to spare me, or even because of his love for me. But only because at last he too believes." She gazed from one to the other, her whole being alive with it. "He knows now that this is not shame that has befallen me, but honor. That I am honored above all women.

"Joseph's house is nearly finished," she told them, "it lacks only a portion of the roof. We'll sleep there this night. And we'll go into his house together, not with bowed heads, Mother, but proudly, knowing how great a thing has befallen us. Both of us. For no matter what people are saying, they are wrong. This child that I carry is the child of no man, but as I told you in the beginning, the child of him who created us all. The child who is destined to be our deliverer."

In the silence they could hear the children still arguing, the shrill whine of their tops on the doorstone. Salome had begun the churning, there was the slosh of the coming butter in the skins. Esau passed by the window, leading the goats to the rain-filled trough. A rich scent of animal and earth came into the room. And it was all so homely and dear and familiar—how could she expect them to understand? How could she leave them even for Joseph? Yet he was coming, her dearest, her chosen one, who was also even as she, chosen by God. A great excitement of love and pain and wonder flamed up in her.

"What did your aunt have to say of all this?" Joachim asked.

"Elizabeth knew. For she cried out at sight of me that my womb was blest, and at that moment her own child leapt. The child that is likewise destined to be a great and holy man."

Elizabeth. Hannah blanched. Her own sister then, who was older and wiser and intimate with godly things, accepted this. A part of her scoffed, a part of her fell prostrate almost in terror, wondering: Could it be? could it possibly be? "I wish it otherwise," she said. "I wish that God had chosen some other one."

"Then you believe?" Mary cried. "Mother, you do believe?"

"Would that I could." Hannah sat on the floor beside the chest, plucking fiercely away at the chaff—how it clung. "Would that I dared believe."

"Father? You didn't question this when I first told you."

"No," he said, "it was somehow easier then. Before I'd had time to think, to question, to reason."

"To listen to me," Hannah said.

"Yes, to reason and to listen to reason. And yet now that I have seen you—yes, Mary, it's easier for me to believe this marvel than to believe that you have sinned."

"Thank you, Father. If even one of you ceases to doubt, then my heart will be at rest."

Jealousy wrenched Hannah again. The old alliance, shutting her out; now this mystery. She could only grope blindly along its edges, like Esau. What was it, what was it? Would the door never be opened to her, the light come streaming through? No, no, she shrank back from it, her whole practical nature thrusting it away.

She could feel Mary's large beseeching eyes. "Oh, Mother, I beg you to try, for your own soul's peace."

"I don't know, I don't know," Hannah said. "I only know that I'm wretched and afraid." She sprang up, began to give cryptic orders for the packing of the baskets, for she heard the commotion in the yard. Joseph had arrived. He had put off all semblance of mourning, she saw, shocked. He wore his best raiment of many stripes with a scarlet collar at his throat and a girdle to match. He was dressed as a bridegroom! Together he and Joachim loaded the ass that he had brought. They worked busily, passing few words. There was something touching about their earnest endeavors with Joseph so dressed.

The women too worked in haste and silence, a tension between them. "Are you sure you won't come down later, Mother, to eat a celebration meal with us?" Mary asked.

"It's too late. I've already ordered Salome to start the preparations for our own meal."

"Then goodbye. Though I'll see you often," Mary said.

"Yes, yes, it doesn't matter, we'll see each other often." Hannah kept her voice casual, turning her dry cheek for Mary's kiss. She watched them set off together, the tall youth in his gallant garb, her daughter beside him, walking heavily with her burden, yet her face that was upturned toward his enrapt.

Hannah clutched at her aching throat. She spoke sharply to the children as she plunged back into the house.

XIV

"I CAN'T go," Hannah protested. "My head—it might as well be beaten with a mallet. Can't Salome stop the children's noise?"

"They're only excited about the wedding," Joachim told her, standing above her couch. "And Salome's still at her cousin's."

That's right, Salome had been there all day. She was elated about serving as one of the bridesmaids instead of Mary. Reluctantly, wrenched by the irony, Hannah had let her. After all, Salome would never have the joy of thus serving her own sister. . . . No wedding for Mary. The stinging wound would give her no surcease. But it wasn't the wedding that mattered, she kept telling herself, it was what people were saying.

Hannah never showed her face at the well herself, but the stories came back. Her sisters-in-law were only too eager to tell her: That Mary had betrayed Joseph with a peddler from a passing caravan. That Cleophas had had his way with her—at least so he was hinting. That Mary and Joseph had been carrying on for years—Mary's plight had been the reason Joachim had consented to the betrothal. Not that the aunts believed the rumors, they claimed. In fact they were outraged, united in an effort to protect the family name.

And all the while they spoke, Hannah could only sit frozen, for once in her life too stricken to reply. Well, she had it coming. How they must have resented her boasts, and how they gloated over her now. She could have almost laughed at her own situation if the sheer pain of it had not reduced her to a witless, enfeebled thing.

Then one day, to her own further grief, her spirits revived. It was the day Cora had come to invite Salome to attend the bride. "Since poor Mary is no longer eligible."

Something in her tone broke Hannah's defensive crust. "Don't speak so of your brother's daughter," she retorted. "Poor Mary, as you call her, is happier than any maid in Nazareth."

"Happy?" The aunt was plainly amused.

"Yes, happy," Hannah insisted. "In spite of all those evil lies. Happy in the knowledge of her own purity, her own wonderful marriage. Happy because Joseph is such a fine husband. And because. . . ." She knew that she spoke in frenzy and in folly, but she could not stop her own desperate tongue. "Cora, you're a good Jewish woman." She leaned nearer across the table where they sat pitting dates. "Actually a far more devout woman than I. Like your brother, you know that there are certain prophecies to be fulfilled. Mysteries—things that can't be explained."

Her mistake was evident at once. Cora stiffened. "Mysteries? What are you saying?"

"Yes, mysteries." Unable to retreat, Hannah blundered on. "Especially one."

There was a second of stunned silence. Then Cora said, "Hannah, you can't be serious. Or you are ill. This thing has gone hard with you, you've been under a strain, and you've been brave. But it's no secret that the whole business with Joseph has been a grave disappointment, and this—this later complication a cause for deep sorrow and yes, shame." Her voice was concerned. "And your kinsmen have supported you throughout. But I fear you'll find that support at an end if you go to such lengths as to imply . . . as to claim. . . ."

"Why not?" Hannah demanded fiercely. "With Jahveh all things are possible. If the Messiah is to be born to a virgin why not my daughter as well as the next one?"

"Or even more than the next one?" Cora asked with asperity. Then she laughed outright. "Hannah,

Hannah, your reputation as a proud mother is well known. But I warn you that to go so far as to claim that your child has been chosen above all others is too much. It won't make people feel more kindly toward you, and it certainly won't make things easier for Mary and Joseph."

For this Hannah had no reply. She was wild with frustration, riddled with regret. Yet it was too late to make amends. She could only plead, half-defiantly, "Say nothing of this, I pray you. I know what I know," she insisted, "but you're right, it would be hopeless to try to persuade others of such a thing."

The sister-in-law arose to depart, tall, unctuous and triumphant. "Don't worry, it's the last tale I'd care to spread abroad about my niece."

Her tone was so patient and yet so scathing that Hannah couldn't bear it. And what if Cora did yield to the temptation to whisper what Hannah had been so mad as to claim? Yet she would almost have run barefoot in the streets proclaiming that selfsame thing: "My child is innocent, my child could not sin. She is privy to some blessed thing."

Could it be as she claimed? *Could it be?* No, no, haven't I learned, even yet, the bitter consequences of such fanatic pride? . . . And Hannah covered her face and wept at the irony. That she would try to force others to believe that which she herself dared not believe. . . .

"I can't go," Hannah said that night of Deborah's wedding. "I can't, it's too much to ask."

"You must," Joachim ordered. "Already we've hidden our heads too long. To absent ourselves from the marriage of my own sister's child would be only to confirm the wildest stories. If you truly love Mary you won't make her lot harder by giving people more to gossip about."

Hannah dragged herself from the couch. The room swayed, she had to clutch the windowsill for support. "If she had been an obedient loving daughter we would never have come to such a pass."

"Hannah, what's done is done and there's no going back. Come now, put on your brightest raiment, it will make you feel better."

She staggered to the clothes chest, resenting him and his willingness to subject them both to the coming ordeal. He loomed behind her in his bright robes, both her deliverer and her enemy, almost as he had seemed that night so long ago when he had carried her into her own bridal chamber. She fought away the memory—that hour of breaking. But though the body might be broken, the spirit never.

"I'll make ready and go," she said. "Not for Mary's sake or to still the gossips but for you, my husband. Because obviously it will please you to witness my suffering on this night when your sister's child is being wed instead of our own."

If the blow struck home he gave no sign. "Then make haste."

Hannah shivered, bathing in the brackish water that had grown cold with waiting, then fumbling about for her clothes. How drab and poor they would appear before the finery of the others. She stood a moment, feeling baffled and defensive, feeling afresh her ignorance of the subtleties of draperies and stoles. It hadn't mattered before; spare and almost boyish as she was she had spurned such trappings as more suited to the dull matrons of Nazareth. And then there had been Mary, so exquisite an adornment in herself.

Hannah set her teeth. She crept, on impulse, into the adjoining chamber and took up the mirror of polished metal. She saw, in a kind of fascination, her own bony cheeks and haunted eyes. She drove Mary's forgotten comb through her hair; it was no use, she could not comb beauty into herself, and some of the gray strands clung to the teeth like a desecration. She turned to the case of cosmetics. All girls kept these scented pots of color. Sneering faintly at herself, yet with a trembling sense of performing some rite, Hannah scrubbed roses into her wrinkled skin. How grotesque she looked, like a gaudy ghost going to some festival of the damned. Yet she felt that she must so sustain herself or her sick and quaking limbs would not carry her forth at all.

There now, she was ready. It was the best she could do,

and no one would pay attention to her, anyway. All eyes would be focused upon the bride, and the proud family of the bride.

Her husband looked at her with great tenderness and pity when she came down, but said nothing. The children were filled with their own excitement. They had been dashing back and forth all day, carrying flowers, stuffing themselves; now they reported that their aunt's house was already bursting with guests and the courtyard overflowing. "Hurry, hurry, or we won't be able to see the bridegroom knock!"

They gave her a spray of myrtle to carry and Hannah clutched it, the scent of it harsh and sweet. She felt herself being half-led, half-shoved along. The street was filled with guests bearing torches that lit up the trees so that they sprang at her like wet yellow mouths, belching sounds of merriment. The tymbals were playing, and the lyres. A crowd of youths surged up, already far gone in wine. Aaron was a popular fellow and they shouted his name in fond jests. Hannah could smell their breath as they made way for her and her family, shouting, "Step aside, these are kinsmen of the bride!" Despite the courtesy, Hannah's skin crawled, for she heard, or imagined she heard, a backwash of comment followed by laughter. How dared they? She turned, longing to claw them with her bare hands, only they had vanished around a corner.

The house of Cora and Nathan was indeed aswarm. Some people had mounted lamps on poles and these dipped about the courtyard like winged birds of fire. There was a tarry smell of smoke from the torches along with the perfumes and spices and oils. Their brother-in-law spied them being jostled and ignored and came expansively toward them, his pert homely face also rosy with wine. He was hearty with happiness, clutching Joachim by the shoulder and steering them inside.

"Cora, wife, come, come, your brother has arrived," he called. And she left off her assertive last-minute adjustings of her daughter's veil and greeted them effusively. She could afford to be generous, kissing them and exclaiming over Hannah's robe which she could see had been hastily donned, it was so wrinkled, and glancing at the two pearls over which she had once quarreled with Joachim, for they had belonged to her mother and it didn't seem right that they be handed on to a crude little urchin from Judea. Well, but her husband could afford to buy her jewels—they flashed now on her hands and in her wads of ornately piled hair. She exuded forgiveness and glory.

"Come see Deborah, she's just down from her chamber. Forgive me for saying so, but did you ever see such a beautiful bride?"

"No," Hannah muttered, "no, never." She choked on her own jealous love. The words were not merely the elaborate politeness required. "Our niece is radiant, she's fairer than the crest of Mount Hermon at sunrise." And it was true.

Deborah sat on a raised bench decked with flowers and glistening palm fronds. She reigned there, cool, bemused, a trifle imperious, half-hidden in the gem-shot lavender veil. Her gown was white with a sash of gold, embroidered with flowers and pearls to match her sandals. Her slant green eyes darted about, afire like the emeralds in her myrtle crown. She was all harsh bright sparks and she was very beautiful, but she also seemed disdainful, anxious only to have the whole thing over with.

Her mother regarded her with a candid objectivity. "But more than that she has always been such a good girl. And Aaron's such a fine man. Who knows but what this union might produce the hope of Israel?"

Hannah flinched and turned away. "The hope of Israel," Hannah echoed, though she felt strangled. It was the polite thing to say at weddings. Cora had meant nothing by it.

"The hope of Israel!" some others standing nearby took up the phrase and lifted their cups to the bride, who gave a vaguely contemptuous little nod and lowered her eyes. Joachim did not join in the toast. His grizzled jaw was working; he set down his cup.

Dressed in white the bridesmaids foamed about the little dais, holding their lamps aloft. They were singing the ancient wedding songs. Salome was among them, enjoying herself. Let her, Hannah thought, and raked such consolation as she could from the child's slight loveliness.

Let Salome at least draw pleasure from these doings. As for herself, she was here, she had been forced to come, let her enjoy herself as well. For life was harsh and the grave was always close, so why not celebrate when you can? Rejoice, drink the soothing wine, and toast the honorable, if rather pudgy, bridegroom when he comes.

Hannah's rouged cheeks began to flame; she could hear her own voice ringing out, joining the songs that praised the virtues and beauty of the bride, who had never been the equal of her Mary, but who was unsullied, unscathed, and so could sit cool and remote on a flower-decked throne awaiting the arrival of her mate.

"Your hair is like a flock of goats, moving down the slopes of Gilead. . . . Your cheeks are like halves of a pomegranate behind your veil. . . . My dove, my perfect one, is the only one, the darling of her mother!" people chanted. There were tears in Cora's eyes, Hannah saw with sympathy and a kind of incensed bafflement—for how was it that other women could feel so about their ordinary offspring? And then Hannah's heart was stirred by the music and the wine and she turned and flung her arms about her sister-in-law.

"Oh, Cora, how fortunate you are!"

She felt Cora go tense in the embrace. A little croak of disbelief escaped her. And turning, Hannah saw a slight commotion in the doorway. The music had stopped, a startled silence washed through the crowd. "Mary!" someone whispered. "It's Mary and Joseph."

Oh, no, Hannah thought. But she felt a spurt of defiant gladness as well. For how beautiful Mary was, framed by the doorway to the courtyard, her face shining with that old radiance that had caused people's heads to turn. And behind her stood Joseph, a trifle diffident, uncertain of their welcome, but never so gravely handsome, as if these past weeks had lent new dimensions to his sensitive face.

No one spoke, the embarrassed crowd drew aside as they entered, Mary bearing her burden high, like a queen. The virgins had stopped singing; exchanging troubled glances, they lowered their lamps. The married women began to murmur, some of them looked uncomfortable. "Such nerve," someone muttered. "How dare they show up here?"

"Hush, be careful," a neighbor warned. "That's Hannah, her mother, standing there."

"Well, let her hear. If a daughter can't be trained to keep out of trouble let her at least be trained not to soil a wedding feast when she's up to her chin with child."

Hannah had gone limp. Now slowly she was braced to tiger strength. Her fists knotted, her lips drew back. Bridling, she turned and would have rent the speaker limb from limb but she felt the restraining grip of Joachim's hand. "Stop," he ordered beneath his breath, "We cannot spoil our niece's wedding."

Our niece's wedding! That he could think of anyone save his own child at such a moment seemed the final outrage. And she began to keen and wail within, and rock her little one against her breast: Oh, Mary, my baby, my little lost bird, why have you been so foolish as to expose yourself? These idiots, these jackals, they would never believe the truth if it were shouted from the housetops.

Nathan came striding in from the garden. He looked at his wife, who was plainly upset. This was Deborah's doing. She adored her cousin, no matter what. Evidently she'd bidden Mary to come but said nothing, no warning —oh, she'd always been a sly one. And this marriage to Aaron whom she only tolerated, whom she almost despised—was this Deborah's way of punishing them for their choice? Oh, what were children coming to any more?

As for Mary and Joseph, if they had any respect for their relatives or their parents they wouldn't have come. Yet here they stood, so comely both of them; under any other circumstances they'd have graced the occasion. There was something almost noble about them, making a mockery of their humble state—Joseph a mere carpenter, Mary a woman in disgrace. It would be too cruel to bid them to depart. Deborah would never forgive them. And Mary's parents had already been through enough, Cora reminded herself with a mixture of acrimony and family loyalty.

Yet something else restrained her. Something she could not explain. An uneasiness smote her, a staggering concern. Hannah's claim. Hannah's preposterous hintings, which Cora had squelched, and rightly, as the last-ditch inventions of an overwrought woman well-known for an exaggerated passion for her child.

And yet, the sweet light that flowed almost tangibly from Mary. And Joseph, who stood behind her, one hand lightly cupping her shoulder. The gesture was loving, loyal, that of a heartbroken man who would support his beloved regardless of all the world. And yet more . . . so much more. Something that baffled and rocked the aunt; that look of secret suffering and gentle commitment on his face. As if something had died within him and something new been born.

She wanted to cry out with it, to demand an explanation. She wanted, curiously, to prostrate herself before it. She was exalted and repulsed by it and she rejected it with all her being. This was her daughter's wedding; there was no place for it here.

Deborah had sprung to her feet, hands outstretched. "Joseph! And Mary, my cousin. Oh, I thought you'd never come." Bending, she threw back her veil almost gaily for Mary's kiss.

At this the crowd murmured afresh. "These modern girls, have they no shame?" "It's bad luck, her first child will be stillborn. . . ." But a new commotion diverted them. Word had come from the courtyard, "He's on his way, the bridegroom's almost here!"

The news sent people running for doorways and into the garden to see the procession. The maids hastily regrouped, holding aloft their lamps that sputtered in the gusts of air from all the rushing about. The music could be heard drawing nearer, a bright tinkling of flutes and tambors and lutes. People did not resume their singing, they waited in a murmuring suspense, for the knock of the bridegroom on the richly ornamented door.

At last it came—*boom, boom, boom!* Mighty and demanding, almost comical in its urgency, and yet holy as well—the male for his mate. And people laughed and sang his praises as he entered in his swishing robes of Oriental splendor, grinning rather sheepishly under his fat turban that was so jaunty and gay with flowers. Plump and perspiring he stood before her with shy moist passionate eyes and a dimple in his round chin. He was shorter than Deborah when she stepped down, her face demurely hidden behind her veils.

But he bore her away in triumph and honor, accompanied by the joyful procession of groomsmen and maids. And half of Nazareth trooped after them to the fine house he had built, where the wedding feast was to be held. There would be singing and dancing and toasts most of the night before they would be finally led to the bridal chamber, there to join their bodies in the hope that out of them might come forth a son who would be the saviour of them all.

XV

MARY and Joseph left early.

Behind them they could hear the sounds of merriment that would continue half the night. A quarter moon lay on its side in a metallic sky. It was circled with a shining band and within the arc burned a sole bright star.

"The circle means the cold will be upon us soon," Joseph said.

Mary pulled her cloak more tightly about her. "Yes, only too soon. Winter will be fully upon us when the little one arrives."

Joseph reached out and drew her nearer. No one was abroad to see. He wanted to reassure himself with her closeness, lost though she was to him. She was so precious, doubly precious now in her pregnancy. Precious in the very burden of disgrace that she had put upon him. That was his weight to carry about and he must bear it as gracefully as she bore the growing burden of the child. He remembered the sly looks tonight when he made his excuses, "My wife is tired." He knew some of the men were thinking, "And besides he longs to get her home for himself, huge though she is. A man who wouldn't wait for his own wedding canopy. . . ." But that didn't matter, only Mary mattered. The pity was that there was no way to spare her, for whatever was said to his discredit reflected on her.

She said, "I'm sorry if I spoiled it for you."

"You could spoil nothing for me, Mary. You are my life."

"Then I have spoiled your life."

"No, no. It is not your doing. It was simply my fate to love you. You who are also the beloved of God." They walked along in silence, still conscious of the music and voices drifting down. Human everyday sounds, lively and tantalizing with the celebration of purely human love. . . . And the bride and groom. Were they growing eager for their hour? How soon would Deborah be led to her couch, stripped of her finery and made to lie down to await her husband in the still throbbing music of the darkness? And the groom, slightly drunken, flushed and perspiring, his garland askew, his pudgy hands outstretched. When? When? How soon?

But he must not have such thoughts. Such evil thoughts. The Lord had chosen him for this honor and this trial. Would he have been selected if he had not also been strong? Yet he was not strong, he knew wretchedly, as surely God knew only too well. Why then, why?

Joseph lifted his aching throat. "Perhaps that circle of light in the sky is a good omen for our cousins. It's like a wedding band."

Mary followed his gaze, aware of the band on her own finger. Married and yet not married. It was all so strange, pure and cold and strange, yet with the little being in her belly burning as boldly as that single star.

"Let's hope they'll be happy, Joseph, even though there is no love between them such as yours and mine."

His heart broke. He said, "Love has seldom been considered important to a happy marriage in Israel."

"Perhaps one day all that will change. This child that is even now rollicking about within me—I feel that he will change so much. Not just things like freeing the Land and making all the world realize there is but one true God, but things that affect people like us, people who know the meaning of love."

The meaning of love. The meaning of love. . . . He walked along beside her, not understanding. He was her partner in this thing, her protector, and he had not lost her—that must be enough. But his heart was raw.

"If it were not so," she said timidly, "if it were other-

wise, my darling, why would the Lord have wanted us to
be the earthly parents? Why wouldn't it have been better
to put his child into the keeping of others who don't feel
so strongly about each other? Even such as Deborah and
Aaron?"

Joseph laughed shortly. "Who understands the ways of
God?" And he thought: The meaning of love. For a man,
at least, isn't the meaning of love fulfillment and not
denial? This denial. This particular denial. Might it not
be an exquisite form of punishment worked out for him?
Yet a holy child, the Lord's own son! Such a responsibility
would never be entrusted to a man whom God wished to
hurt. Mary was right, he saw through his confusion and
pain. They had been chosen because they loved each
other so much. So that this child, whatever his destiny,
might begin his life in a home where there was love.

And perhaps desire was only one part of love. Perhaps
denial was important too. The death of self in order to be
born anew in the happiness and safety of the beloved. . . .
Desire and denial. They wrestled in him as he walked
along beside her on this night of the wedding with the
sweet sensuous music raining down. And although
Joseph could accept denial with his intelligence and his
will, yet his passion, his nerves and tissues and blood,
all that was essential to himself as a man, cried out.

Their cloaks blew about them in a sudden gust of wind
as they approached their house. Unbolting the door,
Joseph said, "I must see about laying by more firewood.
It will be a cold winter I'm told."

"And I must get busy and sew more clothes for the
baby. I want to have everything ready against the hour
when it comes."

Joseph gazed at her in the moonlight, so small and
trusting. "Mary, are you afraid?"

"Not so long as you are with me."

He was startled. A column of joy surged up in him.
He would have expected her to refer instead to God.

Joseph was now very busy in the shop. For a time
work had been slack. Many nights long after Mary was
asleep he had lain worrying. How would he support her
and the child, let alone aid his widowed mother if people
were so offended they no longer patronized him? He

tossed and turned or got up to study the Scriptures by the glow of the night light in its niche. He was careful not to wake Mary whose small shadow was thrown against the wall. Mary wrapped in her mystery.

His faith floated in and out of him. He made futile attempts to grasp it where it hovered somewhere in the region of his breast, as if he could somehow clutch it, implant it there forever and be at rest. But always, when or how he could not say, it coasted off. He would find himself dry, empty, drained and resigned, avoiding prayer, either formal prayer or that instinctive calling out upon something stronger than he was—something powerful and reassuring.

Then the farmers began to come in. They wanted their tools readied for the spring. He fancied a kind of sheepish apology in some of them. People forgave easily in Nazareth, or they simply forgot. If he had deviated from the proprieties, well so had many of them. "And how is your wife?" they asked.

"Oh, fine, fine," he responded as proudly as if the coming child were his own.

It was at such moments that the sweet mists of God blew in. He could relax a little as he went about the challenge of his tasks. It was as it had been when he was building his home. He was fashioning something meaningful once more. He was working for love, whether for love of God or of his wife he could not have said. But he whistled as he worked, and in his being almost more than in his mind, he prayed.

Snug in her house, Mary heard the thunder and the pelting rains. "Listen to it, isn't it glorious?" she said to Timna, who often came to sew and spin with her.

"Yes." Timna cocked her white head, her blue eyes reminiscent. "Jacob loved the rain." She always managed to turn the conversation to him. Forgotten were his imperfections, she had adored him and now he was gone and she dwelled on him.

With Timna, Mary felt in harmony, at peace. She had dreaded what the scandal might do to their relationship, yet if anything Timna had seemed to love her more. "Oh, my child," she had cried in her gentle, dignified

way, "how glad we all are that you have come home!"
As for the baby, her only regret was that Jacob had not
lived to enjoy it. "He'd always looked forward to having a
grandson to teach his trade."

His trade? A carpenter's trade for the son of God?
Mary wondered. Yet she dared not speak of it. Timna
accepted this child as the son of her son. To inform her,
"This is not Joseph's baby, dear Mother Timna, but the
child of the living God," would be both cruel and shocking. Timna would have been forced to reject it, as Hannah
had rejected it. As countless others would, no doubt, reject it. Human passion people could comprehend. But
the passion of God for man—no, it was too appalling.

A flame of portent licked through Mary. In the protective gesture she had seen her aunt make, Mary cradled
her bulging sides.

The rains finally ceased and the cold came down.
Joseph tightened the cracks in their house and went up
the hill to make fast the house of his father-in-law as
well. Mary wove extra blankets for the baby, and
swaddling clothes of the softest camel's hair.

Her confinement would be upon her sometime in December. Women watched her with kindness now and plied
her with tales. Unlike the weaklings of Egypt they prided
themselves on easy births, yet they gloated too in their
suffering, for was it not so ordered in the very beginning?
Mary must be sure to put a knife under her pillow to cut
the pain. Drinking purple aloes mixed with hot wine was
good, powdered ivory if you could get it was better. Old
Mehitabel, the crone at the well, slipped her a dead
scorpion wrapped in a green rag. "Pin it to your skirt,"
she whispered, "it will drive the devils of pain away."
Mary took it fearfully, yet she could not affront the eagerness to help that sprang from those rheumy eyes.

To help. To ease the birth a little, perhaps to share in
its glory. Where did all this passion for birth come from,
this lust for coming life?

She stood on the mountainside one day with her basket
of faggots and dung for the fire. As far as she could see
the fertile hills went rolling, flanks tawny, becoming
lavender where they melted into the sky. They gave off a
pallid sheen, like the flesh that stretched taut across her

own belly, shielding its tumbling life. Their eternal rhythms echoed its curve, the shape of her body that cupped and held the child.

And the sky merged with the hills, resting now after their summer labors, yet already rich once more with their hidden burden of life. All the throbbing, pulsing, germinating seeds. "Be fruitful and multiply!" The ancient command would be fulfilled, for the spring rains and sun would bring them leaping forth, all the flowers and grasses and grains and little furred, winged things that now slept so peacefully. How joyous it all was, and how awesome. Life sprang out of the earth and out of a woman's belly and had its little span of time upon that earth, and then shriveled up like the weeds of the field and died. But the earth and the sky flowed on forever.

Were they then the only permanence? The only things fashioned by the hand of God that he loved enough to make eternal? Or was there something more, something that he meant to give the world through his coming child?

Close though she felt to Timna, as Mary's hour drew nearer she found herself wanting her mother. More and more often she climbed the hillside to be with Hannah for a while. "So you've come," Hannah would say flatly, belying the pleasure in her eyes. "Here, knead the dough and set it near the oven to rise. After that I've some flax to dye." It was good to be near Hannah in the old way, being ordered about. It was curiously like being a little girl again.

One day when they were at the dyeing in the yard, she asked, "When my time comes you will serve me as midwife won't you, Mother?"

Hannah turned from the steaming kettle, stick in hand. Her face flushed almost as crimson as the stuff bubbling in the pot. "Do you really want me? What about Timna?"

"She isn't the midwife you are. And I wouldn't feel safe with anyone else."

Hannah began stabbing and stirring the yarn in the vessel. "All right, if that's the way you feel." She wiped her hands on the tucked-up skirt of her tunic. "And I— I hope it will go easy with you, my child."

"I'm not afraid," said Mary. "God will be with me."

"He'd better be!" The new threads sank into the mixture—all hot and scarlet like blood, like woman's blood that the Lord had made for the sport and pleasure of man, and the ultimate agony of begetting man.

"Mother, Mother, must you always speak so?"

"I'm sorry, I have no gift for words like you. I mean only that since this is his doing, if indeed it is the miracle you believe, why then will you have need of a crude servant like me?"

"I don't know. There is still so much that I don't understand. As you say, another miracle may happen to bring this divine child forth from me. Yet I must be prepared, since I don't know." There was a look of patient bewilderment on Mary's face. "It's the not knowing that's hard. It's that, only that, of which I confess I'm afraid."

They were closer after that. The air between them was heightened and sweetened by this coming event which now concerned them both. Thus when Joseph came up one night to join them for the meal on the Sabbath Eve, they were astounded at his news.

Word of a decree from Caesar had reached Nazareth only a few hours ago. Hearing it angrily discussed in the shop, he'd flung his tools down and gone out to read the proclamation for himself where it was displayed on the notice board. "New taxes are going to be levied throughout the entire Roman world," he told them in a quiet outrage. "And to make sure nobody fails to pay up, they're going to take a new census. They've ordered every adult male citizen to proceed at once to the place of his birth to be registered and counted. For me that means Bethlehem."

Bethlehem! The family stared at him where he stood drying his flushed perspiring face and his hands. They needed no explanation; his parents had lived there when he was born, his birthplace was the one thing Joseph had in common with Hannah.

"But you can't go," Salome voiced their astonished protest. "You can't leave Mary."

"He's got no choice." Joachim moved to the corner where the sacred scrolls and instruments of ceremony were kept. The house was fragrant with the foods that the women had been preparing all day; it was to have been a happy evening. "None of us have." He was scowling, his voice fierce. "To defy those accursed swine would mean being thrown into prison. As if our taxes weren't enough to break our backs, now they must count us like beasts of the fields."

"Father, no," pleaded Esau. "It's not good to feel such hatred. Not on the Sabbath Eve."

Even as he spoke, two final blasts from the trumpets came thrilling through the night, signaling the time for the women to light their Sabbath lamps. A hush fell, and Esau knew that his mother was lighting theirs. He could smell the oil, feel its warm glow; he knew that all over the village other lamps had begun to sparkle, the Sabbath to shine. Mary had described it for him many times; it was like the starry skies. And he knew that bitterness and anger were clouds condemning all to a darkness worse than his. No, no, the Sabbath Eve should always be radiant when his sister had come home.

"In thy light shall we see light," he could hear his father praying. The sweet smelling wine was poured, there was the cool taste of it, the tinkling of the cups, and they strove to be at peace, reciting the sacred words together. But anxiety was upon them, and afterward, instead of discussing the Scriptures or singing psalms or telling stories, they could speak of nothing but this latest insult, with its terrible complications.

"I'll have to prepare for the trip as soon as the Sabbath is over," Joseph told Joachim. "I should leave early in the week. Fortunately my brothers can register here and look after the shop." He gazed wretchedly at Mary, who was helping Hannah clear the table, the only work they might do and not break the rules of rest. "As for Mary, my mother will look after her while I'm gone."

Hannah turned swiftly from the cupboard. "We'll look after her," she said, and for a moment she could not conceal her exultation. To have him out of the way at such a time! To bring the child into the world with her own hands, be the first to know it, love it; and for Joachim to be the first male to consecrate it by holding it upon his knees. Amazingly, it all seemed arranged for her benefit, a late but undeniable squaring of accounts.

But Mary had shaken the last crumbs from the cloth and crossed the room to stand by Joseph's side. "I want to go with you," she said.

"Mary, you can't. My beloved, you can't."

"He's right." Hannah sprang at them. "It's unthinkable. The mountains are treacherous in the winter and the nights are freezing. You might lose the child."

"I cannot lose the child."

"And what if your time comes upon you somewhere out in the wilderness among the jackals? Or somewhere along the road." Hannah was in a frenzy. She accosted her husband, who was regarding his daughter with a strange, fixed expression. "You tell her. Tell her she must not do this foolish thing."

"We will take shelter," Mary said. "We will be safe."

"Mary. . . ." Joseph gripped her hands. "Mary, you had better listen to your mother."

"Joachim, speak to her," Hannah beseeched him. He must support her, surely he would not yield to Mary when so important an issue was at stake. "You're her father, she'll listen to you."

Joachim ran a big trembling hand across his grizzled jaw. Slowly he shook his head. "She must do what she must do."

"I must go with my husband," said Mary. "I must journey with him to Bethlehem."

XVI

JOSEPH had let Mary sleep as long as possible, but now he must rouse her. "If we are to be off before daylight we must get started."

She fought her way up out of the blessed oblivion. She could feel his strong hand lifting her, a strength beyond hers supporting her, and she gave herself over to it, still dreamily, leaning her head against his breast. "Oh, Joseph, forgive me. . . ." For she was usually up before him as a good wife should be.

"You will need your rest, my beloved," he said, and kissed her hair. "Dress warmly, it will be very cold until the sun is fully up."

She shivered, bathing herself. The bread that had been put on the coals to bake last night smelled hot and good. Gratefully she knelt by the oven, feeling the heat on her face and the hot loaves against her thighs as she carried them in her apron to the table. Then she summoned Joseph, who was outside loading the donkey.

They ate hastily, bound by a sense of urgency and yet a queer elation. They had never made a journey together before. And before their return the baby would have surely arrived. When? Where? How? The very concern that underlay it all, the thrill of fear deep in the vitals, added to the challenge. For they were young and strong and in love and buoyed up by the sheer adventure of going forth alone together to face whatever lay ahead.

Mary tidied up, though her mother had said she would come in later to do it. The queer taut elation remained. Yet now something held her; the little house held her. Stay, stay, it begged. Your first home of your own. . . . The warm fire glowing. The dear familiar cups and bowls. The betrothal gifts, and the lovely table Joseph had made. When would she see them all again?

Yet she must go.

Joseph was making numerous trips for things to further load the donkey. He had strapped a tent across its back, forming a saddle on which Mary could ride. To its sides hung paniers containing dried foods, cooking vessels, clothing. Now he added tools, for he had no idea how long they might be gone; he would probably have to find work before they were ready to come home. They would have to stop at the well to fill the water bags, and they'd better get there before the others began to arrive.

It was growing lighter, they no longer needed the torch that burned beside the door. The outlines of the house grew clearer and Joseph felt it too, its permanence and safety, but more, the dearness of this place that he had worked on so hard and now must leave. He put an arm around Mary's shoulders and they stood gazing upon it a moment thus. "Don't worry," he tried to cheer her, "it will still be here when we get back."

He went to stamp out the torch. The sky was gray now, laced with pink. A cock crowed. Hannah and Joachim were coming up the path to see them off, Hannah's teeth chattering with the cold. Her eyes were like burned cinders, her voice had gone hoarse from pleading with Mary not to go. But her first burst of selfishness had ceased to goad her, her only concern was now for her daughter.

Fighting back her own tears, Mary kissed her mother's wet cheek. Then Joseph lifted her onto the donkey. Heavy as she was, he lifted her with ease, Hannah noticed, taking such consolation from it as she could. And for the first time she acknowledged what her husband had maintained: If any man could take care of Mary in her coming ordeal, that man was Joseph.

"Goodbye, be careful," Joachim said gruffly. "If you can join up with a party along the route you'd better do so, there are often robbers in the hills. And wait," he trudged beside them a few steps, "take this, you'll need it." He pressed a few dinars into Joseph's hand. "For the little one," he said.

"We'll be all right," Joseph said cheerfully. "Don't worry. God will be with us."

"Yes, yes, God will be with you." He must let them go, and he stood, one hand upraised. "God be with you and keep you, my children."

They progressed down the street, the hooves of the ass making a hollow music on the deserted cobbles. They were shadowy figures in the white mists of the morning, they were like something out of a dream. And Hannah stared after them, gnawing the fist that was pressed against her lips. "God help them," she whispered. *"Oh God, help them!"*

"He'll help them," Joachim said. "For he is leading them on this journey, he is taking them to the City of David, which is Bethlehem."

"Bethlehem, where I was born. What a pity all my people are gone from there, they might have given them shelter."

Her husband continued to gaze after the laden donkey that appeared and disappeared in the floating veils of fog. " 'But thou, O Bethlehem,' " he quoted from Micah, " '. . . though thou be little among the thousands of Judah, yet out of thee shall he come forth unto me that is to be ruler in Israel. . . .' " His voice shook, even as he felt his wife's hand trembling on his arm. " 'Therefore,' " he went on, " 'will he give them up, until the time that she which travaileth hath brought forth. . . .' " He could not continue, Hannah's fingers gripped him.

"Bethlehem! *She who is in travail.*" And as the great knowledge awoke within her, began to beat and break within her, Hannah's face likewise broke, dissolved. "My God, my God," she cried, and lifted its anguish to heaven, "wherefore have you denied me this truth so long?"

Wordlessly, Joachim drew her to him.

"I knew, I must have known . . . but I dared not . . . after all my vanity and pride. . . ." Far below the road emerged and as Hannah stared, the fog lifted for an instant, and the parents could see them clearly, their daughter, so small upon the burdened beast, and the tall man who led it.

"I must tell her, I must catch them and tell her before it's too late!" She broke from him and began to run, frantically calling her daughter's name. But Joachim caught his wife and restrained her, wildly though she wept. "Let me go, this much comfort at least I can give her. I *believe*. Oh, Mary, I too believe!"

For four days they traveled, south through the old towns of Nain, Sunem and Jezreel, then eastward across the boggy plains of Esdraelon until they reached the Jordan; then southward through its valley until they must climb again into the bleak hills of Judea. "I wish we dared go directly through Samaria," Joseph told her as they plodded along. "It would be so much easier for you, but it would be too great a risk."

Mary nodded. The enmity between the Samaritans and the Israelites had been growing worse. These eternal hostilities, why must they be? Would the time never come when men and nations could live in peace? Or was that the true significance of the miracle she carried? The Messiah. Perhaps through him these terrible conflicts would be settled; he would bring mankind together in love of their God.

She smiled at Joseph. "I am in your keeping. As long as we're together I don't care how long the journey takes."

She rode along beside him, uncomplaining, either of the cold dry east wind which lashed grit in their faces and made them cringe in ther cloaks, or the fierce contrast of the *khamsin*, blowing its hot stifling breath from the desert. The skies were clear and cloudless after the drenching fall rains, but the nights were intensely cold. Despite the dirt, the jolting, all the discomfort, Mary smiled a great deal, half in her pleasure at simply being with him, half in a reverie of the coming child. She smiled faintly even as she dozed—as she was dozing now, on this day which Joseph hoped would be nearly the last one of their journey.

Joseph's feet were sore, his whole body unutterably

weary, but he knew he could not be half so miserable as
she. He halted the donkey and stood for a moment gazing
upon her where she sat, head forward on her chest, one
hand braced to support herself. He stood wondering if
there were anything he could do to make her more comfortable. The marvel of her electing to come with him
seemed more than he deserved. "Mary?" He wasn't
aware that he had spoken, but she started and gazed at
him blankly for an instant. "Mary, have you any idea
how beautiful you are?"

She laughed. "Oh, Joseph, dirty and disheveled as I am?"

He laid his cheek against hers. Then he took a handkerchief from his girdle, and, pouring a little water from
one of the bags, proceeded to wash her dusty face, if
only cool it a litle. "Would you like me to lift you
down so that you can stretch?"

"Yes, I need to walk about a bit." He set her down
upon the hard hot pavement, and she stood there trying
to take in her surroundings. "I must have slept. Where
are we?"

"Not far from Jericho. She, there's the river. By nightfall we should be there. Perhaps beyond. And tomorrow
night, if all goes well, we shall sleep in Bethlehem."

"I hope so." She had not realized how weak and
trembling her legs were until she stood. Her body ached,
her back was one fierce cramp, and the child was threshing about so that it was hard to speak. She drew a deep
breath, still determinedly smiling. "The sooner we can
reach Bethlehem the better it will be."

"Are you all right, my beloved? Are you well?" he
asked anxiously.

"Yes: Yes—it's only riding so long. Come, I'll walk
beside you."

"Very well then, I'll ride," Joseph laughed.

"Would that you could. Poor Joseph. Would that you
had a camel to ride, or a horse like the Romans."

"Would that you were right, for then I would be rich
and able to provide so much better for you and your
child."

"Our child," she said. "This child that the Lord has
vouchsafed into our keeping. Oh, Joseph, just because it

is my body that will bear him does not mean that he is any less your child than mine."

"I didn't father him," he said quietly. "Nothing can ever change that. Don't think I'm protesting, Mary. It is a thing that is beyond protesting. Yet even you must agree that there's no way to change that fact."

"No." She pressed his hand, trying to think how to comfort him. "And it matters to you. You would be less of a man if it did not matter, and I—surely I would love you less. And yet. . . ." She groped for the words to express it. "In many ways he will be more your son than mine."

"More!"

"Yes, more," she insisted. "A father is so important in Israel. A son needs his father to teach him the ways of the world, and of God and the Law. Once I have borne and suckled this child my task will be largely finished. But yours, Joseph, yours will be only beginning."

"He may not need a father's training. He who will come to us as the very son of God."

"Perhaps he will need it more." For a minute there was only the sound of the donkey's hooves on the stones. They could smell the river, now swollen from the rains, and see the cranes that waded its opaque gray-blue waters. "He—the one who is to lead Israel out of her troubles—surely he will have to be very strong and wise. And I . . . I don't know much about it, but I feel in my heart that he will come to us innocent and uninformed, a child like any child, needing guidance from us as well as from the one who sends him. Both of us, Joseph, but you especially. And that's why you were chosen. For you *were* chosen—your honor is as great as mine."

She spoke with such conviction that a thrill of hope ran through him. He knew that she was seeing this only as she wished to, because she loved him. He knew that he would never be as significant in the eyes of God as Mary, nor would he have it so. But her words had inspired and consoled him, given him new purpose, added an unanticipated new dimension to his destiny.

The man who ferried them across the river was a coarse, rollicking fellow who cursed the Romans as he poled his tipsy craft, but also sang their praises for improving his business. "It's almost as good as feast time. I'm getting so rich I may soon have enough to pay my taxes! What's your destination, friends?"

"Bethlehem," Joseph told him.

"Oho, Bethlehem. That's where everybody seems to be heading. All the towns are crowded, I hear, like grain sacks bursting at the seams, but Bethlehem, City of David and all his kin—that's the worst. That David," he whooped, "greatest king we ever had, especially with the ladies. Now me, if I was to take another wife or even a concubine, assuming I could afford 'em, my wife would not only break my head, I'd be read out of the synagogue. But oho, not old David, not him!"

Joseph and Mary exchanged amused glances. "Times have changed." Joseph steadied her as the craft bumped the opposite bank. "How much?"

"Two drachmas for you and the beast." The man glanced mischievously at Mary. "No charge for the lady, though for her I should probably charge double."

Mary laughed. "Thank you. God be with you."

"And with you. May it be a son." The man leaned frowning on his pole. "I trust you have kinfolk to stay with in Bethlehem?"

"Not any more. We're planning to stay at the inn."

"The inn? You'll be lucky to find a corner for the ass at the inn!"

Joseph lifted Mary back onto the donkey and strode along at a faster pace. If things were that bad the quicker they got to Bethlehem the better. Sleeping in the open had not been too hard; he had kept a fire going and seen that Mary was well wrapped. But he knew that her hour would soon be upon her. What, literally, would he do if the birth pangs began without shelter or someone to attend her? True, he had seen animals born. But Mary was no animal. What's more, that which was to come from her was a being so significant that it staggered the imagination. And she had been entrusted to him. He too had been chosen.

Mary too was concerned. Every instinct warned her that her time was not far off. And it must not happen before they reached Bethlehem. Bethlehem, as fated and foretold by the prophets. Therefore, she reasoned, it could not happen elsewhere. Yet anxiety warred with that blind conviction. What if the city were as crowded as the ferryman said? Where would they go if there were no room for them?

Even so, the sheer high spirits of the man had invaded theirs. Partly to conceal their anxiety, they laughed again at his jokes and at their own. The worst heat of the day had passed, the world seemed exquisitely cool and clear. And that evening as Joseph was making camp he snared a partridge which he blessed and bled and roasted over the coals. Mary had already started the quick bread which she baked for them each night. It always tasted of smoke but it was delicious after the cold dry bread and figs they had eaten at noon. Tonight they were ravenous, and the unusual treat of the meat made the meal festive. They sat beside their fire eating and watching the stars come out.

"Our last night on the road," Mary said wistfully. "For some reason I almost hate to have this journey end."

"Yes, it's been good, just the two of us like this." Now that it was nearly over Joseph too had a strange wish to prolong it. Even its ardors. The grit on the face and in the teeth, the endless glare of the pavement, the sore feet, the muscles that ached from sleepless nights lying on the hard ground watching over her, his Mary. Something was ending here, this night. A phase of their life was going.

He fed the fire another load so that it crackled and sprang high, and then he put down a pallet of cloaks and skins for Mary and rolled her up in them. "Warm enough?" he asked and she smiled back, "I feel as snug as a caterpillar in its cocoon." He knelt to kiss her before he wrapped himself in his woolen cloak and lay down by her side.

They had never been happier, or the heavens more beautiful. The sky was almost too crowded with stars; now and then one darted off in bright escape. The constellations drew their jeweled patterns, crisp and clear. They could hear some shepherds singing on a nearby hillside and see the eye of their campfire glowing like a hearth. The voices drifted down to them, and the occasional plaintive crying of the sheep. It was companionable having them so close, it was like having neighbors by their star-canopied home.

Drawing nearer for warmth and holding fast to each other's hands, they fell asleep.

XVII

SUNRISE found them again on their way. They tried in vain to recapture last night's mood. But a sense of urgency was upon them; they were nervous before the events impending. The taxes, the census, the birth. Gone was the sweet bond of aloneness, plodding so immutably toward that which they did not understand but had not as yet really feared. Now as their goal loomed closer, they felt poor and ill-prepared and far from home. For suddenly from sideroads and hillsides other people had come streaming. Leading or riding camels, on mules or donkeys, some on horseback, a number borne on litters carried by sweating slaves, but most of them on foot, they came, all intent to get either into Jerusalem or on to Bethlehem.

The press was so great it was scarcely possible to see the Temple in the distance when at last they reached the outskirts of the Holy City. But by then Mary was too miserable to care.

"Hurry! Oh, Joseph . . . hurry," she begged, when he paused for the fourth time to give her a drink of water and wipe off her streaming face. Her cheeks were ashen, her lower lip was clenched. He could see that she gripped the bundles piled before her until her knuckles were white.

"Darling, I am hurrying. I'm doing the best I can."

"I know, I know. Forgive me. It's . . . just that I . . . I don't know how much longer. . . ."

"Then let's stop," he cried. "Mary, if your pains are beginning we can't go on, we must get help."

"No. No, we've got to go on to Bethlehem!"

"But that's at least six more miles. And at this rate it may be nightfall."

"Then I'll wait. Somehow I must wait." She gave a long shudder, then relaxed, regarded him with clearer eyes. "I'll be all right," she promised. "I've heard that it sometimes happens this way. You get a spasm or two and think surely the labor has started, then it stops. It's sometimes a very long time."

Nonetheless, Joseph was distraught. He pleaded with those in his path, trying to maneuver around them with the heavily laden donkey. "Please, it is urgent, my wife is ill."

"Then let 'er stay home where she belongs." A roar of laughter went up from a group of men, though others muttered and bade them be still. Except for several painted harlots there were few women in the mob. Only men were being rounded up to be counted and most women had had the good sense to stay behind.

It was a little better once they were beyond Jerusalem. It was much cooler here, but the donkey was cruelly burdened. He could move only so fast, especially since the road now climbed again into the barren hills. Mary could only hold on, eyes closed, teeth set, and pray. "Help us, help us. Delay the pains, oh God, or when they come don't let me show my suffering. . . . And help my poor Joseph. And this beast, this poor little beast who's carried me so far—dear Lord, help him too." She could feel its wet heaving sides, and now and then when it tossed its head foam flicked onto the steaming road.

This day the sun shone pale and chill, minus comfort, metallic. Gusts of stinging grit tormented the cheeks and eyes. Joseph pressed on, straining. Again the road was clotted with people and their mounts, their litters or their carts, all of them weary, impatient. The smell of garlic and oil and sweat and dusty clothes together with that of beasts was almost overpowering. Mary had to fight nausea now, along with the grinding anguish that began to gnaw slowly at her back, then in waves at her very vitals, so that she would have doubled over if she could, clutch-

ing herself and moaning. But she must sit erect, hanging
on, grimly hanging on though people jostled her, nearly
knocking her from her seat. . . . God—dear merciful God
in heaven, please help us! Bring us to our refuge soon!

They were not too far now from the Bethlehem gates
where a mass of humanity surged, anxious to have their
goods weighed and be done with the tax collectors sta-
tioned there, so that they could enter the town. A couple
of Roman centurions on magnificent horses rode about
trying to keep order. "Don't crowd, get in line now, get
in line, get your belongings ready. The tax collectors will
take you each in turn."

The donkey had halted. Mary sat dazed, limp from her
last bout with the agony, trying to rest, to regain her
identity before the monstrous thing assaulted her again.
Dimly she was aware that Joseph had left her side. She
could see that he was saying something to the centurion
and this astounded her, and yet it did not either. Nothing mattered, nothing except that she hang onto herself
until they managed, heaven knows when, to get through the
gates and into the inn. The inn, the inn, the bed at the
inn . . . dear God, please let there be a bed at the inn. . . .

She saw the centurion suddenly wheel his horse about
and wave his whip above the crowd. "Stand back, out of
the way, let these people though! You fools, where are
your manners?" Many fell back, surprised, as he pulled
up beside her. "Are you all right, lady?" he asked, taking
off his helmet and mopping his brow where the iron
weight had left a deep red mark. He was very young, his
anxious blue eyes did not match his harsh voice, he
seemed embarrassed.

"Yes," she gasped. "Yes, thank you. Once we get inside . . . into the inn. . . ."

But when he had broken a path for them and led
them forward and ridden on, the crowd closed in upon
them. They resented his having put these Galilean
bumpkins at the head of the line, they muttered and
shoved. Joseph stood scarlet but adamant, trying to protect their place. And Mary suffered afresh for what he
was enduring on account of her. Oh, help us, help the tax
collectors to hurry!

But the process of weighing, measuring and assessing

the value of possessions that were being brought into the city, proceeded slowly. The collectors at the gate got a percentage, and they made sure that nothing, no garment, no trinket, no grain of meal, was held back. It was an eternity before the party ahead of them was finally motioned on and Joseph was called. "Next! Unload and be quick about it."

Joseph had already unstrapped the paniers and lifted down the bundles. All must be exposed, all their poor little possessions. Even—and this was most outrageous and hurtful of all, the lovingly wrapped packet of swaddling clothes. "Is that all?" The tax collector was a large-nosed contemptuous man of about thirty. He exchanged an amused glance with the other collector as he fingered their goods and slapped them onto the scales.

"Yes," said Joseph tightly.

"What about that thing your wife's sitting on? I presume it's your wife?" he joked, while the crowd tittered.

"Just an old robe that serves as a tent and to keep her warm at night," Joseph said, again tightly.

"Let's have it."

"Please." Joseph's contempt surpassed that of his tormentor. "Can't you see that my wife is in no condition to climb down? If there is a grain of decency in you don't disturb her."

"Let it be then," the man brazened it off. "We'll take your word—one drachma for the old robe. That'll be five dinars altogether. Pay up, pack up and move on."

With unsteady hands Joseph brought forth the coins. Five dinars! Out of the twelve they had brought for the trip. It was robbery. He flung the money onto the table and savagely stuffed the things back into the bags. But at least they had cleared the gates and could find a place for Mary. He forced a smile as he strapped the paniers back on. "It won't be long, my dearest. Be brave, I'll soon have a place where you can rest."

She nodded, too grateful to speak. A place. Oh, thank God. Just any place away from people, from staring eyes and shouting voices and stink of flesh. A place where she could give way to her agony at last.

Again the donkey moved forward beneath her, through the gates, into the hubbub of humanity just beyond. The inn stood to the left, a sprawling moss-grown structure with a large courtyard in front and a row of blackened ovens in the rear. The yard was crowded with people unloading baggage, tethering their beasts, or leading them through the low doorway that led to the stable beneath the inn. From the back came the smell of smoke and roasting meat, where cooks tended the spits and serving maids darted about.

Joseph saw at once that the fears of these last tortuous miles were to be realized. Trying to hide his consternation, he tied the donkey and hastened inside.

The innkeeper was busy serving wine, a squat wheezing man who had no time for Joseph's appeal. "I'm sorry, we're full up, haven't an inch to lay a cat in, nay nor a mouse. You'll have to do as the others; find yourself a friendly yard to sleep in or go back outside and sleep in the fields."

"We can't. We've already paid dearly to enter the town. Nor can we sleep on the earth this night." Joseph grabbed the man's beefy arm, causing him to slop wine down his grimy apron. And though the man was angered he could not escape the desperation in the young face. "My wife is in labor. She is about to bear a child. You must give us shelter, at least for a few hours."

"But I can't," the innkeeper wheezed. He gestured to the people pounding their mugs for service. "Can't you see for yourself? There's simply no room. I'm sorry, lad, but I can't perform miracles."

Miracles, Joseph thought in a flash of bitterness. Let the Lord produce one now. "You must," he repeated. "You must help us."

"Well, there is the stable. It's full of creatures and people already, this one below us, but if you don't mind the stink and the noise. . . ."

Joseph's heart sank. The choas was deafening, not only all around them but from below, where he could hear beasts stamping and voices raised in drunken laughter or raucous argument. "Is there nothing else?" he begged. "My wife must have privacy."

The innkeeper was gone. But as Joseph plunged back to the entrance, despairing, the man was suddenly wheezing at his side. "Wait. There are some caves toward the

back where we store things and stable a few animals when
we're crowded. It's quieter there and warm, you'd be
alone there. Just circle the inn and go down the path,
you can't miss it."

Joseph thanked him. But he was heartsick as he
hurried back to tell Mary. A stable! That God had chosen
him to look after her, and the best he could provide was a
poor cave worse than that in which his parents had lived.
A humble cave of a stable.

But she was in the grip of such pain there was no use
wasting time apologizing. "Come," he said gently. "The
inn is truly full as the ferryman warned, but you'll be
alone, my beloved. I'll make you a soft bed on the hay."
Once again taking the donkey by the halter, he hurried
it forward, flinching each time the poor beast stumbled
and jarred her, praying only that the distance would not
be far.

The rocky pathway was strewn with dung. It pitched
downward as it circled the inn and led to the low but
ample opening that marked the first of a series of caves.
As he approached through the gathering darkness he could
see that even here they were not to have complete privacy,
for a group of grizzled Bedouins had built a fire before it
and were cooking their evening meal. It lit up their faces,
some old and weathered, some mere boys, and played on
their veiled heads and their robes. They were laughing
and talking as they squatted to dip their bread into the
stew, or strode about preparing to bed down for the night.
They paid scant attention to the little group that plodded
into the cave's yawning mouth.

Inside there was the mealy smell of oats and the tang
of the animals tethered in the semidarkness. The fire outside guided their footsteps, past the dark shapes of stolid
oxen and cattle or the forms of small patient donkeys,
knees locked, already asleep. At last, at the far end,
groping about, Joseph found what he sensed to be a vacant stall. Hands shaking, he got his lamp lighted and held
it high. The place was indeed vacant, with one lone
manager, a number of tools strewn about, and much clean
straw. A kind of storage room. But the straw in the
manager was old and rancid. Hanging the lamp in a niche,
Joseph cleaned the manger out and pitched the straw

aside. Then, working swiftly, he gathered up armloads of the clean dry rustling straw and spread it in the manger. Upon it, to save time, he flung down his own cloak.

Then, turning to Mary, he held out his arms. "I'm sorry, my dearest," he muttered as she slid down. "It's the best I can do."

"Thank God," she moaned softly. "Oh, Joseph, thank God for it and for you." She leaned against him, her forehead cold with sweat. Then in little gasping steps she moved toward the place where at last she could lie down. "You must go and fetch a midwife," she panted. "It may be hours before the baby comes, but I must have a woman by my side."

"Yes. I should have thought of that before, I should have inquired at the inn." Again the shock of his appalling ineptitude. Fool, fool. Now he would have to leave her alone and go plunging back into the night.

"Don't worry, I'll be all right." She touched his stricken face. "The pain has stopped altogether," she said, surprised. "Perhaps I can sleep a little."

"I'll not be long, I promise. I'll find someone. Sleep, my darling, it's been such a terrible day for you. Sleep and rest."

Leaving the lamp behind, he set forth, feeling his way frantically along the stalls. Idiot, blunderer! A stable, among oxen and asses and not even a woman with her. All this warning and I didn't even have the wits to ask about a midwife.

"Joseph!" He halted, frozen, just as he was almost to the opening where the herdsmen moved about before their fire. "*Joooo-seph!*" It was a scream too horrifying to believe. He whirled and ran.

She was sitting upright, her legs dangling over the stall, gnawing her fists, the tears streaming down her face. "Joseph, don't go, don't leave me! Joseph, it's unbearable, I can't stand it."

"Mary, Mary." He cradled her in his arms, crooning to her and rocking her until the hideous convulsion ceased. Oh, God, he thought. You God. *You God*—if you are a god who performed this miracle—why are you doing this to my beloved?

"I'm sorry," she whispered at length. "Only I got so frightened when it began again and I was alone." She pushed back her tangled hair. "What will we do?" she cried. "You know the ancient taboo; it is not fitting for a man to gaze upon a woman in childbirth."

"Yes," he agreed, beside himself. "And even if it were not so, I know nothing of what to do to help you, my beloved."

"Go and fetch some water," she said. "Some hot water if you can get it. We will need it. Go to those herdsmen at the door and see if they can give us some. But don't be long," she begged. "Go no further even to fetch a midwife."

"I'll send one of them for one," he said. But even as he ran he heard her moaning and knew that the cruel thing that tore at a woman's body to bring forth young was stretching forth its claws again.

The herdsmen who were strumming their lutes or sprawled about drinking wine reared up as he burst into the circle of light. "Help me," he said. "Have you any hot water left from your meal? In heaven's name help us, my wife is far gone in childbirth and she needs water and a midwife."

"My friend, the water we can share with you," one of them said, "but there are no midwives among us." There was laughter, but it stopped as they saw Joseph's face. A man rose, tall and dignified in his striped robes, and lifted a steaming pot from the coals. "There is also some barley soup, it is nourishing and still hot. Perhaps that will be of some comfort to your wife. Here, I'll carry it for you and light your way. Meanwhile. . . ." He kicked one of the slumbering boys. "You, Joab, rise up and go into Bethlehem and see if you can find a midwife."

The youth rose, yawning and surly. It was plain he had drunk too much and considered this a joke. There was no time to argue, he must get back to Mary. Carrying the water and followed by the tall shepherd with the soup, Joseph led the way.

The smothered cries from within the little cubicle halted both of them. "Thank you, my friend," Joseph said grimly, and motioned him aside. "If we need anything further we'll call you."

He stole back in, stood where she lay writhing. He had known that women suffered, had heard his own mother on nights when the younger ones were born. But this was Mary, his Mary, and the thing that tortured her clawed into the dark pit of his own bowels even though it was not his child that she struggled to bring forth. Perhaps the anguish would be less if it *were* his child. Thus he stood while the sweat poured down his contorted face. No man must see a woman in childbirth, that he knew. Yet he could not leave her. And perhaps this was his further punishment for whatever sins he had committed, both in loving her so much and in failing her. That he must stand helplessly by while she cried out in her travail.

"Joseph . . . oh . . . *Joseph*." It came from between her clenched teeth. He could barely hear her, and he fell to his knees beside her, let her grip his hands and pull upon him, pull with all her strength. And dazedly, in their mutual agony, it seemed to him that something was being uprooted within him. Self. The last vestige of self. Was this then the meaning of love? To die to self in order to be reborn for the beloved. To spare her. Dear God in heaven to spare her! To share it. To more than share it, to take it into his own body and bear it for her, and in the process to die and to be reborn.

"Yes, my dearest, my best beloved?"

"If I die in this, if it destroys me utterly, you must know one thing. I did not sin. You are the only man I have ever loved."

"Hush, my blessed, hush." That this could be uppermost in her mind at such a time seemed to him unutterably pathetic. And that he could have doubted unendurable. "I know how pure you are. God forgive me for doubting even for a minute. I was the one who sinned." He stroked her matted hair, plucked wisps of straw from it. His voice was choked. "And you won't die. God would not allow it."

She relaxed a little against his shoulder, lay back dozing. The pain had given her respite and his words had comforted her. Easing her back upon the crackling bed, Joseph rose and swiftly began unloading the donkey. He would need a basin, bowls, linens, so many things. The midwife must come! But whether she did or not, he must be ready. And he knew that the donkey must also be desperately tired and hungry and must be cared for.

Pouring a little of the hot water into a basin, he washed his hands. Then he took a dipper of the soup to Mary, and lifting her carefully once again, persuaded her to sip a little, for it had been hours since they had eaten. "You will need your strength, my darling."

"Yes," she whispered, "for the child. I'll need every ounce of strength for bringing it forth. And attending to it." She drank the entire ladle and bade him have some too. "And you, Joseph, you too will need your strength before this night is done." She lay back, considering. "The midwife—have you sent for her?"

He nodded. "Surely she will be here soon."

"Yes, surely." She was speaking half to reassure herself, half to keep him from worrying. "I wish it could be my mother," she said wistfully. "Although I'm sorry I cried out so for her in the beginning. It was silly and childish, for I am a child no more, I'm a woman. With a woman's job to do."

"Would to God that your mother could be with you." The heat of his words caused her to lift her head. They regarded each other, facing the truth. "Or some woman. I can't leave you, Mary. And if the midwife doesn't come —I'm but a man, without knowledge of these things."

"Don't be afraid." She gripped his hand. "We're forgetting something. That this is God's child and God will not abandon us. Weak and human as we are, God has chosen us to be his servants. Surely he will help us."

God's child. She was right. Ignorant and inexperienced though they were, God would not fail them. God would let nothing happen to his own child, nor to her who delivered it.

"I must think," Mary said. "While I am still clear-headed I must instruct you. You must build a fire and keep the swaddling clothes warm. And the water hot. There must be warm water for bathing the baby. And a knife, you must dip it in very hot water before cutting the cord. I have learned that it drives away evil spirits that might harm the child."

"A knife?" Joseph gasped.

"Yes, it must be done. You must do all this if the

midwife isn't here. And the cord must be tied securely with dried gut. I put a piece, together with the knife, in a little parcel, just in case the birth should occur somewhere unexpectedly. And the salt for rubbing the child is with it."

Joseph's head was beginning to whirl. All these things, these human physical things—would it come to that, actually? Despite all else, her swollen body and now the pangs of labor—even so, it seemed to him blindly, somewhere within his being, beyond even the area of thought, that this which had begun as a miracle would conclude as a miracle. Not so much to spare them, Mary her suffering or him his incredible tasks, but simply because God's son must come forth in a manner more fitting than to be hurled from a woman's bloody flanks.

He gazed about. These lowly surroundings—the oxen and sheep, the little donkey braying piteously for its food, the smell of dung and hay, the cold rock walls glinting in the light of the fire that finally, in desperation, he was able to coax in the pit he had dug beneath a chink he had noticed when they first came in—this humble setting which was the best that he, Joseph, could provide —even so, he thought and prayed, wiping his face in relief as at last the acrid smoke began to rise—even so, God's own angels would surely fill the place at the last and lift up Mary and draw from her loins the blessed being without blood or further agony.

The dung and straw and such sticks as he could scrape together, began to blaze, lighting up the chamber. And through the chink in the wall he could see one brilliant star, fixed and new. As if the Lord himself had set it there to watch over them. The smoke obscured it, but when the wind shifted, there it was, sparkling.

The night wore on. Joseph fed and bedded down the donkey, tended the fire, and hovered over Mary. Now and then he dozed and dreamed and sprang up wildly, guilty and sick with alarm whenever she began her fearful moaning. "Help me! Help me, Joseph. Oh—God—help me!" Yet he could not help her. Even though he grasped her hands as she commanded, and pulled upon them until it seemed that he would literally tear her in two, yet he could not help her to bring it forth and stop

her agony. And God, the God that she called upon in her
anguish, as women had always called upon him, heard her
not.

And his face ran sweat and his heart became black
within him. And he remembered his mother crying thus
pitifully in childbirth while his father paced the fields
and wept. And he wondered at the God who could thus
betray his own creatures, and what kind of a so-called
god it was who decreed such torture even in the bringing
forth of his own son.

"You—God!" his spirit challenged. "You—God.
Where is your miracle now?"

The pain was the only reality. The pain had become
her master and the god she served. Beyond the pain lay
the dim world of the stable. The firelight that threw
flickering shadows across the rough rock walls. The steaming kettle, the vaguely sensed shapes of sleeping beasts in
neighboring stalls. And sometimes very far away, sometimes seeming close, the rumble of male voices in the
yard. And the presence of Joseph was a part of that
strange small homely world that surrounded her private
universe of pain. She was conscious of him moving about,
bending above her, supporting her, and suffering for her
so that she fought to still her cries. But she could not.
Pain was her lover, her husband, her master, her god,
smiling, insistent, forcing the outcries from her with whip
and kiss and brutal embrace and mailed fist and chain.
Yet she must remember that this was no demon that was
the author of her torment, but the bloody grip of God.

And she thought of the beasts being led to be
slaughtered at the cold marble tables of the Temple. They
were moaning now, moving closer in their condemned
files, moaning plaintively—or was it only the low mooing
of the cattle in the next stall?

"Joseph, forgive me!" For it was not the cattle that
she heard but the brute moans and bellowings that came
from her own cracked and bitten lips.

"It's all right, cry if it helps."

The hooves of the poor doomed cattle drove on, over
her, crushing her in their path, yet she sought to reassure
them: Never fear, sweet cattle, I will bring forth a new

kind of offering to Jehovah so that one day you will go bawling to the knife no more. . . . And she sought to reassure the child: Never fear, sweet child, let me not frighten you with my screams. Come forth, come forth in triumph out of suffering.

Suffering! A tremendous excitement filled her along with the agony. There was some secret here, if she were not so weary she would understand it—the secret of suffering. Truly to know the Lord God you must go down into the pit with him, be burned at his fires. . . .

The fires licked at her savagely. God help me, spare me! But she must go with the cattle. They had come charging back for her and were goading her to greater effort with their fierce horns. They were dragging her to the altar with them now, and the god of her pain was driving them all ferociously on. And the high priest stood there waiting to offer up the sacrifice. But it was not the priest, it was Joseph who bent near in love and reverence, telling her, "I can see its little head. You must strive harder, beloved. Bear down, bear down."

She obeyed, gratefully. There was a great ripping and flooding and burning, and he came forth out of her, out of Mary, his mother. Thus in blood and pain he came into the world, this son of God who was also man and the son of man.

And Joseph lifted him up for her to see. And they looked upon him together and marveled at him, his wholeness, infinitely small and red and perfectly formed. And when he squirmed in Joseph's arms and uttered his first cry, the thrill of all mankind ran through both of them, for this was life, human life, and they knew that a miracle had been achieved.

XVIII

Mary lay drowsing, with the child in her arms. Joseph had cleansed it and rubbed it with salt as she directed. When it came to swaddling it, however, he carried the cloths to Mary. It was she who placed the newborn cornerwise on the square of linen and folded it up over his tiny sides and feet. Then, with Joseph's help, she made its little harness of swaddling bands to bind it so that its limbs would grow straight and strong.

So now she lay drowsing while Joseph busied himself at tidying up this small nest that had become for a space their home. How beautiful it was. He had taken the bloody straw from beneath her and replaced it with clean sweet hay. He had bathed her too and brought fresh garments for her. He had brushed her matted hair. And then he had brought the swaddled child for her to suckle. She could feel it tugging at her breast as she dozed. So tiny to be so vigorous, so new to be so hungry! How greedy for life it was, it must assert itself, it must be fed. Feed me, it demanded, groping about with its blind little new mouth.

How comical it was, actually. She smiled in her half-sleep and pressed the hot little bundle closer. Yet what bliss, to direct the nipple to the lips, to be the source of its sustenance. Ecstasy flooded her, the ecstasy of the new mother who finds herself with the child safely cradled in her arms after the long ordeal. The only reality is this wonder, this sense of harmony and love so intense it is scarcely to be endured, and the tears escape the eye-lids and roll foolishly down the cheeks.

And so Mary rested on this night that her child was born. And Joseph kept watch, near exhaustion himself, but too excited to sleep. There was a little of the barley soup left and he realized that he too was ravenous. He heated it over the coals, and sitting on the dirt floor, drained the cup. It was delicious after his long fast and the struggle to help his beloved. New strength began to flow through him, and with it an exaltation that bordered on Mary's. He need berate himself no longer. He had not failed her. Her son had been safely born, and he had helped to bring him forth. So that made him in a new and wondrous sense his son too. They were sleeping there quietly now, his wife and child. His little family. And, unable to restrain himself, he shielded the lamp and held it above their faces, if only to witness the blessed sight of it in this moment of his rapture.

And as he stood thus he was startled to hear a low rumble of voices, the sound of approaching feet. Fear gripped him, a passion of protectiveness. Like a lion before its den, he went to bar the door. No harm should come to them, none should even disturb their peaceful sleep. He could see figures carrying torches, though behind them through the mouth of the cave such light streamed that it seemed the sun was already high in the skies or that the herdsmen must have rekindled their great fire.

To his relief he saw that the man who led the group was the one who had earlier given him aid. "Hush," Joseph whispered. "Don't wake them. My wife and new-born son are sleeping."

"Then all is well with you, my friend?" the herdsman asked softly. His long narrow face seemed pale in the glow of the light, his eyes were filled with doubt and amaze-ment. "The child has been safely born?"

"Yes, thanks be to God. A man-child is even now rest-ing with his mother. Pray be quiet."

"Then it's true!" There was a smothered outcry, a stir of excitement, the others pressed forward. Among them were several shepherds who had not been with the group in the yard, men who had come a long way. "We told you this is the place!" one of them said to the Bedouin. "The star led us to it. We have followed it all night, to this very stable, and it stands even now above the door." He begged Joseph, "If you are the father, pray let us come in if only for a minute, that we may see with our own eyes the glory that the angels told us would be waiting in this holy place."

"Angels?"

"A whole chorus of angels," the man said breathlessly. "As we were tending our sheep on the Jericho hills. This lad saw them first." He thrust a boy forward, and to Joseph's astonishment the child fell to his face. "He thought at first he was dreaming, then the rest of us awoke from the music and the light."

"We have traveled for hours," another pleaded. "Please let us come in, if only long enough to deliver the gifts we have brought." And Joseph saw that indeed each one carried something his arms.

"Joseph?" Mary had roused up and was blinking in the strange light that seemed to have claimed the night. "What is it?"

"These men," he told her, shaken. "They are shepherds. They claim to have been guided to this place by a mysterious star. They—they wish to see the little one."

"Then they must be cold and tired," she said. "Bid them come in." She sat up, there on the hay. Startled, half-frightened herself, but smiling, she covered her breast and lifted up the holy child. And the shepherds stole in fearfully, humbly, and laid their gifts at the foot of the manger. Rude gifts hastily assembled— some rabbit skins, a sack of figs, a kid, a newborn lamb. And with shining, transfixed faces, they gazed upon the sleeping child, or fell down upon the straw and worshiped him.

For forty days the rude little stable was their home. And each night the great star stood over its entrance. Joseph had never seen such a star, flaming now purple, now white, now gold. Its light illuminated the countryside. Dazed, he told Mary, "I'm afraid there will be others coming to see the child."

"Let them come," she murmured. "Oh, Joseph, isn't he lovely? Just look at him—see, his eyes are open, he knows us! He's trying to smile."

"Foolish—all babies smile like that, they don't know what they're doing."

"Oh, but this one does. Our baby does."

Their baby . . . Joseph bent over her where she stood unwinding its swaddling bands. She did this several times a day to change it and exercise its limbs. Timidly at first, but now with confidence, she poured a little oil into her hands and massaged the tiny squirming body, the flailing fists, the curved kicking legs. Then she dusted it with powdered myrtle leaves. The scent of it, ineffably new and tender, stirred Joseph deeply. He bent nearer and offered one of his fingers, and the child clung to it in a thrilling intensity of trust. It tugged, striving to direct the finger into its mouth.

Joseph laughed, over the pain of his blind adoration. His child. If not the child of his loins, yet it was still the child of his love. He thought of the ancient taboo, that no man should witness a woman giving birth. Yet God had surely led them to this place where no other woman was. The star outside confirmed it. Had that too been a part of God's plan—to include him thus?

"My son," he said, smiling. "No, no you must not try to eat the finger, my precious son."

The fire glowed day and night, clucking softly, for Joseph went forth each day and brought back fuel for it. And he brought bread and juice and water, and sweets which they ate, often secretively in the still of the night, like children on a holiday. And with them, the core and flower and focus of their existence, was the baby, new, small, helpless, who yawned and woke and gazed at them with his blank blue liquid eyes, and suckled and slept again. Or cried, so that they would take turns walking him up and down while the other rested.

There was the snap of the fire, the rustle of the hay, the kick of a hoof in a neighboring stall. The starlight poured through the chink of window, joining the yellow eye of the fire to throw long shadows. They could hear the voices of people coming and going in the courtyard. Music and laughter and raucous shouting floated down

rom the inn. Camels brayed, harnesses clanked, there
vas the thump of baggage. All, all made a kind of music
or the strange, lovely, half-waking dream.

And sometimes it was interrupted by the coming of
visitors, as Joseph had predicted. For the shepherds had
spread the tidings. And some came who were only curious
or skeptical, but some came who, like those shepherds,
marveled and went away rejoicing.

Joseph stood one night at the stable door. He had been
to the well for water, but he could not go in just yet. The
night was cold and clear, it was exhilarating and yet
peaceful to stand for a moment before joining his loved
ones inside. From this little distance he stood savoring it,
the sweet communion of the stable.

They had made the place more comfortable. The innkeeper's wife had come down, incredulous before the star.
She was a fat, bustling, loquacious woman, childless
poor thing, and she had fallen in love with the baby.
She had urged them to stay. "You will be hard put to
find better quarters in Bethlehem," she told them, accurately reading their poorness. "Remain here at least until
the time of your purification." She had brought down a
table and bench from the inn, and a brazier to augment
the fire in the pit. Now it too glowed through the long
cold nights. They had tethered the ass in another stall,
swept out the straw and strewn fresh rushes on the floor.
The little family had been snug as three mice in a nest.

And now the forty days had passed. Tomorrow they
must take the little Jesus and travel to the Temple, there
to redeem him with an offering. After that, Joseph reasoned, it would be well to come back to Bethelehem and
find work until the baby was old enough to attempt the
treacherous journey back to Nazareth. Would the star
follow them? he wondered. Would it continue to blaze
above their heads like a torch to light the way?

Where now, star? he thought. Guide me, lead me.

A quiet joy filled him. Wherever they went they
would be together, he and Mary. And the child that had
leapt into their lives together. The miracle of that smote
him with new significance. For the miracles we beg of
God are seldom those we receive. The miracle that had

come to them that night was the miracle of birth itself.
The living child, fashioned out of nothing, a mystery of
love, yet swelling and growing and coming forth as blood
and bone and hungry mouth and crying! Would the
miracle have been less if he had indeed planted the seed
in Mary? Or any greater had God sent an angel down
as he had implored and lifted it without pain from her
body? No—no, the miracle, he saw now as he stood
regarding the flaming star, was life. The baby. God's child
—or any child. For is not every birth a mystery and
every child the child of God?

Taking up the cool bulging skins, he was about to go
in when he heard the pluck of approaching hooves and
the jingle of harness, and saw, flowing slowly down the
pathway from the inn, three camels. He paused, curiously repelled and attracted by the serpentine necks and
undulant heads festooned with tassels, the arrogant grace
of them as they moved, and the commanding elegance
of their riders. Rich merchants, evidently, dark princes
from some far country. And it flashed through his consciousness that it was strange they had not summoned
a servant to stable their mounts instead of themselves
riding down from the inn.

Joseph turned hastily, not wishing to be seen, and was
about to duck into the cave when one of them called
out to him. "Wait! You there in the doorway." The
camel drew nearer. "Tell me, is this the place where the
new child lies?"

Joseph stood rigid, silent in the grip of a terrible apprehension.

"Of course it is, it has to be." The second rider was
making a gesture of triumph toward the star. "See, it no
longer moves."

"But—a stable!" The third rider drew abreast. "Surely
this is no fit birthplace for a king."

Joseph's heart had begun to beat in heavy strokes.
Obviously these were men of travel and learning, men
on a vital mission, and he was afraid. A great foreboding
rose up in him, and a fierce rebellion. What did such men
want with his child? Were the dread momentous things
hinted at so darkly in the prophets already about to be-

gin? He would not have it. Not yet, not yet! The child
was not ready; his little life had only just begun.

He stood blocking the doorway as the strangers prepared to dismount, rapping the growling beasts on the
neck so that they folded their thin legs to crouch.

"Why do you ask?" Joseph demanded. "What do you
want?"

"To see him. Is there not a newborn child within?"
Joseph hesitated. "Only my wife and son."

They regarded him. One was tall and handsome, with
a curling black beard and teeth that flashed white in his
swarthy face. The other two were fairer. All had the
look of wisdom and splendor about them, humbling
Joseph, a sense of purpose and wills that were not easily to
be denied.

"You are the father then? Of this holy child?"

"My wife has borne a son," he said. "I am the father
of a month old son. And is not every child sacred in the
sight of God?"

"Yes. Yes, truly," said the tall one after a second.
"But the stars have foretold this event for years. We have
studied the stars. We are Magi from Persia and Chaldea,
philosophers and physicians, and we have traveled for
weeks following the star that stands over this doorway.
It has become the sole purpose of our existence, my
friend—to see him, if only for a few minutes, this child
of yours who is to change the course of all history.
This one who is to become King of the Jews." The voice
was grave, at once stern and imploring. "Surely you
would not turn us away?"

Joseph gazed into the stranger's impassioned eyes. And
he knew that it was ended, the peaceful dream of the
stable with the child as only a child at its center and
heart. For cradled there in the clay manger lay all the
portent and the promise, the man of destiny.

"Wait," he said brusquely, "I must go and consult my
wife."

Mary had been packing for the trip. The remains of
their evening meal still lay on the table, while she attended the baby. He was laughing and crowing as she
bent over him, changing his bands. He seemed to rec-

ognize Joseph when he entered, to gurgle and glow wit
new delight. A sweet desperate pain drove through Joseph'
breast. "I'm sorry I was gone so long," he said. "Bu
there are strangers at the door insisting they must se
him. They are wisemen, Mary, come all the way fron
Persia and Chaldea, they claim."

Mary gasped. And she too was bewildered and sudden
ly stricken. "Wisemen? Then you must not keep then
waiting." She looked about at the confusion. "Thougl
what will they think of us?"

"Mary, it is the baby they are pressing to see." H
caught her hand and they regarded each other a long
moment. "He who is one day to be King of the Jews."

Mary closed her eyes. She too had almost forgotten, o.
set the truth aside. Now she was forced to remember al
that was back of him. All the suffering and hope that hac
led to this moment. And all the threat and promise tha
lay ahead of him—this innocent little being, kicking anc
chewing his fist, unaware of his fate. She took him up
and kissed him; blindly then she put him down anc
began preparing the boy so that he should not be founc
wanting in the strangers' eyes.

"Bid them come in."

In a few moments she could hear the pound of sandals
and the swish of robes as they approached; it was like
the ominous rush and pound of some majestic but overpowering sea. They filled the room with their turbaned
strangeness, their exotic smell of spices and perfume.
But one by one they knelt at her feet, there in the straw,
and kissed the hem of her gown. And they gazed long
upon the baby, who smiled at them with his great liquid
eyes and strove within his bindings, as if to reach out to
them. And they laughed gently, and opening their embroidered shawls, presented their gifts—jars of precious
myrrh and frankincense, a bolt of silk shot through with
gold, a ruby in a velvet case.

"For the king," they said, rising unsteadily and brushing
at their eyes. "For the hope of the ages. And for you, his
blessed mother. . . ." One of them draped a cashmere
shawl about Mary's slight shoulders. "And you, his father.
. . ." A leather bag of coins was pressed into Joseph's
hand. "Use it to lighten your load. For it is a heavy

load you have been elected to carry, and a long journey that you will surely have to make."

"How so?" Joseph asked. "Tell us," he begged, "you who are wise. What lies ahead for the child and for us?"

The men exchanged troubled glances. The tall Persian spoke. "For one thing, make haste to leave this place. You did well to question us. There are those in the land who would come not to worship but to destroy a rival king."

"Herod?" Joseph blanched.

"Yes, Herod, the madman. Foolishly, we stopped in Jerusalem to inquire where the child might be found." He smiled faintly. "Even so-called wisemen can make mistakes. For he seemed unduly interested in this king we sought. He made us promise that when we found him we'd return and tell him."—at Joseph's start—"Don't worry, we'll return to our own country another way. But the news will spread, there will be others who will send the information to him. Take the child and go, don't stay here another day!"

"We are leaving for Jerusalem tomorrow," Joseph said anxiously. "We must present the child at the Temple, for the day of my wife's purification is at hand. Whatever the danger involved, that must be done."

The Chaldean physician spoke up. "Go, then. Many infants are brought to the Temple every day, it's the last place Herod would think to look for him. But whatever else you do, don't return to Bethlehem."

Night now, deep night and all was still.

Now and then a dog barked somewhere, a hoof stomped, a swallow went fluttering across the ceiling. Except for these sounds the stable was silent. Yet Mary could not sleep. Careful not to disturb Joseph, she got up and stole about, doing last-minute things for the journey. Then she crept back and gazed upon the face of the slumbering child. It lay so still, was it breathing? She bent her ear to the hot bundle; she could feel it move inside its cocoon of wrappings, the lips made sucking movements, and her own being relaxed.

"Mary?" She turned, startled to see Joseph sitting up on his pallet on the floor. His eyes were large with alarm. "Is everything all right?"

"Yes. I was only looking after the baby."

He flung off the robe and began striding about, poking the fire, turning the wick of the lamp higher. "I can't sleep either. At least I didn't think I was sleeping but I must have been because I had a dream just now. A vivid dream. An angel stood beside me and repeated the wisemen's warning." He was breathing hard. "Mary, they were right, we will have to flee. After the presentation tomorrow we can't come back here or even go home to Nazareth. The dream made that very clear. We must take the child and flee into Egypt."

"Egypt!"

"Yes, the land of our people's exile. We will have to wait there until it's safe to come back."

Mary stared at him as he heated milk to calm himself. "Joseph, are you sure?"

Sure? He could scarcely steady the vessel he was so shaken. Who was sure of anything any more? All, all was a dream and a miracle. To be born at all, to love and be fulfilled, or to love and be denied. Where was home? A house he had built on a Nazareth hillside . . . or a crowded stable . . . or an everlasting highway? Did man ever really wake and know truly where he was at any given moment, or if he lived and breathed at all, or only dreamed his own existence? For all, all was a mystery— where it began no one knew, and if it ever ended, even at the grave, no one could say.

"Yes," he said grimly and sipped the milk from the gourd. "Yes, we must do as we are told." For, sorrowing, he saw that this was the only truth now. Forces beyond themselves had brought them to this moment, and would surely guide and guard them in the hours that lay ahead.

"Then we won't be able even to see my aunt and the little John?"

"No, Mary."

"I had looked forward to it so. I wanted the cousins to meet. I did so want to show her our lovely baby."

"I know, Mary."

"Oh, Joseph!" She ran to him in her bare feet and flung herself against him, and he held her close and wrapped his garment about her to shelter and comfort her.

"Joseph, I'm afraid. I want to go home. Home to our parents and friends in Galilee. Home to our house." Suddenly—"I want to live as other women, I want to love you as your wife and for you to love me as my husband."

He caught his breath. . . . *"But know her not until she has borne this holy one."* . . . *Until!*

It was too much, it was more than he dared contemplate right now. Yet her words gave him a source of strength and joy he would sorely need. "Hush, we mustn't think of such things yet. For now, for a long time, Mary, the child must be our only concern." He kissed her tenderly and stroked her hair. "We have a long hard journey ahead of us, as the wisemen said. And we must be thankful that they came to warn us. And their gifts —the money will help take care of us and the child. If we are driven to it we can even sell the ruby."

"No, it belongs to him. And the precious silks and oils." She drew away, wiping her eyes. "We will put them away for him, unto the day when he shall truly be king."

Again the conflict bore in upon Joseph. King yet lowly. God yet man. Born of a virgin in human fear and suffering, as all men must be born. Why? Why? . . . Was it to demonstrate the eternal majesty and mystery of being? What a crude and wonderful thing it is to emerge out of a woman and live for a little while upon this planet, whether as king or god or slave. And God the author of it all, in whose image all men are made. God, in his desperation to draw men back to him, willing to be born and perhaps even to die in the bittersweet manner of men.

"Somehow I can't think of our son as a king," Joseph said. "At least not a king who will mount a throne one day and rule the world." He went and stood by the child who stirred in its sleep and whimpered and slept again. "But rather as a king who will somehow change men's hearts."

Mary followed, and he saw that she was weeping quietly but terribly, from somewhere deep in her soul. "Oh, Joseph, our poor baby! I love him so. I would almost renounce the honor of being the chosen one if only this child could be simply our child and not subject to . . . to what both of us know must surely come to him."

"Hush," he whispered. "Hush, Mary, be still." He spoke brusquely even as he soothed her, trying to deny what now for the first time he too must force himself to face. "Why, he has a glorious fate awaiting him. God's own son! I spoke wrongly a moment ago, he will be a glorious king, greater even than David, for his kingdom will be all the world."

She was staring at the baby, across whose sleeping face a shadow now hung. It was only the shadow of a wagon tongue propped against the wall, yet she saw it, the dark and terrible shape of it drawn across the helpless form of her little son.

"No," she said quietly, out of her private agony of knowledge. "The prophets have already spoken of his fate. He will be no earthly king. He will be a man of sorrows whom the world will despise. He will be the scapegoat driven into the wilderness to carry away the people's sins. He will bear the whole burden of their guilt upon his shoulders. He will be led up onto a hill to be slaughtered for that guilt; he will be the sacrificial lamb."

"Don't, Mary, don't! I can't bear it, you can't bear it. He will not be forced to bear it. The prophets were often madmen claiming revelations that came from the devil and not from God."

"He will be slain," she went on as if in a daze. "They will crucify him in the manner of thieves and Zealots. That Zealot I once saw upon a cross. . . . They will make him a cross and force him to carry it for the guilt of our falling apart from God. See—the shadow of that cross is upon him now."

"Stop!" For now Joseph saw it too, and the cry was wrung from his very bowels. In anger and anguish he went to the offending shaft and carried it the length of the stable and flung it into the yard. When he came back he was trembling but more calm. Mary, however, was crouched beside the manger, her head pressed against it.

"Forgive me." She lifted her wet tormented face to

his. "But oh, Joseph, the pains that I suffered to bring
him forth, what will they be compared to the suffering if
this thing be fulfilled?"

"Mary, Mary." He lifted her up and held her like a
child. He strode with her to a bench and set her down
upon it, and then he warmed a cup of milk for her and
bade her drink it. And as she did so he stroked her hair
and plucked the wisps of hay from it, as he had done
that night of her travail. And he whispered softly to
her until she was quiet, and then he sat beside her, holding her hand.

"Hush, my love, my little wife," he said. "Does not
every mother who bears a son know that he must die
one day? Aren't there already a thousand crosses upon
the hills of Judah? Doesn't every man who walks this earth
carry his cross with him every day?"

He turned and looked a moment at the manger. "This
is our cross, Mary. Yours and mine—for you know how
much I love him too. But this is our cross—to know
that our son's hour will come and we can't stop it.
To live with that certainty every day of our lives. But
this is our blessing," he told her. "To know that in his
living and his dying he will be lifting the yoke somewhat
for all men. Life with its burdens will be more tolerable.
There will be hope. Not only for the freedom of Israel,
our own people, but all people who are enslaved.

"And hope for the tormented spirit, Mary. To have
some link, some proof that the God we worship really
cares about us. Not to have to *fight* God any more, not
to be estranged from him." Joseph's face was working,
he was struggling to make it clear. "That too is suffering,
perhaps the worst suffering of all. Somehow through this
child all this will come about."

"But he's so young, so little and young!"

"Yes, he's just a baby now—our baby, unaware of
this great plan." His voice broke, it was a second before
he could go on. "Pray God that he will be a long time
knowing. But when he becomes a man and takes up the
work that has been designed for him, we too must be
ready, Mary. And so we must accept it. Accept it now.
We must not struggle against that secret knowledge, we

must accept it and grow in courage toward that hour. So
that we won't be found wanting, Mary his mother. Mary
—my wife."

He lifted her chin and gazed into her stricken face.
Outside a cock crowed, signaling the coming day. The
darkness was lifting, the room emerging from the shadows. Through the chink above them a pink glow began
to bloom. And it seemed to Joseph that he knew now
why it had been his fate to love Mary—perhaps with a
greater love than man has ever been asked to give a
wife. For that love was akin to the love personified in
the child: *Sacrifice.*

God so loved the world that he would give up his own
son. And that son, that poor doomed son . . . he too would
love the people in it so much that he would be willing
to give up his life.

To suffer that others may live, as Mary had suffered
in birth. To deny oneself for those who are dearer to us
than life. That is the true union of those who love. And
that—that in the end was what would bring man back
to be united with his God.

"I love you, Mary," Joseph said. "This child is truly
a child of love, sent to us because we love each other
so much. And the home that we will make for him will
be one of love. Remember how you once told me that?
Our love will help us, my darling. It will enable us to
grow together in courage and strength, so that we will be
worthy of this great blessing that has come to us in this
stable in Bethlehem. Worthy of having him entrusted to
us, for even a little while."

Mary nodded, though her eyes were wet. Bending her
head, she kissed Joseph's rough hand. Then she arose
and set about getting the morning meal. For it was daylight now, and they had a long, long journey ahead of
them.

ABOUT THE AUTHOR

Marjorie Holmes is the author of the highly successful I'VE GOT TO TALK TO SOMEBODY, GOD; LORD, LET ME LOVE; and a host of other books, novels, and magazine articles. The *New York Times* described her as "an American phenomenon," and the *Washington Post* as "the housewives' patron saint." For twenty-five years her column LOVE AND LAUGHTER was a popular feature of the *Washington Star*. She also wrote the column A WOMAN'S CONVERSATIONS WITH GOD for *Woman's Day* magazine. She has taught writing courses at the University of Maryland, Catholic University, and Georgetown—all in the area of Washington, D.C. She was born in Storm Lake Iowa, where she attended Buena Vista College, before graduating from Iowa's Cornell College. She has traveled widely, visiting Israel a number of times to do research for her novels. She is the mother of four grown children. After the death of her first husband she married Dr. George Schmieler, a physician from suburban Pittsburgh, where she now lives.